DISNEP

THE QUEEN'S COUNCIL

REBEL
ROSE

EMMA THERIAULT

AUTUMN
PUBLISHING

Published in 2020
First published in the UK by Autumn Publishing
An imprint of Igloo Books Ltd
Cottage Farm, NN6 0BJ, UK
Owned by Bonnier Books
Sveavägen 56, Stockholm, Sweden
www.igloobooks.com

1120 001
2 4 6 8 10 9 7 5 3 1
ISBN 978-1-83903-631-6

Printed and manufactured in the UK

For all those who dream of adventure in the great wide somewhere.

Vincit qui se vincit.

He conquers who conquers himself.

PROLOGUE

O rella had come to the castle cloaked in the skin of
an old beggar woman.

She had cast a pitiable figure by design – hooded,
wrapped in rags and soaked to the bone by the sleet that fell
like daggers from the blackened sky. Blessed with foresight
as she was, Orella had never been so haunted by a vision. A
bloody revolution was coming for France, as it had come for
America and would one day come for the Russian Empire.
Death was marching for many thousands of people. She
had no choice but to try to spare the people of Aveyon.

In the castle, the prince behaved just as she had foreseen
he would. He rejected her request for simple shelter in
exchange for a blood-red rose. She recognised the pain in
him – the sharp loss of his mother's love and the aching
absence of his father's, the sudden orphaning that left him
unmoored in a world he barely understood, the weight

of a kingdom on his untested shoulders. His cruelty was a shield, one that had grown around his heart, turning it to stone. Others might believe the prince would grow out of the unkindness that festered in him like a disease, but she knew better.

Without her interference, armies of men would march on charred ground, fighting over whatever scraps and rot remained of a ruined world. She had done what she could in Versailles to no avail. If she similarly failed in Aveyon, the kingdom would be a dark catalyst for the rest of Europe and beyond. This time she could not falter.

She knew it was coming, but still her heart cleaved when he rejected her a second time, sealing his own fate. She shed the skin of her disguise and let her true form fill the room. Orella was a flame in the dark, all at once as ancient as the earth and as young as the first blossom of spring. She read fear in his eyes and the word he whispered on his lips. *Enchantress.*

She was not an enchantress, but it suited her to allow him to believe she was. In truth, she was both more and less than one. Her powers were greater, but her purpose was more narrowly defined. Appearing as she was to a prince was not something she ever thought she would have to do, but Orella's gift would not let her sit idly by.

The prince begged for forgiveness, swearing he could change, and it was only then that she saw a glimmer of the goodness he kept hidden, and of the king he could become.

But promises born out of fear do not carry the same weight as those born out of love. A twist of her fingers transformed the prince, confining him to a monstrous form that would force him to change his heart. Another twist placed a powerful spell on the castle and all those who lived within it, erasing them from the minds of those outside it. She didn't relish it. She wanted to tell him the curse had a purpose, to warn him of the fire she had seen burning through France and the reign of terror that came after it. But she had already meddled too much.

Instead, Orella left him with the only gifts she could conceive of: a magic mirror to anchor him to the world he was leaving behind, and the rose she had offered him, now enchanted to ensure he did not tarry.

As she left the castle, Orella was besieged by a flickering vision of a girl in a blue dress with a white muslin apron wearing a crown on her head – sometimes the girl's body was burned, sometimes it was whole. It was too tenuous a thing for her to read clearly; too much could change before it came to be. But the crown on the girl's head told Orella that she had at least achieved what she had come to the castle to do.

She had set them on a path; Belle and the prince would have to do the rest.

CHAPTER ONE

TEN YEARS LATER – JULY 1789

Once upon a time, a cursed prince fell in love with a headstrong girl, and together they saved a kingdom. But that was in the past, and all Belle could think about as her carriage rumbled over the cobbles of Pont Neuf was the future.

Paris was just as she remembered it – so frenetic, chaotic and choked by smoke that it threatened to overwhelm a girl more used to rolling fields and worn-down markets.

She leaned out the window to take in the city after days of monotonous countryside. Lumière continued to sleep hunched over in the corner – the same position he had spent most of the journey in. Behind her, her husband's hand clasped her skirts as if to anchor her to him, but she could not tear herself from the view. Outside, the city was so viscerally alive. The bridge teemed with people of all sorts – bouquinistes with their stalls of old books and pamphlets; mountebanks on raised platforms, hawking their vials of curatives; jugglers doing their best to impress the grisettes on their way home after a hard day's work. Belle watched with grisly fascination as a barber yanked a tooth from a poor soul's jaw, gaining purchase by placing his foot on the wall of the bridge behind them. And under it all, the murky Seine still glittered in the afternoon light as Parisians littered the embankment, seeking respite from the summer heat by its cool waters.

Belle revelled in it now just as she had long ago, when she first saw it all from the back of her father's wagon, wedged between his inventions. She had tried and failed for so many years to convince herself that it hadn't been so grand, and that life in Aveyon hadn't been so comatose in comparison. She had strived to remember only the filth and stench of Paris, and those remained, but beneath them was a city of people and industry and enlightenment, of poets and philosophers, and of scientists and scholars. It was a city that valued knowledge, no matter where it came from, unlike her own sleepy village of Plesance, where Belle was taunted for being different. In her mind, Paris became the kind of place Belle dreamed of running to, before she met Lio and the course of her life changed forever.

She drank the city in, scarcely able to contend with everything happening outside the carriage. "You know, they say the police know a man has left Paris if they haven't seen him cross Pont Neuf in three days."

"Oh?" Lio was absent-minded and still, preferring to sit

back and let Paris pass him by.

She glanced over at him. "You weren't lying when you said it has no hold over you."

He gave her a quizzical grin. "What?"

"Paris," she said, leaning towards him. "I feel as though I might burst out of my skin, but you're—" The words died on her lips as her ears rang in the sudden muffled quiet of the carriage.

He looked out to the busy bridge and sighed. "Paris is host to a lot of my unhappy memories." He watched her smile fade and reached out for her hand, thumbing her palm. "I am happy that you're happy, Belle. Perhaps we can make new memories here."

Belle hadn't ever thought herself to be the marrying type, but after she broke the curse that bound the man she loved and set a kingdom free, marriage hardly seemed a challenge at all. Her time in the enchanted castle had changed her. When Lio proposed in the library he had gifted her, surrounded by her father and the family she had made for herself, saying yes had been the most natural thing in the world.

Now the curse was far behind them, and while Belle did not regret choosing Lio, she hadn't entirely realised the consequences of that choice. She had never imagined a life spent in a castle, or the duties that came with marrying a prince. But she and Lio needed to build a life together, and Paris was to be the first stop on the grand tour of Europe that Belle had always dreamed of. Cogsworth had, of course, bemoaned the time wasted and the unseemliness of a *prince* touring the Continent, but Belle was adamant that she see everything she could before the walls of Lio's castle closed around her for good. She needed one last bit of adventure she could cling to. Lumière had chosen to accompany them for the beginning of their journey, eager to visit the kitchens of Paris's most celebrated restaurants. Cogsworth had made him promise to behave, but everyone knew that was asking a lot of Lumière, who was as dedicated to mischief and revelry as he was to his duties as maître d'hôtel, or master of the house.

Lio shook off his melancholy mood. "Is it everything you remember it to be?"

"Paris has not changed," she concluded with a sigh. "I'm the one who's different."

"A princess, you mean?"

She pinched his arm lightly as the carriage turned onto rue Dauphine. "Not a princess." Belle's refusal to take the title marriage to Lio would have afforded her was a touchy subject between them.

He mercifully let it go. "But certainly not the girl you were then."

She turned her attention to the wallpapered panel of the carriage, tracing the embossed flowers with the tip of her finger, unwilling to let him see her smile falter once more. She didn't know how to explain that she would always be that girl, that no titles or fine clothing would change her. In her bones, she was a poor, provincial peasant who had risen far above her station. Sometimes she worried her life was made up of illusions – to Lio, she was a girl worthy of a prince and a kingdom, and to herself, she was a girl who could tame her restless spirit and be happy with stillness. She wondered which of their illusions would shatter first.

She buried the unpleasant thought as Lio changed the subject. "Should we go over everything again?"

Belle grimaced. Visiting the court of Versailles was not something either of them wished to do, but it was a necessary evil. Aveyon was a principality, and its rulers had sojourned at the French court for centuries at the will of the king of France. It was a mutually beneficial relationship that Lio wished to restore. But he had been absent from court for ten years, bound by a curse that erased him from the minds of those who once knew him. Neither of them knew where he stood with King Louis – he might be irreparably angry with Lio, or have forgotten him altogether. But ignoring the problem solved nothing. They would have to face the king of France eventually.

She could tell her husband was nervous, so she tried for levity. "To begin with, we do not speak to someone of higher rank unless they have spoken to us first. Which reminds me, where does a prince étranger fall in terms of rank?"

Lio shrugged. "Well below a prince légitimé or a prince du

sang, but above most nobles."

"And what about the wife of a prince étranger?"

Lio cocked a brow at her. "That would depend on whether she took the title of princess, which would have afforded her a great deal more respect than if she hadn't."

She refused to take the bait. "So to be safe I just won't speak to anyone." Lio rolled his eyes, but Belle pressed on. "Are you sure your cousin can secure us an invitation?" The court of Versailles was a beast of protocol and etiquette, and Belle was certain she would never fully understand it.

Lio waved a hand. "He's a duc, Belle."

"And you're a prince," she replied flatly.

He pressed his lips together. "He's a duc who has ingratiated himself with the court of Versailles for many years. He knows the ins and outs, and if anyone can get us an audience with the king, he can."

A younger, more naive version of Belle would have assumed that the prince of Aveyon would have had no trouble securing an invitation to court. But the older version of Belle understood that the court of the king of France was mired in layers of complexity and convolution designed to control the very noblemen who made it up. There was a chance that even with Lio's cousin's intervention, they would be barred from it. The rules of Versailles had been laid down by King Louis's grandfather and could not be discarded. They had to behave impeccably, lest they be turned away for good.

She voiced their most pressing concern. "Are we prepared enough for your cousin's questions?"

When Lio at last shed the curse that had bound him, his kingdom awoke to a world that had forgotten its existence. Lio's staff had returned to their true selves and found their families, who resided outside of the castle, had not even noticed they were gone. Mostly they wove back into their normal lives without having to explain where they had been for so long. It was as though the curse had covered Aveyon in a blanket of forgetting, and when it was gone, the blanket had simply been lifted. Mercifully, it seemed that the world outside of Lio's castle was willing to accept them back into it without question.

But despite how relatively easy it had been to craft a story believable enough to satisfy a kingdom, Belle and Lio worried his cousin – once as close as a brother to him – might prove to be an exception.

Lio kissed the back of her hand in a show of confidence Belle wasn't sure she believed. "Of course we are, and once this business with the king is sorted, we'll be on our way, I promise you."

Belle looked at her husband, studying the face she had only known for a few months. She nestled her head against his chest and listened for the heartbeat she had known a great deal longer. "It shall be our first test."

If they could lie convincingly to Bastien, duc de Vincennes, perhaps it meant they stood a chance of doing the same to the king of France.

CHAPTER TWO

T he carriage rumbled into Paris's richest enclave, and Belle's breath caught in her throat. Nothing like it existed in Aveyon, where you'd expect to find the manors of Aveyon's nobility dispersed throughout the countryside, small islands of opulence, isolated and surrounded by modest villages. France's nobility resided mostly at Versailles. To try to live separately from the king's court or even leave it briefly spelled disaster for lesser nobles. Only the richest and most powerful of France's nobility maintained homes in the city, which they visited sparingly. Each one was larger than the last, squatting like miniature castles on the clogged streets of Paris.

"You know, I thought the mansions in Saint-Germain would seem smaller now that I'm older, but somehow they've only grown in their intimidation."

Lio looked out to the row of hôtels particuliers that passed in a blur. "Yes, but to hear Bastien tell it, you'd think he was living in a hovel rather than a townhouse."

Belle sat back and looked at Lio. "Was he always so—"

"Spoiled? Arrogant?" Lio fidgeted in his seat. "Truth be

told, we were a lot alike as boys. Growing up together made us rivals, and my uncle only encouraged that. I hope we've moved past it." A darkness took over his features as he remembered the cruel boy he had been before. No matter how many times Belle reminded him of his changed heart, Lio let years of guilt weigh down upon him, bearing it like Atlas bore the heavens on his shoulders.

Belle tried to reach through the shadows of his past. "How long were you fostered in your uncle's home?"

"Some five years, beginning when I was six."

Belle paused. "Six is young to be taken away from your family." Belle couldn't imagine ever having left her father's care. After her mother died, they only had each other. She and Maurice had been forced to learn how to live without her, and their relationship was stronger because of it.

Lio adjusted his collar, a finely embroidered thing. "My father insisted I be raised closer to Versailles. I think even then he was concerned about Aveyon's relationship with France. He was trying to make me into someone who felt at home in King Louis's court, instead of someone who felt at home in Aveyon. And then…" He trailed off, and Belle knew better than to push him. "And then my mother died. She was gone before I even knew she was sick. I returned for her funeral, and when my father tried to send me back, I refused. At least in Aveyon I could walk down corridors we had walked in together, I could go to her chambers and run my hands over her gowns.

15

I abandoned the name my father had given me, refusing to be addressed as anything other than Lio. Did I ever tell you why she called me that?" Belle shook her head. "From birth my mother called me her petit lionceau, her little lion cub." His expression was half a smile, half a grimace. "Only my father ever called me by my real name. Over time it was shortened to Lio. To go by anything else felt like I was dishonouring her memory. It seems insignificant now, but I was more connected to her after she died than when I was away in Paris. I knew I would lose that if I went back to my uncle's home. My father was desperately angry with me, but I thought we'd have years to repair our relationship." His gaze drifted back to the homes they passed. "I didn't think I'd be made an orphan within the year."

Not for the first time, Belle thought of the enchantress who had cursed Lio and she felt rage simmer in her gut. He had been a boy left alone in the world, wounded and angry, and the enchantress saw fit to punish him for it. But Belle and Lio had grown accustomed to dancing around the topic of the curse, so she said nothing.

Silence stretched between them as they came to a stop at the largest hôtel particulier she had seen yet. One would be forgiven for thinking they had left Paris proper and emerged at a country estate. Once they cleared the immense gate, they arrived at a vast courtyard of smooth, pale pink stone. Artfully pruned shrubs and small trees were dotted throughout, mingling with the Grecian statues that lined the perimeter and the thick Romanesque columns that supported the home itself. It was absurdly ostentatious even on a street full of magnificent homes. But Belle could hardly judge such extravagance now that she herself lived in a castle.

Lio gently shook Lumière awake. The maître d'hôtel swallowed a snore that became a yawn. "We're here already?"

"That's what happens when you sleep through a journey, my friend."

"Ah, but sleep was my only respite from the constant declarations of undying love." Lumière winked and then hopped out of the carriage to begin attending to their luggage, a task he had taken upon himself from the start, despite their insistence that they could more than manage it themselves.

Belle stepped down from the carriage, emerging into the oppressive heat of the sun, and was struck by how much warmer the summer was in Paris. Aveyon's forests and mountains kept the temperature in the kingdom relatively mild no matter the season. The seasons in this part of France, by contrast, could vary wildly. She knew that the kingdom had just experienced a harsh winter, and the droughts of the year before had left France's farmers to contend with failing crops and hungry bellies.

Liveried men stood guard between the columns, perspiring in their thick uniforms under the hot sun.

"Surely this level of protection isn't necessary for a duc so heavily ensconced in the safety of Saint-Germain?"

Lio looked to the guards and sighed. "No doubt Bastien uses them as a show of his status."

Belle paused. "I must say he sounds lovely."

Lio grinned. "If you look past the arrogance and superiority, he's quite charming." He pulled her close to him. "Just remember, I was once as wretched as my dear cousin, and you still managed to fall in love with me."

"Be careful, I might take my chances with the duc."

"Good luck with that," said Lio, nudging her gaze to the townhouse's front door. Emerging from within was a man who could only be the duc de Vincennes. He cast a wealthy figure: his wig was curled and powdered the same pale white as his skin, ruffled lace cuffs poked out of his salmon velvet overcoat, an elaborately embroidered collar reached high up his neck, and his grey knee breeches gave way to cream-coloured socks and ended in a heeled leather boot. He carried a walking stick with a carved ivory handle as he clattered down the stairs to greet them, his jewelled rings glinting in the sunlight.

"Dearest cousin," he called out to Lio, removing his cocked hat. "Welcome to my humble abode. It has been a long while since we've been graced by the presence of a prince." His tone was just sarcastic enough to suggest he thought Lio's title to be a great joke. By then, Belle and Lio had reached him on the steps. "And this must be your bride. I must say, her name hardly does her justice." He reached a hand out for Belle's and brought it to his lips. She could see that he was fine-looking underneath all the paint and artifice.

She resisted the urge to withdraw quickly. "It's a pleasure to meet you, Bastien."

His smile faltered for a fraction of a second before he recovered and placed his hat back upon his head. "And you, Belle." She could hear the absence of the title he would have said if she had not addressed him so. He thought it an insult to be informal with her, but she preferred it that way. He gestured with his cane to Lumière and their coachman and frowned slightly. "How odd that you've come without a retinue, Cousin. We were expecting a crowd." He pulled at his collar and squinted up at the sun. "No matter. Shall we get out of the heat? Perhaps some champagne to cool us?"

"Can we beg the same for our companions?" Belle asked.

Bastien paused as if he didn't understand the question. He looked to Lio, who merely smiled. "If you insist," Bastien said. Belle was surprised, but she understood that the way they did things in Aveyon might not be how things were done in Paris. She looked to Lumière, who shook his head at her as if to say she shouldn't even bother, but she wasn't about to back down from the idea that everyone in her employ be treated with respect.

The duc signalled to one of his servants to help Lumière with their luggage. The maître d'hôtel turned to them and bowed low, his movements fluid and graceful.

"Unless you need anything else from me, I have a whole city of dishes to sample," he announced with both a signature flourish of his hand and a mischievous wink.

"Enjoy, Lumière," said Belle.

Bastien looked at them, struggling to understand their dynamic before giving up. He then guided Lio and Belle into his palatial townhouse, and Belle was immediately struck by the interior. She had heard tell of mythical Versailles, and from what she could see, it seemed Bastien was doing his best to emulate France's monument to extravagance. Everything was gilded – from the furniture to the light fixtures to the crown mouldings. The walls were covered with mirrors and portraits and wall hangings of richly stitched brocade, and a liveried servant stood at every threshold, ready to open the door and dip into an efficient bow. Bastien led them on a tour through the labyrinthine home, each room grander than the one before, pointing out which tables had been procured by Bastien's mother from Madame de Pompadour, explaining the differences between Greek- and rocaille-style furniture, and pausing to insist that they appreciate the gilded laurel garlands on what he called a Riesener original cabinet.

"He's Marie Antoinette's favourite ébéniste," he told them, waiting for them to be sufficiently awed and impressed, and tutting when they did not appreciate it enough. "His pieces are notoriously difficult to come by. This cost a fair deal more than I am willing to admit," he added, by way of explanation.

Lio let out a low whistle that Belle recognised as an attempt at placation. She swallowed a laugh as they continued on through the halls.

Belle quickly fell behind as she studied the frescoed ceilings, the intricate crystal chandeliers, and the innumerable marble statues. She had thought Lio's castle back in Aveyon the height of opulence, even when it had fallen into disrepair. But all it had on Bastien's home was its size; the duc's residence won in every other respect.

It took her a few false turns to find Lio and Bastien again. They had come to rest in something of a parlour, perhaps an office, though the duc did not strike her as someone particularly married to his work. The walls were lined with bookcases, and a large mahogany desk sat heavy in the centre of the room. Bastien was over by a cart bursting with bottles of liquor, pouring champagne into thin flutes. He offered one to Belle when she joined them, and she took it out of a sense of politeness. He turned back to pour one for Lio and began to speak.

"You know, Cousin, each time I tried to visit your quaint principality, something went horribly wrong." He faced them and handed Lio his flute. "Carriages lost wheels, catastrophes cropped up out of nowhere, maidens needed rescuing. It was as if fate was working against me."

Lio took the flute and pressed a hand to his chest. "A good

thing too, Bastien, as I was grievously ill."

Belle did her best to settle her hands as she listened to Lio tell the lie they had come up with when they realised that, because of the curse, everyone outside of the castle had simply forgotten about their prince for ten years.

When she and Lio defeated it, memories came flooding back through the kingdom and beyond, memories of the spoiled orphan prince of a kingdom left to fester for ten years. It meant they had a lot of questions to answer, but it wasn't as if anyone could know the truth. An illness seemed as close to honesty as they could get without informing everyone that Aveyon had been ruled by a reclusive beast for a decade.

Bastien quirked his brow. "My letters went unanswered."

This is our first test, Belle reminded herself to stop from panicking. If all went well with Bastien, the rest of their plan could come to fruition.

"Meaningful correspondence was out of my reach, Bastien. I was—"

"Ill, I know." He drained his flute. "Thank God and the king for your eventual recuperation, Lio. I'd wager most individuals never recover from a ten-year illness." He studied them both, perhaps looking for a crack in their defences. Belle smiled as serenely as she could manage, and something seemed to shift in the duc. He raised his empty glass in the air. "To good physicians."

Lio's shoulders dropped, but Belle didn't think Bastien

noticed. He raised his full flute in reciprocation. "And to family."

"Old and new," Bastien added, standing and walking to the champagne cart. "I want to know everything about your whirlwind romance, Cousin, but that can wait. First, you must tell me what interest you have in Versailles. You certainly haven't expressed any in the last ten years."

Lio cleared his throat. "I wish to reassert my allegiance to the king. I owe him as much after my time away from court."

Bastien looked back at them. "Versailles is not as you remember it, Cousin."

Lio nodded. "I am not surprised to hear it, as I have not been to the palace since I was a boy."

Bastien poured more champagne. "King Louis has likely forgotten all about your humble principality. So much has happened here since you last visited. Are you sure you wish to poke the bear, so to speak?" he asked over his shoulder.

Lio's smile was tight. "I remember Louis to be a reasonable man, Bastien."

He turned dramatically on his heel to face them. "The treasury is empty, Cousin. France is drowning in debt after supporting the blasted American Revolution. Surely you heard of the unrest of the Third Estate?" It had only been some months since Belle and Lio and Aveyon had emerged from the curse, but diplomacy had not been a priority in their kingdom for a long time. They had heard small rumbles of what Bastien was referring to, that the Third Estate, France's peasant class, was suffering, but Belle and Lio had not paid them any special attention. Belle felt foolish, and Bastien sighed at their ignorance as he sat down. "Louis is in desperate need of money, and he tried to obtain it as he always has – with taxes. But this time, he wanted the nobles and clergy to pay their share. Unsurprisingly, they refused." He swung his legs up onto the desk before him and folded his arms across his chest. "Out of desperation, he convened the États généraux for the first time in nearly two hundred years. Needless to say, that did not go well." He waved his hand lazily. "It was perceived as an attempt to control the outcome, and as a result, the Third Estate is calling themselves the National Assembly now, claiming to represent not the *estates* of France, but the *people*. They are demanding a constitution be drafted." He chuckled and rolled his eyes. "How very American."

"How bad is it, Bastien?"

Bastien smiled wickedly, like a man rich enough to feel removed from it all. "Well, it certainly isn't *good*, Cousin; we are in the midst of a financial crisis. And King Louis just sacked Jacques Necker, ever the stalwart finance minister, so now *everyone* is angry: rich, poor, noble, peasant. It wasn't the canniest of moves, if you ask me."

"Perhaps we should postpone our visit to Versailles," Belle suggested.

"Oh, it's too late for that. Doubtless word has already

spread through court like a pox. A prince étranger, returned from the dead!" Bastien pulled an emerald ring from his finger, the jewel the size of a quail's egg, and spun it lazily on the desk. "You'll be the talk of Versailles. I would be surprised if a messenger wasn't on the way already with an invitation from Louis. He will wish to evaluate you." Lio glanced at Belle, who did her best not to shrink under Bastien's words. The duc sensed their discomfort. "I can accompany you, Cousin. Louis has a fondness for me, to say nothing of the queen." He winked at the veiled suggestion. Belle suppressed the desire to gag. "I can help to soften the blow of your extended absence, but if I'm to go to all this trouble, you must at least attempt to fit in at court. To start with, you'll need a new outfit if you wish to cross through even the gates of the castle, and a hefty amount of powder in that hair if you don't wish to deeply offend the courtiers."

Lio stiffened. "Perhaps I could borrow from you, Bastien."

Bastien evaluated him lazily. "Perhaps." He shifted his gaze to Belle and steepled his fingers under his chin. "Am I right in assuming you were, up until very recently, a commoner?" Belle fidgeted in her gown, a robe à l'anglaise that had seemed so fine to her when Madame Garderobe had presented it. The gown was made of striped blue-and-cream silk, with the softest lace peeking from above the bodice, covering her neckline. The sleeves were tight and fell to just below her elbows. Bastien ducked his head to catch her eye and smiled sympathetically. "It's not just the gown, Belle. You wear your former status on you like a brand."

"How dare you—" Lio started.

Bastien held up his hands in mock surrender. "It is not an evaluation of her character, Cousin. But you'd be feeding her to the wolves in Versailles." He looked at her almost tenderly. "I mean no offence, Belle, but you do not belong in King Louis's court. The courtiers would sniff out your weaknesses and exploit them before you'd even have a chance to curtsy."

Belle nodded, but Lio was indignant. "Belle can do whatever she pleases. If anyone has a problem with her, they can answer to me." She was sure no one else would notice how, in anger, his voice still slipped into something akin to a growl. But Belle had lived with the Beast longer than she had lived with Lio. She could pick out the parts that lingered still, but she would never tell him as much.

"And what of the king, Cousin? Or do you forget that your duty as a prince étranger was to marry for political gain and not love? Weren't you all but betrothed to a lesser Habsburg from birth?" Bastien's hand fluttered over his embroidered collar. "I think perhaps it would be best if news of your marriage came as a happy surprise after you're back in the king's good graces, wouldn't you agree?"

Lio opened his mouth to argue further on her behalf, but Belle placed her hand on his arm to stop him. "Lio, please. I don't even wish to go."

All of Lio's bluster left him at once. He turned to look at her fully. "Are you certain?"

She waved her hand at him. "Yes, I was dreading it the whole way here. I'm happy to have a reason to avoid it, and I'd much rather spend my time in Paris on foot, visiting the places I remember my father taking me to, and exploring new ones."

Lio frowned. "Bastien just finished telling us that Paris is in turmoil."

"Oh, mon petit lionceau, you are so provincial." Bastien rolled his eyes. "The Third Estate is nothing. Merely rabble-rousers without anything better to do. The most they've achieved is the forcible seizure of Paris's tollhouses, so unless Belle has a cartful of taxable goods entering the city, I doubt she'll even much notice their presence." He laughed sharply. "King Louis has everything under control. The city is perfectly safe, I assure you."

Belle watched as the duc's smile slid from his face the moment Lio looked away. It was the sort of quirk her mind would have latched on to were she not tired from her journey and bursting at the thought of reacquainting herself with the places in Paris she remembered her father taking her to, to say nothing of exploring new ones.

And so she tucked away the duc's curious expression, promising to revisit it when there wasn't a whole city of delights waiting for her.

CHAPTER THREE

Lio left with Bastien for his chambers in search of something more appropriate to wear to meet the king. A servant guided Belle to their apartments, where she was happy to have a moment alone with her thoughts.

The bedchamber was as sumptuous as the rest of Bastien's home. Belle's feet sank low into the plush carpet that covered most of the floor, as elaborately woven as the richest tapestry. She wandered absently to the full-length mirror anchored to the wall to study the dress she wore, the one Bastien had insulted. To her eyes, it was the finest thing she had ever seen, finer even than the gown she had worn when she married Lio in the breathless days following the breaking of the curse. She had donned it that morning at the inn where they were lodging, having picked it specially for their entrance into Paris. When Lio had seen it on her, he couldn't disguise how happy it made him to see her so finely attired. To him, it was a step towards the acceptance of her new role. To her, it was armour, a signal to the rest of the world that she could belong.

Now she realised it was just another illusion, and not even

an effective one, for Bastien had seen right through her. The world of the French court was not her world. She would never fit into it.

She tore off the gown, desperate to be rid of the artifice. She dug through her trunk, searching for the plainest dress she had packed, buried deep at the bottom. She pulled it over her head and relished the familiarity. It was blue like the gown she had discarded, but the fabric was cheap muslin that she covered with a thick white apron tied around her waist. In Paris she knew the style of dress was actually popular. It was called a chemise à la reine, named after Queen Marie Antoinette's fondness for all things pastoral. Only, Belle truly had fed chickens and washed laundry in hers. She thumbed the stubborn stain that had never come out, the one that Gaston had given her when he splashed her skirts with mud after his ill-fated proposal.

Lio's voice made her jump. "Don't be mad at me, but I think I prefer you like this." She looked up to the corner of the mirror to see him standing in the doorway behind her, dressed for Versailles.

"Only if you won't be mad at me when I say you look ridiculous." A curled white wig covered his beautiful chestnut hair, thick white powder coated his warm skin, and his outfit mirrored Bastien's in its extravagance and quality. He wasn't her Lio any more – this Lio belonged to Versailles.

He approached her bashfully, joining her to stand before

the mirror. "I don't even recognise myself."

But despite her misgivings, she could see how princely he looked, how easily he would be accepted by Versailles's courtiers, and how different they really were, standing side by side.

Lio seemed to read the discord on her face. "It's only temporary, Belle." He pressed one hand to the small of her back and used the other to gesture at himself. "All of this will be gone as soon as I'm back in King Louis's good graces, I swear to you."

"It fits you so well, mon coeur," she remarked.

He pulled on the lapels of his forest-green frock coat. "It would seem we are built the same, Bastien and I."

"No, I mean the whole thing. You look like a prince."

He raised a brow at her. "I was a prince before I put on a wig and powdered my face."

"Yes, of course." But she couldn't shake the feeling that Lio was inching closer to the person he was supposed to be, and all the while she had been straying further from her true self.

Lio changed the subject. "Are you excited to explore Paris?"

She tried to shake her worries away. "Very."

"And you're sure you don't want to come with us to Versailles? Because I don't care what Bastien thinks. If you want to come, you're—"

"I promise you I don't." She reached for his hand. "It's better this way."

Now Lio wouldn't have to be ashamed of his common, provincial wife, and Belle wouldn't have to pretend she couldn't hear whatever insults were lobbed her way. She was always going to be more comfortable in the streets and markets and gardens of Paris.

Bastien appeared in her doorway, freshly powdered and with a garish beauty mark painted on his cheek. "The carriage is ready." His tone was ominous, and Belle couldn't help but laugh at his severity.

Bastien gave her a questioning look, and she took a deep breath to suppress her laughter. "Oh, come, now. It's Versailles, not prison."

Bastien sniffed. "Oh, but the king's court is its own kind of prison, Belle." They began to descend the grand staircase. "France's nobility is in chains, madame. They may be gilded, but they are chains nonetheless."

Belle was quite sure any number of France's working class would have happily been shackled by the gilded chains of the nobility, but she held her tongue as they exited the duc's home. Bastien immediately ducked into the awaiting carriage while Lio paused, taking Belle's hands in his.

"We shouldn't be too long. King Louis must have matters to attend to that are more pressing than a wayward prince étranger."

Bastien laughed coldly from within the carriage. "Don't be so sure, Cousin. You may find that Louis has plans for you yet."

Lio rolled his eyes and pulled Belle a bit closer. "To hell with the king and his plans," he whispered in her ear. "We've got plans of our own."

Bastien poked his head out of the carriage window. "Would you like us to drop you somewhere, Belle?"

The thought of spending time in an enclosed space with the duc was unappealing, to say the least. "No, thank you, Bastien. I'm happy to explore on foot."

He looked her up and down. "Yes, I'd imagine you are."

Belle made a face at him as he disappeared again. Lio squeezed the hand he hadn't relinquished yet.

"Honestly, Lio. I'll be fine. Look." She pulled a book from the deep pocket of her dress. "If I find a garden and a patch of shade, my day will be made."

Lio kissed her forehead. "Wish me luck with Louis."

She opened her mouth to tell him he didn't need it, but paused. The truth was, Lio would need a great deal of luck to make it through Versailles.

"Good luck," she whispered, truly meaning it.

Lio grinned, but she could see the worry that hid behind his smile. He stepped into Bastien's carriage, and the footman closed the door behind him. The horses started up, and soon the carriage was winding down Bastien's laneway.

Belle's heart hammered in her chest as she watched them go. Breaking the curse had tethered her to Lio in ways she didn't yet understand. When she watched him die as the Beast, defeated by Gaston's dagger and hatred for something he didn't understand, a part of her died with him. And when she wept over his body, she whispered in his ear the truth she had been denying. He came back to her as Lio, his body whole and his mind sound, and that part of herself that she lost was similarly restored. They pieced each other back together, and now they were bound as one.

She felt sick when she thought of him facing the trials of Versailles alone. *Not alone,* she thought. *He has his cousin with him.*

But Belle still didn't know what to think of the duc de Vincennes. She wasn't sure if he would be an ally to Lio or if he had ulterior motives. She supposed it was best to assume that everyone in Louis's court did. She certainly didn't plan to make friends with any nobles now that she had married one.

The carriage disappeared from sight, and Belle tried to smother the worry that roiled in her gut. She was in Paris, a city that had lived on inside her heart since she left it, the place she had dreamed of when she felt the constraints of her provincial life most acutely.

It wasn't as if there was anything she could do for Lio now.

• • •

A weight lifted from Belle's shoulders as soon as she walked through Bastien's gate. It was like stepping into another world. His courtyard was so insulated that the noises of Paris didn't reach it, lending it a false sense of tranquillity amid the chaos of the city. She hoped Lumière was enjoying his time to himself. She had a feeling he had more than a few past paramours to visit.

Despite the filth of the streets ruining her boots and hem, Belle felt more like herself than she had in weeks. Back home, she had become something larger than Belle. Whether they knew she broke the curse or not, the people of Aveyon viewed Belle as their saviour. Some thought she had rescued them from an inattentive, reclusive prince; far fewer knew she had broken the curse that had been drowning the kingdom for a decade. Everyone wanted her to be their princess, to embrace her new role to the fullest extent.

But she couldn't bring herself to do that, not yet at least.

This trip was to be a reprieve. Here she was anonymous, just someone going about their day. Her plain dress made her invisible. She could enjoy Paris the way she'd always imagined, before returning to her new life and hoping it fit her better after some time away from it.

She turned onto rue de l'Université and spotted the Seine in between buildings. She was heading to the Palais-Royal, armed with the piecemeal knowledge she had collected from travellers through Aveyon who told her Philippe, the duc d'Orléans, had opened the gardens to the public some years before. Belle had heard tell of the exchange of ideas that occurred there, and of the bookshops and cafés tucked into the covered arcades that surrounded the gardens. She had spent long nights imagining herself there, attending salons and taking part in lively debates with a more open-minded crowd than she could find in Aveyon. Each step she took was like walking through both a memory and a dream.

"Madame." A woman stepped in her path, reaching a hand out in front of her. "Could you spare a sou? My children are hungry." Her skin was a sickly pallor, and the dark circles of exhaustion under her eyes were deep. Two children hid among her skirts, hunger shrinking their forms. Belle couldn't prevent the memories of her childhood from flooding into her mind. She had once known the ceaseless gnawing of an empty belly. When her mother was sick, Maurice had used every bit of money they had paying for physicians and tonics to no avail, since her illness took her anyway. Belle and her father went through a season of lean nights – sometimes sharing only a heel of bread and some watered-down broth – both feeling the pain of losing Belle's mother more acutely than their hunger pangs. Spring came, and at last Maurice was able to bring one of his inventions to a nearby fair and sell it for half of what it was worth in order to fill their bellies.

She reached for her coin purse without hesitation and handed the woman a twelve-livre coin, enough for her to feed herself and her children for the days to come.

The woman's eyes widened in disbelief, but she accepted

the coin quickly. "Mon Dieu, thank you, madame, thank you."

Belle wanted to say something, but the woman and her children vanished into the crowd like wisps of smoke, and she stood still for the first time since leaving Bastien's home. The chaos of Paris continued to swirl around her, but beneath it, on the edges, she saw poverty unlike any she had seen before. Exhausted mothers and wailing babies, emaciated men, orphaned children, all collected on the seams and in the alleys of the city. Each of them wore their starvation plainly – in the number of ribs poking through thin tunics, in the shadowed clefts of skin pulled too tightly across collarbones, in the cheeks sunk deep into their skulls.

Without thinking, Belle wandered into the closest alley and began passing out the coins from her purse. She tried to talk to each person she met, but she was soon swarmed by children with outstretched hands. She was happy to press a coin into them, but she wished she could do more. Money was a temporary solution; these people needed long-term aid, work, shelter – things she couldn't readily give to them. Guilt ate away at her. She was married to a prince and yet she had no power to end their suffering.

A shout echoed down the alley, scattering the children. Belle turned to see a group of soldiers armed with muskets nearly as long as they were tall. Their blue coats and red collars and cuffs with embroidered white braids marked them as Gardes françaises.

One of them stepped closer to her. "Madame, are you all right?"

She scoffed. "Why wouldn't I be?"

He gave her a pitying look. "One can never be too careful with needy peasants."

And then she realised that he thought her separate from them. She lived her whole life as a commoner, but since she'd married Lio, something about her marked her as different. She didn't know if it was the shine of her hair, or the fullness of her cheeks, but just as Bastien knew she wasn't noble, others now knew she wasn't common. It left her torn between two worlds, neither of which she truly belonged to.

A sudden swell of loud voices snapped the soldiers' attention back to the road behind them. Belle craned her neck to see what was causing the commotion. A large group of men were marching through the street towards the Palais-Royal, armed with nothing but their voices. She couldn't make out what they were shouting, but what they lacked in intelligibility they made up for in passion.

Curious, Belle followed the soldiers out of the alley and found herself swept up into the crowd. She looked from person to person and could find no commonality among them; they didn't all share a type of clothing that would mark their trade or their class. From what she could tell, they came from every stratum of Parisian society.

The sea of people crossed Pont Royal and spilled into the

palace gardens on the other side with startling efficiency. Any soldiers who had followed them were stopped at the gates by red-coated Gardes suisses who turned them away brusquely. Belle slipped in past them, as much a part of the crowd as anyone else, and found herself in a place she had spent years only imagining.

The garden was a throng of people. Groups large and small clustered around tables, shouting over one another to have their voices heard. To her left stood a man on a makeshift pulpit, surrounded by a host of eager listeners. He wore the short-skirted coat and long pantalon of a working man, but he commanded the attention of the hundreds of people gathered around him like someone with authority. Perhaps he was a bourgeois, she thought, one of the wealthier members of the Third Estate. Belle fought her way to the front of the crowd and strained to hear what the man was saying.

"And King Louis hides away in Versailles, caring very little about our starving children, and then he has the audacity to ask us for more. He calls the Estates of France to his palace and pretends the Third Estate will have an equal voice, but we have never been equal! Not even on the foreign battlefields where France's poorest sons fight and bleed and die for freedoms they themselves will never know." He paused and waited for the crowd to settle once more. "We must be united in our opposition; we must not separate until France has a constitution!"

The crowd rippled to life around Belle, but a man next to her spat at the feet of the worker, stunning the people into silence. He looked out of place in his white wig and culottes.

"Canaille," he hissed. *Scum.*

Only a few heartbeats elapsed before the crowd surged forward, united in anger. The man on the pulpit lifted his arms in the air.

"Calmez-vous," he implored before looking directly at the wigged man. "When France is washed clean of la noblesse, it is the Third Estate scum that will survive, monsieur."

Cheers drowned out the nobleman's reply, but Belle caught bits of the threat spilling from his lips. The crowd was tipping towards chaos. All at once, the appeal of the Palais-Royal vanished. Belle wanted to be anywhere but there, trapped in a group of raucous, angry men. She pushed her way out of the centre and hurried from the garden. A passing girl pressed a pamphlet in Belle's hands before she reached the gate. Belle was back across the Seine when she glanced at the front page and realised it was a political pamphlet, not unlike the ones she had hoarded back in Aveyon that had been written by the likes of Jean-Jacques Rousseau, Émilie du Châtelet, Olympe de Gouges and Nicolas de Condorcet. She hadn't read this one before.

What is the Third Estate? Everything.

She recalled Bastien's claims earlier that day, that the Third Estate were an annoyance to the king and nothing more.

Merely rabble-rousers, he had assured them. She looked back to the pamphlet.

What has it been until now in the political order? Nothing.

What does it ask? To be something.

From what Belle understood of French politics, it was a deceptively simple desire. In France, the power was concentrated in the hands of the clergy and the nobility. Peasants had nothing. It had been that way for centuries. But what if they could take some for themselves? What if the Third Estate became *something*?

It would change the world.

It was bold for so-called rabble-rousers, she thought. But Bastien had already told them that the Third Estate had transformed into something new: the National Assembly. And King Louis had thus far been unable to quash it. To Belle, that sounded like power.

On her walk home, she realised she had been wrong. Paris was nothing like she remembered it. The city was a powder keg, and the peasants shouting for revolution in the gardens of the Palais-Royal held matches in their hands.

Belle may have grown up a peasant, and she may not have taken the title that was afforded to her, but she didn't think either fact would be enough to convince the people of Paris that she wasn't like the nobles they reviled.

She was a girl married to a prince. She lived in a castle and wanted for nothing. In that moment, as she thought back to the woman who had begged for coin to feed her hungry children, Belle wasn't sure she could convince herself of it either.

CHAPTER FOUR

On the walk back to Bastien's home, Belle was lost in contemplation.

She found herself agreeing with the pamphlet in her hands, written by Abbé Emmanuel Sieyès. She thought the Third Estate deserved equal representation and that their votes should be counted by heads, not by estates. Belle had read enough of the Enlightenment thinkers to know where she stood on matters such as equality and freedom for all members of society, not just noblemen. And yet, she was married to a prince, so a part of her felt like her voice didn't matter or shouldn't be counted at all.

On the other hand, she wasn't foolish enough to think that the revolution they were calling for would be free of violence. France had been part of the bloody war for independence in America. The men shouting for revolution in the gardens of the Palais-Royal were not shouting for peaceful talks or bloodless transitions. She recalled the threat she had heard earlier: *When France is washed clean of la noblesse, it is the Third Estate scum that will survive.* She was not naive. Belle knew that the Third Estate was expecting violence, just as she knew the king would respond in kind. Once the embers of revolution were lit, nothing could stop it. Aveyon was not like the roiling city of Paris, but borders would not stop a fire such as that.

A guard peered at her dismissively from behind the duc's gate, noting her dress and dirty boots. He was about to leave her there.

"Hello," she called out to him. "I'm a guest of the duc's."

He looked at her incredulously and waved another man over, one she recognised from earlier. They conferred for a moment before the first man opened the gate.

"Apologies, madame," he muttered as she walked through. She didn't have the energy to care that he didn't think she belonged at the duc's manor, not when she didn't think she belonged either.

The house was larger even than she remembered. She meant to walk back to her room but got lost along the way in Bastien's labyrinth of a home. She wandered aimlessly until she found something familiar: the duc's office. She walked in and sat on a plush divan, intending to wait for him and Lio to return rather than pester a poor servant to help her find her way.

It wasn't long before Belle was perusing Bastien's shelves. They were filled with the typical dull tomes one would expect to find in the home of an aristocrat – the recorded lineages of France's noblesse, a pristine copy of Hobbes's *Leviathan* that

Belle was sure Bastien had never once cracked open, bound hymnals collecting dust – and she was unsurprised to learn that he was as boring as she had assumed. She abandoned the shelves. Her feet ached. She was unused to walking as much as she had that day. Her time in Lio's castle had made her soft. She had the feet of a noblewoman now. She made a mental note to tell Lio of her wish to expand the castle gardens so she could tend to vegetables and pigs and chickens like she used to.

She couldn't help but move to Bastien's imposing desk and pull out the leather chair to sit upon it. She swung her legs up onto the mahogany surface like she had watched him do earlier that day and rested her hands on the back of her head. From here, the duc must have felt very powerful indeed. There was a portrait across the room she hadn't noticed earlier. It was of Bastien's father, the former duc de Vincennes, and two young boys Belle guessed were Bastien and Lio, painted sometime before Lio left Paris for good, judging by their ages.

The painting was a fine work and would have cost a fair bit to commission. She could see that Bastien took after his father, though the painted version of the elder duc lacked his son's knowing smirk. Young Lio appeared to be as haughty as his cousin. Belle didn't recognise the look of cold superiority on his face. This young version of Lio was about to learn he had lost his mother. Her heart ached for him, and she found she didn't want to look at it any longer.

When she pushed her knees back under the desk, she

knocked them on the underside of it, releasing a mechanism and revealing a hidden drawer. She paused before her curiosity got the better of her, and she pulled the drawer out to find a hidden trove of documents. On top were papers published by Rousseau, Descartes, Locke, Montesquieu and Voltaire, the philosophers Belle had spent years studying. She shuffled through the papers and noted that a lot of them were revolutionary pamphlets like the one that had been pressed into her hands at the gardens of the Palais-Royal. She was no stranger to pamphlets, but these were authored by people she had never heard of. Information was often slow to trickle to Aveyon, if at all. She had to stop herself from tucking a few into her pockets. She found bound folios labelled *Cahiers de Doléances*, and inside were the demands of the Third Estate, assembled for the États généraux that King Louis had called earlier that year, the one that France's peasants had called unfair, setting off the establishment of the National Assembly. Was Bastien gathering information for the king? Or was he sympathetic to the cause?

She was so absorbed in reading from the trove of pamphlets that she didn't hear Lio enter the room.

"Belle." He spoke from right over her shoulder, making her jump. She slammed the hidden drawer shut and turned. Her husband was ashen, and not just because of the smear of white powder on his face, now faded so that patches of skin showed through. Defeat lay heavy on his bones, and Belle's mind flew to the worst possibilities.

"What is it? What happened?"

He sank into the chair she had vacated and spoke like he hadn't heard her at all. "I remember Versailles being lavish, I remember being stunned by it, but, Belle, mon Dieu, it was overwhelming."

She could only imagine the reception a long-lost prince étranger would have garnered. Lio would have bristled at the gawks and whispers from the hawkish courtiers, to say nothing of the king himself. "Were you the talk of the king's court?"

He shook his head. "I barely saw any courtiers. We were made to wait for Louis in some forgotten set of chambers. I thought Bastien was going to murder the valet who left us there."

"I can imagine." Bastien was not a man accustomed to being forgotten.

"And then Louis was nothing like the Louis I remember. He was soft, weak, paranoid. He didn't care to know where I had been for ten years. All he did was make demands."

"Demands?"

He tore the wig from his head and threw it on the desk. "France is facing a financial crisis."

She waited for him to elaborate, and when he didn't, she placed a hand on his shoulder. "We know; Bastien told us."

"I didn't think it was quite so dire. Bastien has a way

of making everything sound inconsequential. It's a gift, really." He sighed and ran his hands through his matted hair. "It would seem that Louis has spent his reign gifting tax exemptions to disgruntled nobles, while calling on France's peasants to fund America's war for independence. And then he banned promotion to officer from the lower ranks of the Royal Army, effectively preventing any commoner from advancing via loyal service and brave deeds. And he and Marie Antoinette spend and spend and spend without consequence. I don't understand how he didn't see what the outcome would be. It's worse than we thought, Belle, and the king wants my help."

She leaned against the desk and folded her arms over her chest. "With what?"

He pulled at his collar. "My undying loyalty and support in the form of money for his coffers and men to bolster his ranks."

Belle tried to collect her thoughts. "Lio, we can't." It was all she could muster. The idea of sending Aveyonian men to serve in France, a place they didn't know, ruled by a king who didn't give a damn about them, was unthinkable. So few of the men who had left their kingdom to fight in America had ever returned, and if France was tipping towards a bloody revolution, it was up to Belle and Lio to protect their people from it, not offer them up as some sort of payment.

"I know, but Louis is desperate for more troops. He's

convinced that the peasants are going to rise up against him." He said it like the prospect was ridiculous.

"I think they will." She uncrossed her arms and stood. "I think France is on the verge of civil war."

He looked up at her incredulously. "What do you mean?"

"I went to the Palais-Royal today, and it's chock-full of people making speeches criticising the king and calling for revolution. Look." She reached into her pocket and pulled out the Sieyès pamphlet. "I think your cousin is mistaken. I think the Third Estate is about to become *something*."

Lio quickly read over the pamphlet before setting it down on the desk, looking dejected. "I don't think I can refuse him."

"You'd send troops here?"

"I don't want to, but what can I say? The king of France didn't care to know what one of his allies was doing during ten years of silence. All he cared about was my money and my soldiers. What can I do? Refuse him? On what grounds?"

"It's not our fight, Lio, Aveyon isn't like France."

"I know, but as a principality, we're subject to its laws and its king. And Bastien was right: Louis had forgotten Aveyon. Our tax rate has been unchanged for over a decade. If I anger him, he'd be well within his rights to increase the rate retroactively and call upon our people to pay the difference. I can't do that to them."

They sat there in stunned silence, both of them too tired to come up with a clever way out of their predicament. Belle wanted nothing more than to take a long bath and sleep the day away. Perhaps everything would look different in the morning.

"Well, I'm going to need a large tea and an even larger nap if we're going to be up all night finding a way out of this," she said. Lio's face fell. "What?"

"I forgot to tell you Bastien is hosting a dinner in our honour. He invited all of the courtiers I grew up with." He spoke as if the words were poison.

"Surely you don't mean tonight."

"They've already begun to arrive." He took her hands in his. "Bastien cannot resist the opportunity to be the centre of attention. I promise it will all be over soon."

He looked so exhausted by the events of the day that Belle couldn't bring herself to tell him the truth she was beginning to feel in her heart – that it had only just begun.

CHAPTER FIVE

Dinner passed in a blur of high-throated laughter and the occasional sneer from Bastien's numerous aristocratic friends. The immense dining room table all but sagged under the weight of the dishes: tureens of beef madrilène, bisque of shellfish and cold cucumber soup mingled with heaving platters of beef ragout, scallops smothered in puréed chestnuts, salmon en sel and ramequins of cheese soufflé. All the dishes perspired in the July evening heat under the glow of a thousand candles, but thanks to the duc's priorities, the champagne was pleasantly cool.

The only respite she found from the constant inanity of dinner came from her seatmate, Charles Louis, the marquis de Montcalm, whom she quickly discovered was a close friend of Olympe de Gouges, a playwright and activist whom Belle deeply admired.

"Where did you meet the Madame de Gouges?" she asked between bites of ragout.

The marquis dabbed at his mouth with his napkin. "I believe our first meeting was at a salon hosted by the Madame de Montesson. Olympe was as vibrant as one could imagine, advocating passionately for human rights and against the slave trade. She held the room in her thrall."

Belle hung on his every word. "I should very much like to meet her one day."

The marquis smiled. "I am certain that could be arranged, madame."

The prospect thrilled her. She hadn't expected to find someone like Charles Louis at Bastien's dinner, but she was glad she had.

The dinner was a more refined affair than Belle had ever experienced, and it did nothing to prepare her for the barely restrained indulgence that came after. Courses were presented and removed before she even had a chance to work out which of her six forks matched which type of dish, but it didn't matter; she didn't have much of an appetite. Her head ached from the weight of the wig Bastien had insisted she wear, proclaiming the state of her hair to be outside the bounds of acceptability after a day of walking Paris's streets. It was a towering, rolled thing, dyed a shade or two darker than Belle's own hair, with ringlets framing her face. Her itchy scalp begged for mercy, and Belle did her best with the handle of her smallest fork when she thought no one was looking.

Once the last of the smelly cheeses had been taken away, Belle realised that the excesses of the meal were for show. Hardly anyone ate more than she did, leaving ample room for after-dinner champagne and the heartiest meal of the night – gossip.

Bastien paraded Belle around like an exotic animal, introducing her as a commoner turned princess, evidently a novelty none of the guests had ever encountered before. Explaining to them that she was not, in fact, a princess proved tedious.

"But you're married to a prince," remarked a woman with deeply rouged cheeks.

"Indeed I am," Belle replied patiently. "But I did not take a title when I married."

"Why not?" the woman asked, her voice high.

"It's not something I've ever desired," Belle offered weakly, knowing this noblewoman didn't care to know the true complexities of Belle's feelings on the matter.

Lio was across the room, surrounded by friends and acquaintances he hadn't seen since childhood. Her husband had done away with the white paint and wig Bastien had insisted he wear to Versailles, and yet he was still confined to an outfit of his cousin's choosing, and unused to the ruffles and lace of Parisian finery. His discomfort reminded her of the time Lumière had wrangled the Beast into something of a courtly ensemble.

Even rough around the edges, Lio still looked princely standing there among them, shooting her apologetic glances when he could, knowing she was probably tallying all the absurdities she'd been made to endure thus far. He owed her. She had half a mind to demand he present her with another library for her troubles.

The liquor flowed freely, and the guests, while absurd in their conduct, were pedigreed beyond compare. Lio had spent the dinner whispering names to her under his breath.

That's the comte de Chamfort. The last time I saw him he was beating a servant with his walking stick for spilling tea when we were boys.

That's the Mademoiselle de Vignerot, she's been betrothed to an Austrian archduke since birth.

Belle would have rather been anywhere else. Bastien's guests were an unpleasant blend of immensely rich and disturbingly aloof. She knew in any other circumstance they would reject her outright because of her status as a commoner, former or not. But she was *interesting*, and to a roomful of courtiers who spent most of their time in the protocol-laden court of King Louis, being interesting was a far greater virtue than simply being rich or noble. They peppered her with questions about the most mundane aspects of growing up a peasant, and they were utterly enthralled by her answers.

What was it like to make your own bread?

Did you truly mend your own clothing?

You said your father is an inventor? How quaint!

She felt as though she was on display in a museum, but she couldn't escape their queries. So she fought back the best way she knew how.

"Surely I'm not the only commoner you've ever spoken to?" she asked the Mademoiselle de Vignerot, a girl a few years younger than Belle who wore a gown so encrusted in jewels it seemed impossible to breathe in. She had been engrossed by Belle's tales of peasantry for nearly a quarter of an hour while she fanned herself.

"Madame, we do our best to avoid them," she confessed with mock sincerity. "Though if they are anything like you, then perhaps we are missing out." She said it like she knew it wasn't true, and all the ladies clustered around her howled with laughter. To them, Belle was an oddity: a peasant who was polite enough to dine with them without catastrophe. She didn't fit with their preconceived notions of how a peasant should behave, so they treated her like a rarity. It was absurd; Belle herself had grown up with many smart and worldly commoners, and met more than a few ignorant and dim nobles in just one night.

She walked away from the gaggle of them and found a hiding place on the other side of one of the pillars that lined the edge of the room. She took some deep breaths and tried her best to convince herself not to run away from the dinner entirely.

"That bad, is it?"

She turned to find she wasn't the only person hiding from the guests. A tall woman with warm brown skin and tightly curled black hair leaned against the wall with a flute of champagne held close to her mouth. She was close in age to Belle, perhaps a bit younger, but she possessed a commanding posture and wore a dress so simple in its design it only served to make her stand out all the more.

Belle wasn't often lost for words. "I'm sorry?"

"Your guests." She gestured around the curve of the pillar. "Monstrous bores, aren't they?"

Belle's heart warmed at the insult, but she didn't know the woman she was speaking to, and an unkindness lobbed at those she found insufferable could quickly turn into one aimed at her. "I'm sorry—" she started.

"You keep saying that."

Belle cleared her throat and commanded her cheeks not to flush. "I don't believe we've met."

The girl drained the flute. "I'd hardly warrant an introduction." She wiped her mouth on the back of her hand and extended it outward. "I'm Marguerite, the Mademoiselle de Lambriquet, as it were."

Belle took her hand and found herself dipping into a curtsy without meaning to. Marguerite laughed and held her up by the shoulders. "Please, as the wife of a prince, even without your title you rank much higher than a daughter of a penniless duc."

Belle's mouth eased into a smile. "You might be the first person in Paris who has spoken frankly with me."

"That I can believe. Look." She gestured out past the pillar that shielded them. "See that *flagorneur* by your husband's cousin?" Belle guessed the man Marguerite was calling a sycophant was the one she had scarcely seen away from Bastien's side that night, and his only true rival in pomposity. "That is my brother, Aurelian, the marquis de Lambriquet." He was a slight bit older than Marguerite and ostentatious in all the ways his sister was subdued. "He despises Bastien and his *shallow frivolity*" – she pitched her voice to an unbearably nasal tone in what Belle imagined was an imitation of her brother – "but he sees the duc de Vincennes as his surest ticket to our father's title and holdings."

Belle looked away from the peacockish marquis and over at Marguerite. "I'm sorry, when did he pass?"

"Pass? Oh, no, my father is alive and well. He simply refuses to attend Versailles and so he is an outcast with no appointments or influence, taxed to the hilt because he receives no subsidies he would be entitled to if he took part. It is the source of Aurelian's greatest shame." Marguerite's expression was smug as she pulled another flute of champagne seemingly out of thin air. "My brother is hoping Bastien can help sway the king to strip my *ungrateful* father of his title and bestow it upon his son."

"Why would Bastien be able to convince the king of anything?"

She looked at Belle as though the answer were obvious.

"Bastien and Louis are thick as thieves, madame; everyone knows that."

Belle was about to press her for more information, when their hiding place was discovered. The Mademoiselle de Vignerot popped out from behind the pillar and planted her hands on her hips.

"Here she is!" she cried out, clutching Belle's forearm and pulling her back into the scrutiny of the dining room. "We thought we lost you, madame."

"What a pity that would have been," Belle replied, glancing back at Marguerite with a grin. But her tone went unnoticed among her companions.

Mademoiselle Dupont handed her a glass of champagne. "We were just wondering when you plan on making your debut at Versailles. Virginie guessed that you'll be waiting for the autumn so as to give Rose Bertin enough time to craft for you an entire wardrobe, seeing as you'll be needing one."

Belle ignored the insult and focused instead on making her intentions abundantly clear. "I won't be attending court."

The group of ladies fell silent, each wearing expressions of true bafflement. The Mademoiselle de Vignerot spoke first. "But, madame, surely you won't be returning to Aveyon. It is only natural for a princesse étrangère to find a place at court. The queen especially will demand that you are presented to her."

Belle drew herself up a bit higher. "The people of Aveyon

suffered while my husband was ill, so our place is with them."

No one seemed to understand the sentiment. Mademoiselle Dupont spoke as if Belle were a child. "But, madame, Aveyon will seem so small after your spell in Paris. What is it that you will *do* with your time there?"

"Serve my people, of course."

"Yes, but once that is complete?"

Belle didn't know how to respond. She didn't know how to explain to a group of nobles that she didn't want a life that resembled theirs. Charitably, she could understand that Bastien's friends had grown up in a very different world than she had, and that perhaps she wouldn't recognise herself if she had been similarly privileged. But she also thought that the poverty she had witnessed on the streets of Paris that day was impossible to ignore unless the nobles preferred their ignorance. She worried she lacked the diplomacy required to maintain decorum with Bastien's guests.

"Belle is planning to host a series of salons," said Lio, appearing out of nowhere to fill her silence. It had been his first promise to her, in those wild days right after they broke the curse, when they talked feverishly about their most cherished dreams and whispered their deepest fears to each other. Back then, Belle's only fear had been her own ignorance. She had told him of her wish to travel to Paris and attend a salon herself, perhaps one that counted some of her favourite philosophes and encyclopédistes among its members.

He had said her dream was too small and that she herself should host one.

The Mademoiselle de Vignerot smiled politely. "What will the subject be?"

"Oh, everything," said Belle. Her enthusiasm elicited laughter, but she was entirely serious.

The comte de Chamfort cleared his throat, his lips curling into a sneer. "That is very broad, madame. Surely you have a more specific interest? My parents used to attend the famous Bout-du-Banc literary salon in Paris, but that was a very long time ago."

Belle gave him her best patient smile. "I don't wish to be limited, monsieur. My salons will invite scientists, philosophers, inventors, novelists, really anyone in possession of a good idea."

The comte guffawed. "Why on earth would you do such a thing?"

"To learn from them, monsieur. I would have thought the reason obvious."

Marguerite snorted into her glass. Belle sipped her drink as Lio placed his hand on the small of her back. She didn't know if it was meant to calm her down or encourage her.

"Whatever for?" the comte asked with the menacing air of a man discovering he was the butt of a joke. "Everything that is worth learning is already taught."

"To whom?" Belle felt the heat rising in her cheeks.

"Strictly the wealthy sons of wealthier fathers?" Some of Bastien's guests gasped, they themselves being the children of France's aristocracy, but Belle was heartened when she saw Marguerite smile encouragingly. "I believe that education is a right, monsieur, and one that has long been reserved exclusively for the most privileged among us. My salons will reflect the true reality."

"Which is what, madame?" Marguerite prompted eagerly.

Belle's heart rattled in her chest. "That scholarship is the province of any who would pursue it."

The silence was deafening, and she wondered if she had gone too far. It certainly hadn't been her intention to speak so forcefully of her beliefs with Bastien's noble guests.

Charles Louis, the marquis she had spoken with at dinner, gave her an approving nod. "How very modern, madame."

The comte chuckled unkindly as heat rose to his cheeks. He looked to Lio. "You should be careful, sire."

"And why is that, monsieur?" Lio's tone was neutral, but the room stiffened nonetheless.

"It would seem you've married a revolutionary."

Belle nearly dropped her glass. Her instinct was to fiercely defend herself, but she understood that reacting in such a manner would only serve to convince the comte that he was right about her. Women had to be emotionless in order to be taken seriously by men like him, and Belle was nothing if not passionate about her beliefs.

Lio removed his hand from the small of her back and straightened. "Only a monarch truly undeserving of their crown would fear a learned populace."

The comte was dangerously red-cheeked. "I should have expected nonsense like that from a prince willing to lower himself by marrying a peasant."

Gasps reverberated through the room, and Marguerite spoke before Belle or Lio had a chance to.

"She may be a peasant, monsieur, but she has a great deal more nobility than you ever will."

Her response was the perfect antidote to the comte's comment – Marguerite was noble and familiar to the crowd, so her rebuke elicited laughter and helped to defuse the situation. Belle squeezed Lio's hand and hoped he understood her silent plea that he say nothing.

Bastien met Belle's eye and gave her a tight, apologetic smile before clapping his hands together. "That's about as much talk of politics as I am willing to endure. Let's retire to the sitting room and open another bottle, shall we?"

She was grateful when he didn't insist that she follow. His guests were eager to move past that hiccup and followed Bastien towards the other end of the room, leaving Belle and Lio with Marguerite.

"Thank you for saying that," said Belle.

Marguerite nodded. "It was nothing, madame. I've been desperate for an excuse to put the comte in his place ever since he treated my friend boorishly at a garden party."

Lio gave her a small bow and a smile and looked to Belle. "Shall we take this opportunity to escape?"

"Absolutely."

Lio took her hand, and she looked over to Marguerite, feeling a pang of regret at leaving her on her own. Marguerite seemed to read it on her face.

"Do not worry about me, madame." Marguerite winked. "I am used to them."

Lio began to pull Belle away. "It was a pleasure to meet you," she called over her shoulder, knowing that she wouldn't meet another woman like her anytime soon.

"Likewise," Marguerite returned before downing another champagne.

She and Lio raced through Bastien's halls, putting as much distance between themselves and the guests as they could. His hand urged her forward, and when she looked up to meet his eye, they both dissolved into the kind of feverish laughter that could not be explained. But despite the levity that moment of absurdity provided, his anger had returned in full force by the time they were back at their chambers.

"I can't believe he spoke about you like that right to our faces."

They stepped into the room, and Belle opened the windows, hoping the cool air would wash away their hot tempers. "Can't you?"

Lio ignored the question. "And I used to enjoy their company! In fact, this was once my future," he said, gesturing to the room around them. "Could you imagine if I had never left Paris? I'd be as bad as the rest of them. No, I'd be worse, because I rank above them and that sort of nonsense used to matter to me."

"Instead, you're an outsider like me."

"How do you mean?" he asked distractedly.

"Well, I am on account of my being a peasant. None of Bastien's friends are ever going to see me as anything more than an oddity. And you're an outsider because you see things differently now. You're not the boy they knew; you're a man they don't recognise. Something marks you as separate, and they won't ever understand it."

"Because I was cursed." It wasn't a question, and Belle knew she had to tread carefully.

"It's more than that. The curse forced you to change, but the transformation was yours alone."

"Not just mine." He stepped to her and brought her hands to his chest.

Heat rose to her cheeks, but she leaned into the warmth. Lio tilted her chin up and kissed her, sending a shiver down her spine despite the summer heat. She pulled her hands from his and wrapped them around his neck, twining her fingers in his hair, trying to close any distance between them. Every kiss was like their first – capable of wrecking her and healing her in equal measure. A soft growl escaped his lips. She pulled away and looked up, watching as his blue eyes softened.

"I was in that darkness for ten years before you gave me a reason to seek the light," he whispered.

They kissed again.

• • •

The moon shone through the window that night. They were both exhausted, but neither Belle nor her husband could sleep.

"This has to be nicer than ours," Lio remarked, pushing his hand into the plush down-stuffed mattress underneath them.

"I am not surprised to discover the duc de Vincennes has expensive taste in mattresses."

He rolled over to his side of the bed and sighed. "I don't know how I'm going to get out of supplying Louis with troops and aid. With any luck, the Third Estate or the National Assembly or whatever they're calling themselves now will dissolve thanks to infighting and a lack of organisation."

Belle eyed him from across the bed. "They have more support than you think, Lio."

"Really? Everyone I spoke with tonight said they were nothing more than toothless agitators looking for trouble."

"Of course they did. We were dining with France's aristocracy. Did you think they'd lend credence to the people who are fighting for equality?"

"You don't mean to tell me that *you* support them?"

Belle shifted in bed to face him as she selected her words carefully. "I certainly don't support violence as a means to an end, but I cannot deny that I think equality is worth fighting for."

"Of course, but to attempt to force it? To destroy the very apparatus they could use to bring about change?"

"What other methods would you have them use, Lio? Peasants don't have a voice, and when they were finally given one, Louis made sure it was in appearance alone. He fears his own people so much he would go to war with them."

"You're probably right, as usual." He brought her hand up and pressed a kiss into her palm. "But I'm so exhausted I feel numb to everything. We both need to sleep."

Belle was never one to back away from a discourse on equality, but after the day they'd had, she found she was entirely willing to table it for the morning.

Even so, she lay awake long after Lio fell into a deep sleep.

The day had felt as long as a year. They had arrived in Paris only that morning, and so much had happened since then. Belle had been so excited to return to the city that had long occupied her heart, but now she felt a pang to leave it. Paris was making stark the differences between Belle and Lio, the ones they could pretend didn't exist in Aveyon – that he was noble, and she was a peasant, and their kind never mixed.

It had all seemed so simple after they broke the curse, when everything felt like a fairy tale. Back then, Belle would have said that their love would be enough to weather them through any storm, and she still believed it. But she hadn't anticipated that the storms would grow and multiply, or that she would find herself adrift, unsure of what side of the battle line she should stand upon.

A part of her feared that by marrying a prince and living in a castle, she would become someone she didn't recognise, someone like those ignorant courtiers who had access to the best books and educations money could buy but used them to make their worlds smaller.

And then another part of her feared that by resisting the change, she would move further and further away from Lio, and she didn't want that either.

Her heart belonged with Lio, but what about the rest of her?

Where would she be if she hadn't met him, and if the embers of revolution were stoked all the way to Aveyon? Would she be fighting alongside the men and women she had seen in the gardens of the Palais-Royal?

Tomorrow she would tell Lio of her desire to abandon the rest of their journey and make for home. At least outside of the city they could go back to ignoring what made them different. She got up and walked over to the open balcony. The moon lit up her view of Saint-Germain's mansions, but she could just make out the Seine, and beyond it, the rest of Paris, the part that belonged to the peasants.

She fell asleep trying to shake the feeling in her bones that she belonged there too, and that no marriage or title would ever change that.

CHAPTER SIX

The summons came before they finished breakfast.

Bastien sat at the head of the table with a sleep cap on his head and the night before weighing heavy on his shoulders. His guests had kept him up, only retreating to their carriages as the sun peeked above the horizon. He looked a decade younger without his face painted, but he bristled when Belle told him as much.

"That's not the compliment you think it is."

Belle shrugged. "I meant it as one all the same."

He rolled his eyes. "In Paris, the goal is not to look young, but rather to look *rich*."

"Then I guess it is both a compliment and an insult to say you look positively impoverished, Bastien."

He grimaced just as a servant appeared at his side with an envelope on a silver platter. He took it and waved the man away lazily. When he broke the seal, his eyes widened. "Cousin, get up." He wiped his mouth with a serviette. "You must rifle through my wardrobe once again and make yourself presentable."

"What for?" Lio moaned through a mouth full of toast.

"Your presence has been requested at Versailles. Louis wishes to negotiate with you over the next few days."

Lio dropped his fork. *"Days?"*

Bastien waved a finger. "Be grateful Louis is distracted of late. I've seen him summon courtiers for whole seasons." He turned his attention back to the letter and frowned. "He makes no mention of Belle."

Relief flooded her. If he had requested her presence, she wouldn't have been able to refuse, but because he had forgotten her altogether, she had an excuse to stay away. After a night spent with Bastien's friends, Belle had got a small taste of Parisian high society and found it detestable. She couldn't imagine spending any time at all in the gilded halls of Versailles.

But Lio did not sense her relief. "You should come with me, Belle. We are a team, and we should appear as one."

The request wasn't fair, and he knew it. But Belle was in no mood to compromise. "I cannot." The words were perhaps more forceful than she'd intended, but such was her desire to stay far away from the king's court. "I don't belong there, Lio. I will only hurt your cause."

Lio gave her a pleading look. "So I'm to face it alone?"

"You'll have Bastien," she offered hopefully.

"Sadly I am needed elsewhere, Cousin."

"All the more reason for Belle to join me."

Bastien steepled his fingers together. "Lio, I think Belle is right. Bringing her with you would only serve as a distraction. If you wish to negotiate in good faith, I suggest you go alone. And besides..." He paused. "If Belle wasn't mentioned in the summons, there might be a reason for it."

"You mean to say they are snubbing her?"

Bastien shrugged. "Is it really a snub if she'd rather drink from the Seine than join you?"

A crease formed on Lio's forehead. "I worry it isn't safe to wander the city any more. Belle witnessed a mob only yesterday."

"I am absolutely fine on my own," she replied. But the men kept talking.

"Belle will be more than safe here, well protected from any errant mobs."

"I do not require protection from my own people, Bastien." Belle kept her voice level but firm, and Lio's face fell.

"Belle, do you really think—"

"Truth be told," she interrupted, needing him to understand her. "I feel safer on the streets of Paris than I ever could in the palace of Versailles."

"Yes, you've made your hatred of the aristocracy abundantly clear." Bastien took a sip from his teacup. "Curious, then, that you married into it."

• • •

She lasted an hour before slipping away from Bastien's home.

Belle didn't think of it as escaping. She wasn't a prisoner and Bastien's staff hadn't been expressly told to keep her inside the walls. But still she sneaked away from the mansion like someone guilty of a crime far more serious than boredom.

Even Lumière had been roped into keeping watch over her, but she dispatched him with a request that he find her Paris's best macarons, knowing his devotion to the task would keep him away for a few hours at least.

The July heat made the air sticky and the scent of urine and smoke almost overwhelming, but she was happy to be free of Bastien's monument to excess. She didn't have a destination in mind; she was only seeking an escape. She worried if she stopped, she'd come to realise that what she was trying to escape was her new life. So she kept her feet moving and her mind as blank as possible.

She stepped lightly over puddles of refuse, weaving through crowds of peddlers and shoppers, dodging the fast-flying carriages of the rich, hunting for something she couldn't quite explain. She had left Bastien's home without a purpose, but now her steps felt guided by some unseen force. Instinct, she thought, though that didn't quite fit either. Something tugged at her, and she meant to find out why.

The edges of her vision became hazy as she plunged deeper into the city. Paris was not a place that Belle knew well, and she walked through the streets with an unearned determination, her sights set on something she didn't fully understand. She wondered why it didn't frighten her, but Belle had always been achingly curious about the unknown.

The city felt different than it had when they rode their carriage through it. It felt different still from yesterday's afternoon in the gardens of the Palais-Royal. Dressed in the plain gown that rendered her all but invisible once more, she was free to roam where she pleased, but gone was the wonder she had held on to from her childhood. Now Belle knew of the cracks and fractures, of the unrest brewing like a sickness in the crowded underbelly of the city. People seemed to gather on street corners and down alleys in numbers Belle had never seen before. The groups were made up of peasants and sans-culottes, people dressed in rags and those clothed in finer garments. Whispers filled the air. The city was on the cusp of something Belle wasn't sure she wanted to be a part of.

She turned onto a quieter street and stopped mid-stride as though frozen. She looked around, trying to ascertain what had made her come to rest. The buildings were old there, and seemed to stretch and lean over the road, stopping the sun from reaching her down at the bottom. The air was surprisingly cool, and there wasn't another soul in sight – a rarity in a city such as Paris. The silence and stillness struck her more than the chaos she had left a street over.

She turned to the shop immediately in front of her and felt a calmness settle in her bones. She was meant to be there, though she couldn't tell what sort of shop it was from the outside. She walked towards the entrance, her steps tapping on the cobbles and echoing through the street, and reached for the brass handle. At her touch, the door swung open and a bell chimed overhead. An errant breeze picked up behind her, ushering her into the shop.

The first thing she saw was her own face in a hundred different reflections. It was a jarring thing, to see herself so completely from every angle, some distorted and stretched, some cloudy with age, some only as reflective as glass. She watched as her expression shifted from confused to quizzical.

Belle had wandered into a shop of mirrors.

She looked around for a shopkeeper or other customers, but she was alone, and for some reason, that put her at ease. She stepped farther into the shop and let the door close behind her, ringing the bell above it once more. It was hard to determine the true size of the room, but it felt small even as beaming arcs of light danced across the space.

Belle walked over to some shelves in an effort to escape her own gaze but found they displayed a collection of smaller handheld mirrors, each with different, beautifully engraved frames. She was drawn to a silver one that reminded her of the mirror Lio had given to her when he was the Beast, the one that had shown her a vision of her ailing father. Belle's pain had been enough for the Beast to free her, setting them on a path that would end with a knife in his back and the destruction of the curse that shackled the kingdom.

Remembering the moment she lost the Beast was not easy for Belle. She had loved him. She loved Lio too, and though of course they were one and the same, it felt different somehow. The moment the Beast closed his eyes for the last time changed her. And though there were some happy memories from those enchanted months before, she didn't like to think of her time as a prisoner in the castle she now called home. But still the mirror seemed to call to her. Her heart raced as she reached out and grasped the silver handle, raising it up to eye level, half expecting it to show her a vision. But the mirror remained inert – it was not enchanted, and Paris was not Aveyon, and the curse had long been destroyed.

She breathed a sigh of relief and even allowed herself to feel silly for fearing a simple object, moving to put it back where it belonged just as a noise from behind startled her.

"Bonjour, madame."

Belle was surprised to hear a young voice, and even more so a woman's. She spun to find the shopkeeper – a woman only a bit older than she was, dressed in a sturdy gown and practical apron. Her skin was pale but warm, her long hair the colour of rich honey, her blue eyes striking in their depth. The shopkeeper looked on expectantly.

"Bonjour," Belle returned. "I hope I'm not disturbing you."

"Of course not," replied the woman, looking down at the mirror Belle still held in her hand. "What brings you to my shop today?"

Belle was unsettled by the woman's manner – she spoke as though she already knew the answer to her question but was only asking to seem polite. Belle turned her attention back to the mirror, feeling foolish for allowing the object to frighten her. "To be honest, I didn't mean to come here at all."

"Is that so?" asked the woman absently. She looked at the mirror and back at Belle. "You'll have more luck if you make a request of it."

Belle's stomach twisted at the thought. "A request?" But she knew exactly what the woman meant. The mirror from the curse hadn't done a thing until Belle asked it to show her father to her, like it was a conduit for magic. She took a step away from the shelf, but the woman placed her hand on Belle's shoulder, sending warmth through her.

"Much can be discovered in the reflection of one's heart's desire."

Her voice was warm and clear, and the words were a comfort to Belle, though she distantly thought she should be more fearful. A strange quietude had enveloped her, leaving room for the burning curiosity she should have buried. She held the mirror aloft once more and tried to think of a worthy question. She didn't need to see her father this time – she knew Maurice was safe, his letters had said as much, and so was everyone else she and Lio had left behind in Aveyon. She tried to think of something that would be useful to her, something that would set her on a new path. There was so much uncertainty in her life, and now she had a chance to find answers.

The woman was close to her now. "Perhaps, madame, you would like to know what life has in store for you." Her voice barely reached above a whisper.

Of course. "Show me my future," she demanded. It was precisely what she wished to know.

She wanted to see herself content in Aveyon, happy in her new life with Lio by her side. She thought if she could see that version of herself, then it would be easier for her to strive for it, even when she was restless for something more.

The mirror came alive in her hand as glowing tendrils of green light leaked from the surface onto her skin, just like the mirror the Beast had given her on the balcony of the West Wing. Her reflection faded from view, replaced with a vision of the castle she now called home. But there was something wrong. In this vision, Aveyon was burning.

People were marching on the walls with torches in their hands, screaming for blood. It was worse than when she had watched the people of her village mob the castle to kill the Beast. Those villagers were infected with fear, and they hadn't known they marched on their prince. But in the vision, Lio's own people were bent on destroying him.

She felt the heat of the torches, could hear the flames crackling as though she were there on that balcony facing the mob. It was all too much for her to bear. She wrenched free of the mirror's hold on her and took a deep breath like she was coming up for air. But every mirror in the shop displayed the same vision she tried to escape. The footsteps of the mob pounded through her, and their shouts, though muddled, filled her mind.

"No!" she screamed, dropping the mirror to the ground. It shattered into a thousand pieces. She covered her face with her hands, but all at once, the shop was silent. The assault was over.

Her breath came out rough and her head spun. She needed air.

The woman touched Belle's shoulder, and once more a wave of peace flooded through her, only this time Belle had the sense to cling to her dissipating panic, hoping to maintain clarity in the face of that strange magic.

The woman looked at her, a fire alight in her eyes. "What you saw is what will come to pass unless you and Prince Lio return to Aveyon at once."

"How do you know my husband?" Belle started before she had a chance to process what the woman had said. "What is that supposed to mean?" Her voice was hoarse.

"Precisely that," the woman replied. "It is a warning. A way to escape the coming storm."

Belle didn't want to hear it, especially not from a woman wielding a magic that bore a terrifying similarity to the magic that had choked Aveyon for ten years. The realisation that this magic was the same chilled her like an icy plunge, and the fear that had been slowly evaporating set into her bones all at once. She needed to be free of the shop and its strange power. She jerked away from the woman and felt relief as soon as they were parted.

The fire in the woman's eyes was fading, and she did nothing to stop Belle as she backed away. "I don't mean to frighten you, Belle, only to warn you." The woman's expression was difficult to read. She seemed almost hopeless. Curiosity tugged at Belle, but she was already through the door, tumbling out onto the street so quickly she fell to her knees. She stayed there for a moment, hoping for the world to stop spinning. It was all behind her now.

But now the narrow alley was no longer the quiet refuge it was before she'd wandered into the mirror shop. The noise and chaos she'd been escaping flooded her senses, no longer muffled by whatever sinister power had guided her to the shop.

She stood and brushed the dust from her dress, trying to ascertain if there was another way for her to get back to Bastien's home that would avoid the busy street, but she didn't know Paris well enough to feel confident in her sense of direction, and she was still shaken from what had happened in the shop. She just wanted to get away, and the only way out would be back through the mayhem.

She walked with purpose to the street, hoping her path home would be easy. But it was not to be. Just as she turned a corner, shards of glass cracked under her feet. Droves of shouting people marched shoulder to shoulder, waving their guns and fists above them. Acrid smoke filled her lungs, the scent of blood and gunpowder lay heavy in the air. The crowd carried violence with them. Some were wounded – a patchwork of bruises and cuts and scrapes over cheeks and scalps. Some were sprayed with blood that Belle had the sickening feeling didn't come from their own bodies. All of them were caught up in something much larger than themselves, something Belle wanted no part of.

Everywhere she looked, Paris was burning.

Belle couldn't have predicted that the small gatherings of people she had passed on her way to the mirror shop would have grown to a mob in such a short amount of time. She looked up at the sun and saw that it was much lower in the sky than she would have guessed. Was it possible that she had spent a great deal more time in the shop than she thought? Belle recalled the woman and her strange ability to put her at ease, understanding now that it was a kind of magic, and surely magic could explain the gaps in her memory and the passage of time.

She couldn't stay there, clutching a lamp post like an anchor. She had to get back to Bastien's. Back to Lio. Her stomach sank as she realised her only option was to get swept up in the crowd and hope she could pull away closer to Saint-Germain.

So she reluctantly let the crowd take her, feeling the hatred and anger coursing through the people like a wave. The heat weighed down on her, and the stench of the mob was overwhelming. She was drowning. Her lungs burned for more air, but the crowd was too much. She couldn't break free of it, and she didn't know where it was heading.

It was so much more than the sans-culottes calling for revolution in the gardens of the Palais-Royal, or the Third Estate demanding that their voices be heard. It was like Belle had slipped into the mirror shop and the world outside had irrevocably changed.

She tried to free herself from the mob, squeezing past angry men and woman, only to find herself pulled back in. She craned her neck to see ahead. There was a man at the front being led through the streets. He looked like a prisoner – his sweaty hair was pressed to his skull like a wig had recently covered it, his finely embroidered shirt was untucked and torn and speckled with blood, and his cheeks were red with rage.

They came to rest at last before a monument Belle recognised, the Hôtel de Ville, Paris's town hall. The man's captors pushed him to his knees. Belle couldn't make out what was being shouted.

"Who is that?" she asked the woman closest to her.

"Bernard-René Jourdan," she replied, giving Belle a look

that suggested she should have known the answer. "The marquis de Launay," the woman added when Belle didn't seem to recognise the name.

"Why is he being marched through the streets?"

She looked Belle up and down, searching for some sign she was perhaps an aristocratic infiltrator. Her face changed as she took in Belle's simple dress, the spot of mud on the pocket. Belle was one of them – in appearance, at least. "He's the governor of the Bastille. He didn't take kindly to us acquiring arms from his fortress."

So that was where the weapons had come from. The people she watched make speeches the day before had been armed only with their voices, but these people could use guns and cannons to change the world.

The woman watched Belle eye the weapons with disgust. "We didn't have a choice," she hissed. "We need to be ready for when the king sends his troops against us."

"I don't see any troops here," Belle replied, but the woman had already moved on. Another surge pushed Belle closer to the governor, until she was near enough to hear him beg for his life.

"Please, I did as you asked," the governor pleaded as Belle's blood ran cold. Several men held him to the ground. Mud thickly caked his knees. "You swore you'd spare my life if I capitulated."

The man pressing the barrel of his gun to the marquis's

head spat on the ground in disgust. "Just as you swore your garrison wouldn't fire on us?"

There was a thrum in the crowd, a current of rage that Belle could sense but couldn't escape. It didn't matter that the man was a marquis, or that oaths had been sworn to him. The rule of law had been reduced to ash. The crowd wanted blood.

"The marquis shot first!" cried out a man who held Bernard's shoulder down. "We don't owe traitors anything."

The thrum quickened. The crowd turned. Nothing would save him now.

Belle looked away from the mob with their fists and feet and knives and bayonets. She couldn't bear to witness what came next, but she heard it well enough as they took their anger at the king out on a man who perhaps didn't deserve it. Guilt gnawed at her as she pushed and shoved her way out of the thick of it, not caring to orient herself any more than she needed to in order to be free of the mob. The crowd cheered or cried, she didn't know. They were hungry for something, and the marquis was just the beginning, and what scared her the most was the fact that they were as afraid as they were angry. Fear was as much a motivator as hate. Fear made monsters out of men.

She pulled herself up onto the steps of a shop to catch her breath as screams echoed from the centre. She couldn't help but look that way, only to be met with the grisly sight of the marquis's severed head held aloft, his face frozen in wretched agony. She knew with stinging certainty that it was an image that would stay with her forever. She emptied her stomach on the cobblestones beneath her, and when she stood up, she froze, certain that she had seen someone familiar in the crowd.

She paused and swayed, unsteady on her feet as she tried to get a better look. She didn't see the butt of the errant bayonet coming, but she felt it connect to her temple. Belle fell hard to the ground. She held on for a few seconds, enough time to register the taste of dirt and blood mingling in her mouth, and then she was gone.

CHAPTER SEVEN

B elle awoke to the press of soft fabric on her cheek and the rumble of a carriage underneath her. She sat up with a start, trying to understand how she had got there.

"Belle, calme-toi." The last voice she was expecting to hear was Bastien's. The duc sat across from her, resting his chin upon his ivory cane. His skin was free of the garish white paint he never left his home without, his hair uncovered and loose around his shoulders, and his clothing so plain and muted she suspected he had borrowed them from a servant. The outfit certainly couldn't have come from his wardrobe. "Are you all right?"

She wasn't sure. Her dress was covered in mud and specks of vomit, and her head ached like never before. She brought a hand to her temple and felt crusted blood caked into her hair. "What happened?"

"What happened was that I was proven a fool for not keeping you under lock and key."

"Excuse me…" She paused as the carriage spun around her.

"Leaving you free to roam resulted in you almost getting

killed. I found you in the middle of a mob of bourgeois militiamen who stormed the Hôtel de Ville last night demanding arms and, in failing to get them, repeated the same tactic today on the Bastille with startling success." He shook his head and continued. "I presume you saw the marquis de Launay's head on a pike?" He didn't wait for her to confirm it. "It isn't safe to walk the streets of Paris any more, especially not for a woman *married to a prince*." He hissed the last words like she was an unimaginable fool. "What were you thinking?"

"That I am free to do as I please," she shot back, but even as she was speaking the words, she knew they were petulant. He had saved her life, after all. "How did you find me?" she asked quietly.

He sat up straighter and cleared his throat. "I'd been looking for you ever since I was informed of your… excursion." He glared at her and she glared back. "I didn't think I'd ever find you, and what a joy it would have been to explain to your husband that you died in the middle of a mob of the very peasants you spent the morning so fiercely assuring us you could *never* fear. I departed the safety of my carriage to look on foot, which proved to be an exercise in utter futility."

"How did you even know where in the city to look?"

Bastien shrugged, but his cheeks reddened. "You seem like the kind of girl who courts trouble. I simply followed the mob."

Belle studied him. Something about his answer made

her uneasy, but she didn't have the energy to interrogate him further. "And so how did you come to discover my unconscious form?"

The contempt melted from his face. "I—I was accosted by a woman I have never met before in my life, who insisted that I follow her. She led me straight to you, crumpled in a heap in a filthy alleyway." He shuddered. "She was gone before I could ask her how she knew I was looking for you."

Belle rubbed her throbbing temple and remembered the woman in the shop of mirrors, the one who had shown her a terrible vision. The memory was hazy, as though it had happened in another lifetime, but Belle was certain she would never forget the image of her home burning, set aflame by the people of Aveyon. She banished the memory to the recesses of her mind, refusing to believe for one second that it was a vision of the future. No, that woman must have been a peddler of some trickery designed to swindle her.

Still, Belle's spine tingled as she wondered if she was the same woman who brought Bastien to her. But admitting it out loud would mean that Belle accepted that something strange was occurring, and she wasn't ready to do that.

"Lucky for me, I suppose."

"Yes, well, I haven't heard a thank-you yet."

"My apologies, I'm still trying to come to terms with the fact that I saw a man's severed head today." She leaned her head against the wall of the carriage and closed her eyes.

"Did you see... everything?"

She opened her eyes. "I mercifully missed the act itself, but I did get to watch the marquis beg for his life to a crowd of monsters."

Bastien looked at her curiously. "Not all of them are monsters, Belle." He seemed to speak before thinking.

"I'd hazard that taking part in a murder does indeed make one a monster."

"Does that make you a monster, too, then? Since you were also a part of the mob?"

"You know very well I was in the wrong place at the wrong time."

"And so too, perhaps, were others." He adjusted the plain white knot tied around his throat, so unlike the frilled jabots and cravats he preferred. "I'd caution you not to judge a whole group based on the actions of the violent minority. The Third Estate numbers in the many thousands. You fell in with some hundreds. Do not paint them all with the same brush."

Belle thought about what he said for a moment. "I did not expect to hear an impassioned defence of the Third Estate from the duc de Vincennes."

"I recommend walking this earth burdened by the notion that most anyone can surprise you. It will make your life easier."

She had no reply for him. She thought back to Marguerite telling her the night before that Bastien and King Louis were thick as thieves and wondered just how tangled the duc's loyalties truly were. But it was a conversation for another day. Her head was pounding and her body felt close to collapse. "Does Lio know?"

"Of your thrilling adventure?" There was the sarcasm she knew and loathed. "No, Lio is still in Versailles, though I can't imagine he'll be sticking around once word of the storming of the Bastille reaches the king." A flash of sympathy crossed his face as he eyed her wounded head. "Perhaps we'll keep the worst of it from him. We'll get you cleaned up as quick as can be. There's no way Lio has made it back to Paris just yet."

She nodded gratefully. She didn't want to lie to Lio, but she felt the need to spare him the gory details lest he think the worst and assume she had been in mortal peril. Belle knew getting caught up with the mob had been a mistake, just as she knew Lio's concern would be excessive if he were to learn the truth. It would be better for them both if he never knew. She leaned her head against the glass window of the carriage and watched Paris go by in a blur. Now that they had left the Hôtel de Ville behind, the city hardly seemed like it was in the grip of violent revolutionaries.

They travelled the rest of the way in silence. The sun was beginning to set on the horrors she had borne witness to. The day was almost over, and Belle found that she wanted nothing more than to go home to Aveyon. She daydreamed about cataloguing the library, tending to her garden, wandering the peaceful streets. More than anything, in that moment she wanted Lio. She wanted to wrap her arms around him and forget what she had seen, in the shop and in the street. She wanted them to escape from the darkness of Paris. Most of all, she wanted to stop worrying it would follow them home.

When the carriage came to rest at Bastien's door, Belle knew she owed a debt of gratitude to her host, even if he drove her mad. He exited the carriage before she did and held a hand out for her to take.

"Thank you," she offered. "For rescuing me."

The duc looked behind her and winced at the mud she left in her wake. "I'm not sure it was worth the mess."

She held back the desire to smudge dirt all over his face. "I mean it."

"Yes, well, let's hope you're still thanking me in a few moments." He was looking beyond her with widened eyes. Belle turned to find Lio marching out of the stables. "Best come up with a good lie; he looks positively furious."

CHAPTER EIGHT

The last vestiges of sunlight shone on Lio, illuminating the panic and fear carved into his features. As he neared, Belle realised it was an expression she recognised from the Beast.

She looked back at Bastien. "It wouldn't be a lie," she insisted. But she couldn't tell him that lying about what happened to her would be a kindness, given what she and Lio had been through together. Bastien still didn't know about the curse, and Belle and Lio hoped to keep it that way.

"Where on *earth* have the two of you been?" Lio's voice was rough with worry.

He reached Belle and pulled her into a desperate, angry embrace. Belle faltered under the weight of him and was lost for words. He had seen the state of her, so there'd be no convincing him that she'd had a relatively normal day.

"Belle and I got caught up in a fringe protest filled with the dregs of Parisian society. Not a lick of passion among them, barely qualified as revolutionaries." Bastien was using his most practised nonchalant tone.

Lio pulled away from Belle slightly and looked down at her. She tried not to shrink under his gaze. "What are you doing here?" she asked. "I thought you'd be in Versailles for days?" Lio frowned.

"Versailles has been engulfed by chaos. I doubt King Louis has noticed I'm gone." He held her by the shoulders at arm's length. "What happened to you?" He registered the dried blood that had trickled from the wound at her temple and thumbed her cheek tenderly. "You're hurt. What happened? Who did this?"

"No one. I just fell." It was a weak excuse and she knew it. "I'm fine."

"Imagine how I felt hearing the news in Versailles that the Bastille had been taken by revolutionaries, and that the Gardes françaises had either abandoned their posts or joined up with the rabble. Imagine how I felt stealing a horse from King Louis's stables and riding hard the whole way home, desperate to be sure that you were okay. Imagine how I felt" – he took a shuddering breath – "arriving here to find you missing, and none of Bastien's staff had any clue where to find you. *Gone all day,* they told me." He bent down so their eyes met.

She didn't know what to say. The weight of what they thought they had put behind them was back, forming a knot in her throat.

"Really, Cousin, it was a tepid skirmish," said Bastien

flippantly. "We were out of there before anything dramatic got going. Come." He gestured to his servants to open the front doors. "Let's go inside and get cleaned up."

As Lio turned and strode towards the doors, Belle gave Bastien a grateful smile. He nodded in return, giving her a look almost of warmth. She hadn't expected to find a coconspirator in the duc de Vincennes, but it had been a day of surprises.

They made their way through his house and ended up in the kitchens, where they found Lumière tucking into a makeshift feast at the chopping block. He ran over to Belle at once.

"Madame! You had us all very worried." He pulled a thin white box tied with a velvet ribbon out from behind his back. "Here are the macarons, though now that I know they were a distraction, I feel less inclined to give them to you," he scolded playfully.

She was so relieved to find him safe and teasing after the day she had. "Forgive me?" She pushed the macarons back towards him, a peace offering.

"Of course, I could never stay mad at you. Though" – he leaned in closer – "next time, simply tell me what it is you wish to do. You are not a prisoner any more." The words were meant as a kindness, but they struck her nonetheless. It hadn't been so long since Belle was confined to a castle, with the Beast as her keeper. They still hadn't healed from that. It was another thing both of them chose to ignore, hoping their love would serve to patch over that particular pain.

She stepped back to take in the kitchens. The cooks had been peeling potatoes, but they bowed at Bastien and scurried from the room.

Bastien offered her a damp cloth, but Lio took it from his hand and began tending to her head wound.

"It's not so bad," he said. "It looks worse than it is, and I imagine your head is pounding, but the cut is a flesh wound, nothing more."

"Certainly bled all over my coat like it was a grievous injury," Bastien muttered from within a cupboard.

"What was that?" Lio called out to him.

"Nothing." Bastien spun away from the cupboard, holding up a bottle of whiskey in one hand and glasses in the other. "Shall we?"

"Yes," said Lio and Lumière in unison.

The duc began pouring. "Tell us more about Versailles, Cousin." He handed Belle a glass, but she refused him, not wanting to cloud her mind any further than it already had been that day. He shrugged. "More for me."

Lumière nudged a mug of hot chocolate over to her, and she smiled gratefully. The drink was cool enough for her to take a deep sip. After the day she had, it was a most welcome comfort.

She looked up, and Bastien choked a laugh into his glass.

"What?" she asked, wiping her mouth with the back of her hand.

"Nothing," said Bastien. "You've just smeared more dirt all over your face. Here." He handed her his handkerchief. "This will be of no help at all, but I am nothing if not a gentleman. Lio, Versailles?"

Lio took a swig from his glass before pouring the amber liquid on the cloth Bastien had given him and pressing it to Belle's head. She winced, but he held it tight to her shallow wound and took a deep breath to begin.

"King Louis is surprisingly calm; it's everyone else who's panicking. The comte d'Artois, with the support of the queen, is begging his brother to flee the palace and make for Metz, where he would at least have the protection of loyal troops, but Louis is refusing to abandon Versailles. He still believes he can work with the revolutionaries."

"That has the appearance of wisdom," began Bastien. "But I do not believe Louis has the intelligence to pull off that sort of delicate cooperation."

"You think the mob will make for Versailles next?" asked Belle.

"Oh, certainly not," Bastien said. "It is still too early. They may have stolen what arms they could from the Bastille, but even the most rabid among them know they don't stand a chance at besieging Louis's stronghold. But the thing is, the revolutionaries don't have to storm the palace to get what they want. They hold the power, especially now that they are an armed militia. Louis will have no choice but to make concessions to them." He poured himself another glass of whiskey. "Truth be told, Louis is weak. He will not withstand this. He should flee while he still can."

Lumière gave a low whistle as the four of them sat in shocked silence. Belle didn't know how so much had happened in so little time. Even the difference between the morning and the evening was staggering. The image of the marquis's severed head and the vision of the mob storming Aveyon were haunting her already. She did her best to set the false vision aside, but it was the execution of the marquis that was sticking with her the most. She knew there was nothing she could have done to save him, but the guilt over witnessing his execution was heavy in her chest. This was not the Paris she had loved as a child. It was like the fate of the city balanced on the tip of a blade, and if it fell, so too would the rest of Europe.

"I think we should go home," she said quietly, fearing that her husband would disagree. Belle worried he had made promises to the king that he would refuse to go back on now.

Lumière nodded, and Lio surprised her by joining.

"Louis has lost my confidence. We gain nothing by swearing oaths to a king whose own people seek to dethrone him. I don't think Aveyon owes France anything." He looked up to Belle. "We need to get back to our people."

Bastien took a deep breath and brushed his hair out of

his eyes. "Then it's settled. You'll leave in the morning." He downed the rest of his whiskey. "Go to your rooms; I'll have food sent up to you. And I'll see to it your luggage is prepared for your departure."

On another day, Belle might have asked Bastien why his loyalties had flipped so quickly. But she was tired, and it was plausible enough that the only person Bastien was truly loyal to was himself.

"Sire, I will see to the carriage," added Lumière with a quick bow.

"Thank you, Lumière." Lio pulled Belle to her feet and wrapped an arm around her shoulders protectively. She knew better than to tell him she was perfectly capable of walking on her own. "Goodnight, Cousin."

Bastien waved them off, but Belle paused at the doors and turned back, feeling a pang of obligation.

"Thank you, Bastien."

He simply nodded, but she knew he understood that she was thanking him for so much more than sending food to their rooms and arranging their departure. The duc was still a mystery to her, with a web of loyalties and motives she wasn't sure she'd ever understand, but he had saved her that day. She shuddered when she thought of what might have become of her if he hadn't found her in the alley.

And then Belle remembered the woman in the mirror shop. She had to be the same woman as the one who had led

Bastien to her. None of it made any sense, and as much as Belle was curious by nature, she would be relieved to leave that mystery behind her.

●●●

Lio guided Belle through the manor with all too much care, but she let him. Almost as soon as they closed the door to their apartments, one of Bastien's stewards arrived informing them that the duc needed his cousin's opinion on certain matters pertaining to what he had seen in Versailles. He promised to return swiftly, but Belle knew not to hold him to it. Bastien was well acquainted with late nights and likely wouldn't think to spare Lio after the day he'd had. She didn't envy him one bit.

Alone, finally, Belle sighed and sat on the edge of the bed, too exhausted to be concerned about dirtying the fine linens with her ruined clothes. She would have fallen asleep in them if something on the desk hadn't caught her eye. It was a white card propped on a silver tray. As she approached, she saw it was an envelope with her name on it. Belle slid a letter opener through the seal and pulled out a folded piece of parchment.

Dear Belle,

I suspect you abhor titles, so I hope you'll forgive my informal greeting. I deeply enjoyed our meeting last night and your subsequent dressing-down of the comte. It will

be the talk of court for weeks to come. If you find yourself
without engagements during your stay in Paris, I know of a
few salons that might interest you.

I hope you enjoy the rest of your tour of the Continent. I
hate to presume, but I would hope that if I were ever to find
myself near Aveyon, I might burden you with a visit. It is
rare to meet a woman so willing to speak her mind.

Yours most sincerely,
Marguerite

The Mademoiselle de Lambriquet had been a fast ally at Bastien's ill-fated dinner, and once again, Belle regretted leaving so abruptly that she didn't get a chance to know her better.

She didn't waste any time writing a simple reply on the back of the parchment, wincing at the stark difference in their penmanship.

Dear Marguerite,

Meeting you was a bright spot in an otherwise entirely
too eventful trip. I regret that we are making for Aveyon
in the morning. It would have been nice to see more of the
Paris I remember from my youth with you.

Please consider yourself welcome anytime you wish
to visit.

Yours,
Belle

She folded the parchment and put it back in the envelope it came in, scratching out her name and replacing it with Marguerite's full title. She placed it on the tray outside their bedroom door, knowing Bastien's servants would see that it got to its intended recipient.

She then retreated to the bathroom and found that someone had mercifully drawn her a bath, perhaps after catching a glimpse of her sorry state. She dipped her fingers and found the water to be quite hot still. She opened a cupboard stocked with fragrant soaps and oils and chose one that smelled of lavender and honey and poured the lot of it into the water. She stripped out of her stained clothing and made a mental note to burn the dress at the first opportunity before sinking into the tub and submerging completely. It was blissfully silent under the water, a stark contrast to the mob. Belle then spent half an hour scrubbing her skin raw, trying to get rid of any traces of the streets and mobs she had been at the mercy of that day. By the time she was done, the water was grimy and lukewarm, but she was clean. Lio had not yet returned, so she dressed herself in one of the frilly nightgowns Madame Garderobe had insisted she pack and climbed into bed, intending to wait for her husband so they could talk about everything that had happened that day.

She was asleep within minutes. It was a deep slumber, and Belle would have slept well through the night if she had not been awakened suddenly by a thrashing beside her. She sat up with a start.

Lio had been taken by a nightmare.

It had been many weeks since his last one, but Lio had gone through a sort of turmoil that day, one that frightened him enough to dredge bad memories to the surface.

She reached for him out of instinct, and he wrestled from her grasp. The room was dark, but she could make out his body by the moonlight peeking in from a crack in the curtains. He held his head in his hands, his back doubled over in pain. She didn't know if he was awake or dreaming. Sometimes it was impossible to tell.

In Lio's nightmares, the curse had never been broken.

"Lio?" she whispered gently, hoping her voice could pull him back to her. Instead, the cries continued. Experience told her this was a nightmare he could not fight alone; already he was raging against a darkness only he could see. Even if she woke him now, the fear would likely spill into real life.

She sat up and tried again. "Lio." She reached out to him and found his skin cold and damp. At her touch, he shook violently awake.

"Belle." He sat up, breathing in great gusts of air like a man pulled from a fearsome current.

She held her hand out to him. "It's okay. It's over."

He lay back down slowly, still breathing heavily. It took time to reacquaint himself with the world, to shake off the clutches of the nightmare he had left behind.

She could tell a part of him was still dreaming, so she nudged closer until he wrapped her in his arms. His skin felt feverish against her cheek. "I'm here, I'm here."

"I always dream of losing you, but this time I dreamed I lost Aveyon too." His teeth were clenched together. She listened as his heartbeat slowed over time. His hands twined through her hair. "If Louis cannot hold on to his kingdom, how is a beast to lead his people?"

The Third Estate rising up and storming the Bastille, and King Louis's subsequent weakness, had awoken Lio's old fears. "Shhh, you're not a beast any more. And you're not going to lose either."

"I'm sorry you have to see me like this."

She sat up on her elbows and looked at him. It was dark, but there was moonlight reflected in his eyes. "I loved you then, and I love you now. In fact, there isn't a single part of you I don't love completely, so don't say you're sorry to me."

He tugged her back down to lie beside him. "Let's just go back to sleep."

She hesitated. "We should talk about this, Lio."

"It was a nightmare, nothing more. We have a big journey tomorrow."

Belle had been there for some of the darkness that haunted him still, but she knew that didn't compare to living in it every day for a decade. She feared if she pushed him too hard, she'd be pushing him away. So she swallowed her concern and simply kissed his forehead. When he pulled her down and pressed his lips to hers, she couldn't help but wonder if it was an attempt to drown out whatever fear was still swirling in his mind.

• • •

The morning was so steeped in chaos that any plan Belle had of talking to Lio about the night before was immediately abandoned.

They emerged from their chambers to find Bastien's household in total disarray. Servants ran about in every direction, packing up trunks or flinging white sheets over gilded furniture.

"What on earth is going on?" Belle asked Lio, who shrugged.

They made their way to the dining room, only to find it packed away, as though Bastien was leaving for a season at Versailles.

"Oh, you're awake at last." Bastien came up behind them and clapped them both on the back, guiding them away from the room and towards the kitchens. "How did you sleep?" He paused as if for them to reply but immediately ploughed on. "I haven't slept a wink. I've been receiving letters and notes all night. Nobles are fleeing Versailles, led by the comte d'Artois, who evidently has no interest in waiting for his brother to see sense." He ushered them into the kitchens, where two bowls of porridge were waiting for them. "I think the only ones mad enough to wait out the storm are the king and queen and their closest staff. Everyone else is making for Metz, or the Continent, or England of all places. But I would genuinely rather die than set foot on King George's soil, so here we are."

Lio took a spoon to the steaming bowl, and all at once, memories were conjured of the Beast struggling with simply holding the utensil. "Er," he said, "which is where?"

Bastien gave him a pitying laugh. "I'm coming with you to Aveyon, Cousin. It is clearly not safe for noblemen in Paris any longer, and I think it best that I be with the family I have left." He let go of his arrogance and spoke plainly. "I need a place to wait out the storm, and while I'm waiting, I'd like to help you make sure Aveyon is secure."

Belle felt a twinge of uncertainty she couldn't account for – almost as if Bastien might bring Paris's troubles along with him by association. But Lio was thrilled. "We'd be honoured if you made a home in Aveyon, for however long you need."

Bastien beamed. "Perfect. My things will travel after us."

"Us?" Belle asked.

"I thought we could all become better acquainted on the ride to Aveyon." He smiled at her, but it was a wicked smile. "I'll go give Lumière a list of the servants who will be accompanying me." He left the room in a rush.

"You really think this is a good idea?" Belle asked Lio.

"He's a powerful ally, Belle. We could really use him."

She stirred the sludge in her bowl, wishing desperately for fluffy eggs and buttery toast instead. "I suppose you're right."

Lio touched a hand to hers. "I know you don't love him, but he's correct. It's not safe here any more. What kind of cousin would I be if I refused him?"

Belle nodded through a mouthful of horrible porridge before swallowing it down. "All that matters to me is that we're going home."

Belle had left Aveyon hoping it would be a long time before she saw it again. She wanted to travel the Continent with her husband by her side, making memories that had no foundation in pain. But there could be no honeymoon if France was at risk of descending into civil war. And after even a small time away from it, Belle found herself missing home.

Perhaps that was all she needed to calm her restless spirit. Perhaps now she would be content.

At the very least, Aveyon was far away from the turmoil of Paris.

CHAPTER NINE

The journey felt twice as long now that Bastien was accompanying them.

The duc insisted they stay in only the most expensive roadside inns and taverns and would not travel more than six hours by coach each day, almost doubling the length of the trip. Lio did his best to be patient with his cousin, but Belle was ready to strangle him midway through the first day.

The carriage had felt so spacious on the way to Paris, but now it felt as cramped as a coffin. By the time they rumbled up the steep wooded road to the castle, Belle, wrinkled and wearied, thought she might kiss the ground as soon as she was free of it. She pushed open the small window and leaned right out of the carriage, breathing in Aveyon, where the air was thick with the scent of pine and the sun was warm but not punishing. The wind tickled her skin and pulled her hair from the simple braid she had tied that morning.

Her first glimpse of the castle warmed her heart – there were the towers that scraped the clouds, though still dwarfed by the mountains in the distance. Their polished white stones shone brilliantly in the sunlight. She counted the carved angels that sat sentinel on every buttress, and admired the lush gardens. It was all so different from the first time she had seen it, sullied by the curse as it had been.

She was home. It was time to put Paris behind her.

They were greeted by a beaming Mrs Potts and a restless Chip. Even though the curse was long over, Belle couldn't help but expect them to appear to her as they first had – a round bone-china teapot and matching teacup with a chip in its gilded rim. But this version of Mrs Potts was as soft as a kindly grandmother, with pillowy white curls curving around her warm face, and Chip was as jumpy as a colt, his sandy hair sticking out in every direction as his dog, Chou, danced in circles around his legs. They were not the static objects she once knew. They were vibrant and alive, and after the rough days in Paris, it filled her heart with joy all over again to see them as they were meant to be.

A wound-up Cogsworth – moustache twitching – almost as rigid as he had been when Belle first met him – besieged Lio with concerns and plans before he'd properly exited the carriage.

"Sire, we must call a meeting of your advisers at once. The unrest in Paris—"

"Cogsworth, please." Lio looked tired, and older than when they had left the castle several weeks prior. "We are exhausted from our journey and ready for nothing more than a good rest."

"But, sire—"

Lumière deftly stepped between Lio and his majordomo, taking Cogsworth by the shoulders and steering him away from the group. "Wonderful to see you, old friend. Shall we see to the logistics?"

"What logistics?"

"You know, the *logistics*, the ones we must tend to in the castle."

"But—but—" Cogsworth sputtered as Lumière led him away through the enormous front doors. Even as humans, they made a funny pair: Lumière, tall and spindly; Cogsworth, short and rotund. Watching them walk away reminded Belle of the time they played her guides through the castle, and how easily she had slipped away from them.

Mrs Potts came to Belle and Lio and embraced them warmly. "You two were greatly missed."

"Not as much as I missed your cooking, Mrs Potts." Lio beamed.

She grinned. "I was beginning to fear you'd regretted my promotion."

"Never. All it took was one bite of your soufflé to hook me." Lio gave her a warm bow and went to talk to his coachmen.

Mrs Potts took Belle's hands in hers. "Your father sent word that he has left Toulouse and is making his way back here." Maurice had been gone from Aveyon some three months, travelling with his inventions from one town to the next, seeking like minds. Belle was relieved to know he was returning. "He doesn't know how long he will be, given the travel delays caused by the mess in France, but take heart, he will be back soon." She straightened and brushed the wrinkles from her apron. "I'd best get back to the kitchens, love. Dinners of my calibre don't prepare themselves." She winked and left. Belle wandered over to where Bastien was gazing up at the castle with a quizzical look on his face.

"Is it your first time in Aveyon?" Belle asked.

He didn't look away from the stones and tiles. "I came once as a child, but I don't remember much."

She looked up at the tower he was studying. "It must seem so small to you."

He looked to her and offered a tepid smile. "Small isn't so bad." She wondered why this version of Bastien – polite, humble, maybe even kind – remained hidden most of the time. She thought she could even become friends with him if he had left the brash and arrogant Bastien in Paris.

Raised voices stole their attention away from the architecture and back to the coach, where Lio was admonishing two servants.

"I don't care; get rid of them." His tone was pure ice, and when Belle got close, she figured out the problem immediately. In their absence, roses had blossomed in a forgotten patch of garden. They were glorious – blood red with lush, unblemished petals and sharp thorns.

They were also a living reminder of the curse that had nearly consumed the kingdom.

Mrs Potts had seen to it that the castle gardens were rid of any traces of roses as soon as the curse was lifted, but some had evidently been missed.

"All this fuss over some roses?" Bastien was looking between Lio and Belle, trying to understand what was really going on. "You know, maybe I was wrong. Perhaps you would fit in just fine at Versailles, Cousin, where things like errant flowers are deemed worthy of getting upset about. You would find an ally in Marie Antoinette. I once saw her tip an entire steaming plate of filet d'aloyau braisé onto the carpet beneath her rather than waiting for it to cool slightly."

Bastien, of course, had no idea why Lio would never want to see a rose again. Servants began hastily hacking away at the bush, and the duc continued to look between Belle and Lio incredulously, waiting for a response they couldn't give him.

"Is someone going to explain this to me?"

Lio turned away from his cousin and retreated to the castle in stony silence. Belle looked at the duc and sighed. "Roses make him ill." It was a weak excuse, but she couldn't think of anything better.

Bastien watched his cousin disappear inside but mercifully dropped the subject. "You know, it's been a long journey and I'm ready to drown my sorrows in the biggest bottle of champagne you've got."

• • •

They spent the first night back in Aveyon tucked into their corners of the castle, too exhausted to do much more than nibble on the food Mrs Potts had delivered to their doors and wash away the stench and dirt of the journey from their bodies. Belle and Lio danced around the incident with the roses. She was too exhausted and too haunted by everything that had happened to launch into the discussion they both knew they needed to have.

It was one thing to lie to Bastien in Paris. It was another to hide such an enormous truth in their own home, which had until recently been under a veil of magic.

But it could wait. Time was on their side.

They were asleep before the sun set.

When she awoke, Belle was surprised to find it was nearly midday, and Lio was gone. She had slept for so long, and yet she did not feel rested. The weeks they spent travelling had been borrowed time. Now that she was home, Belle had time to be haunted by the violence she had seen in Paris. The marquis's severed head dripping, held aloft by men whose anger would not be slaked by just one death. That was not retribution, she thought. It was only the beginning.

She was starting to understand that the image would

never leave her. The horror of it had made a mark. She felt it in the way her mind refused to quiet, in the way rest eluded her, and in the way the distance between her and Lio grew. Belle already regretted her choice to keep what she had seen that day in front of the Hôtel de Ville from him. It had seemed logical at the time to spare him the worst of it, but now she was suffering alone, and it was too late to tell him without it seeming like a betrayal. She would have to hold that darkness inside of her and hope it didn't break her.

The shadows on her wall stretched as she lay alone in her bed, holding the disparate parts of herself together. She was Lio's wife. Maurice's daughter. A noble. A peasant. Alone. Loved. Distantly, she knew she must get up, but in that moment, she was numb to anything else.

The door opened, and Lio came into the room.

"Belle." His voice was strained. "Are you all right?"

She turned to find him framed in the doorway. "I'm fine," she replied. "Just tired."

He looked away from her. "I know you lied to me about that day in Paris."

She sat up with a start, both ashamed and relieved that Lio had been able to see right through her. Heat rose to her cheeks in a mixture of anger and shame. She threw off the covers. "It wasn't so much a lie as it was an omission." She felt as small as the words were insignificant. It didn't matter the reason. It mattered that it was a lie.

He looked at her at last, eyes blazing with the light of the reflected sun and something deeper. Anger, perhaps. "Why wouldn't you tell me?"

The room got smaller and smaller. "I didn't want to make it any more real than it already was." She fiddled with the blankets that pooled around her. "I didn't want to burden you with something so horrible."

"So instead you shouldered it yourself." He sighed and his anger seemed to break. He walked over to the bed and knelt before her, taking her hands in his. "We have been forced to lie to the world; we cannot lie to each other."

"I know," she started, but lost the words when he brought his hand to her cheek.

"You have seen my darkest moments; don't ever try to spare me yours." He sat beside her on the mattress. "Come, tell me everything."

And so she did. She told him of the frenzied streets, the rage that united the mob, the feeling that she had no choice but to let herself be taken by it. She described how the crowd was as fearful as they were angry, and how disorganised they were. She explained that she didn't think any of them set out that day to kill the marquis de Launay, and that almost made it worse. The thought that the desire to harm could infect a crowd like a sickness and push ordinary people towards a violence they might never have known otherwise... it was almost too much to bear, and it made her all the more fearful that Aveyon could become similarly infected.

But she refrained from telling him about the woman in the mirror shop and her dire warning, which had proven oddly prescient. Belle's memory of everything before the mob murdered the marquis was hazy at best, and she didn't have an explanation for what she had seen. Telling him that the sort of magic that had smothered his kingdom lived on in some way—even if she doubted the veracity of the vision itself, Belle understood that she had been exposed to magic within the shop – would only serve to worry him. She'd seen how affected he'd been by the roses, and this was so much worse.

When she was done, it was like coming up for air after too long a stretch underwater. She still felt the pain of what she had seen, but it had lessened. Telling Lio had softened the worst of it. Belle thought she could live with what was left.

Lio's mouth was a hard line. "We can't let any of this happen to Aveyon."

"No, we certainly cannot."

"Thank you for telling me."

"I'm sorry I didn't tell you sooner." She tucked her head under his chin. "What are we going to do?"

"We've been through worse. We'll figure it out."

She leaned back to look up at him and pulled him closer, needing to know that her lie hadn't driven them apart. He tilted her chin up, and when their lips touched, everything else vanished and all that remained was the two of them, bound as they were by the curse they had broken.

He pulled away, his cheeks flushed. "You need to come with me."

She was a bit breathless. "Where?"

"I've called a meeting of my advisers. There is much that needs to be discussed, and Cogsworth is right – we don't have any time to waste."

"I had hoped we'd talk together first." She had so much she wanted to discuss with Lio before being shunted off to the side of the throne room while six different useless men vied for his attention.

"I know. We just don't have time." Her frown made him smile, infuriating her. "I think you'll like my first order of business." He jumped up from the bed and made for the door. "Dress quickly; we're already late."

She stood and reached for a clean and simple gown, one of many that lined her wardrobe, much to Madame Garderobe's chagrin. "What is it you've got planned?"

He gave her a wicked grin. "Follow me to find out."

• • •

Lio stubbornly refused to give Belle any more details all the way to the throne room. It was driving her mad, but she kept reminding herself that Lio's surprises were almost always the good kind. They reached the massive oak doors, and Lio entered without waiting for her.

Belle paused at the threshold, surveying the room. Seeing all of his advisers gathered caught her off guard. The most powerful among them were: Seigneur Montarly, a thin, reedy man who was a living relic of the ancien régime; Baron Gamaches, a bear of a man whose exalted status had been built on his military victories for Lio's father; and Seigneur Geoffroy, the heir apparent to Montarly's tired sensibilities.

In the months since the curse was broken, at most two of the men had deigned to appear at meetings at the same time. She wondered if it was the French peasants' uprising that had scared them into attending. Aveyon's aristocrats had much to lose, even if Lio's court was nothing at all like Versailles.

She was especially shocked to see Bastien seated next to Lio's chair, a place that conveyed a certain amount of influence, more than she had thought the duc would wield in Aveyon. She noticed she wasn't the only one staring at the duc in his spot of honour. Some of the advisers looked positively incensed. Cogsworth sat off to Lio's other side and gave her a perfunctory nod.

"Belle, join us." Lio urged her forward. She entered the room and felt the eyes of the men who represented all six of Aveyon's provinces scrutinising her every step. They were relics of a bygone era – men who had amassed a great deal of wealth on the backs of peasants, chosen as advisers by Lio's father not because of their wisdom, but because of their lineages and the lands they owned. Like all those outside the castle walls, the men in Lio's advisory had been enchanted to forget Lio had ever existed. They spent ten years without a ruler, living like kings in their lands and holdings, letting their people suffer. When the curse was lifted and memories of their prince returned, they were more than happy to slip back into their roles as advisers if it meant exerting even more power over a kingdom they had all but ignored for ten years. How easy it was for them to forget the ways in which they had spent a decade, but Belle couldn't. She and her father had lived under the yoke of Seigneur Montarly, a man far more interested in hunting and drinking than effectively governing their province.

Lio thought he and Belle should go easy on them, as they had been subject to the curse as well, even if they didn't know it. Belle often reminded him that they were not cursed to neglect the peasants who worked in their fields and households. That wickedness came naturally. She wanted nothing more than to be rid of them, but Lio insisted that they have a place in his rule. He didn't want to wash the kingdom clean of everything his father had done, not when Aveyon was still vulnerable.

Each time they made a sly comment about Belle's standing, Lio had to stop himself from revealing to them that she had saved them all. But he knew enough not to trust those men with his darkest secret, even if it meant they would give Belle the respect she deserved; Belle, on the other hand, didn't give a damn what they thought of her. She hated them regardless and could hardly stand being in the same room with them.

"Belle, I've invited you and Bastien here in the hopes that you will both take a place on my advisory." She froze, caught somewhere between pride and incredulity. "Aveyon would benefit greatly from your, frankly, encyclopedic knowledge, and also from Bastien's political acumen."

The rest of the advisers started whispering furiously. Belle scanned the room and noted that Bastien didn't seem surprised by the offer. She wondered when he and Lio had discussed it, and why she hadn't been present.

Lio looked at her intently, still a hint of a wicked gleam in his eyes. "Do you accept?"

Seigneur Montarly, the oldest of the advisers, cleared his throat so severely his moustache trembled. "Sire, do you think it wise to invite someone so entrenched in the French court to your advisory? In these troubled times, shouldn't we be more prudent?"

"Adding the duc is the most prudent choice. I trust him implicitly, and that should be enough for you." The advisory did not seem convinced, so Lio continued more forcefully, listing off Bastien's qualifications one by one. "He brings a city sensibility to our country province. He's lived in Paris all his life, and he knows the ins and outs of the French court. He has been privy to strategic discussions about the simmering revolution, and he knows where Louis failed."

"You have lost all faith in your king?" Baron Gamaches asked the duc pointedly.

Bastien surveyed him steadily. "What good is a king who cannot protect his own throne?"

Montarly scoffed. "You speak treason."

"I speak the truth. And if King Louis cannot protect his own throne, you can be sure he is not protecting Aveyon."

Lio winced at this, and Belle's blood ran cold. This is what she had wanted to discuss with him while they formulated a plan over the course of several weeks. Rushing into anything felt like a mistake. Bastien was ratcheting up the urgency, and she didn't know if it was out of a sense of pragmatism or desperation.

Seigneur Geoffroy leaned forward. "I find myself in agreement with the duc. Word has reached me of the horrors in Paris. Nobles are fleeing the capital, and Louis is capitulating rather than quashing the rioters."

"We have reports from the French countryside that peasants are taking up arms against their betters and pillaging grain stores. We *must* protect our borders," said Gamaches, as military-minded as ever.

Montarly shook his head. "What is it you are suggesting, sir? That we betray our strongest ally? Do you think we could so lightly put aside the treaty signed by the prince's forebears some centuries ago?"

In the background, Cogsworth went beetroot red at the

thought.

Bastien stood and rested his hands on the table. "The seeds of revolution are spreading whether you would admit it or not. If you choose to remain loyal to a man lost in a mess of his own making, then you are choosing ignorance. You are choosing weakness." He stood straighter. "King Louis will not recover from this. Terror will reign in France long before another king will."

It was the first time Belle had heard it spoken aloud – the end of a reign, the abolition of the French monarchy. Bastien spoke with such certainty that she could sense the room giving over to fear. No one wanted the same for Aveyon, but perhaps for different reasons. Belle and Lio knew they could do better for their people. They wanted to avoid bloodshed and make Aveyon a peaceful place. The advisory wanted to maintain the existing state of affairs. They could be allies for a time, but Belle would relish their eventual dismissal.

Montarly let his fist fall heavy to the table. "If the treaty is void, that leaves our kingdom vulnerable."

"We cannot trust that the rest of Europe will not sense an opportunity to test us," said Gamaches.

The duc sat back down and folded his hands over his chest. "There is an obvious solution." When no one spoke, he continued. "Secede from France and make your prince a king."

Belle expected the room to erupt in objections, but instead, the men around the table were quiet. The vision she had seen in the mirror shop in Paris flashed in her mind – Aveyon's commoners marching on the castle in revolt. She buried it once more, refusing to accept that any part of it had been real.

"I second the motion," said Geoffroy, breaking the silence.

"And I," replied Gamaches.

Lio held up his hands. "Wait, is this really what's best for our people?" He looked over to Belle, but she couldn't find the words to express how she was feeling.

Bastien sighed as though Lio were a protesting child. "You are a prince, Cousin, and have been charged with protecting your kingdom. This is how you must do so."

Geoffroy cleared his throat. "Sire, it is not so illogical a leap. Your people will have also heard of the unrest in Paris and the French countryside, and they all know to fear a foreign conflict. They will welcome your ascendency as a sign of strength."

The advisers murmured their assent. Belle wanted nothing more than to escape the role that was being thrust upon her. There would be no denying a title now, not when her husband was king. She forced her hands to still in her lap, even when every part of her wished to scream, to flee, to disappear. She had been adamant that she would never be Princess Belle, eager to avoid the false trappings that came with a title so flimsy in a principality. But queen of a kingdom in its own right? That was no empty title.

"Then we are in agreement?" Bastien asked.

Each man in the room called out, "Aye." With that, the motion would be passed, and Lio would be king. But no one was speaking, and Belle looked up to find that all eyes were on her.

"Belle?"

Hearing Bastien call her name elicited a strange reaction in her. She had thought she would be treated as a figurehead on Lio's advisory, a mere seat filler to keep her husband happy. But Bastien was including her in the vote. She hadn't expected that. "Sorry?"

Bastien spoke slowly. "Do you agree that Aveyon must secede from France and your husband must become king in order to best serve his people?"

There were a thousand reasons to say no, but none of them held more weight than the reason to say yes.

"I agree," she said, hoping the words didn't come off as reluctant as they felt. Cogsworth caught her eye and gave her a reassuring smile, which was not something she had seen him do since the days of the curse. It didn't fill her with confidence.

Bastien hit his fist on the table. "Then it is done." He gripped his cousin's shoulder. "Vive le roi."

If any of the other advisers chafed to see their newest appointee take on a leadership role, none of them said a word. They merely repeated Bastien's words.

"Vive le roi!" Their voices echoed around the room.

Belle was numb with shock. She did her best to grapple

with the weight of everything that had just happened, but she was coming up short. Lio was going to be king of Aveyon, and she his queen. *The* queen. There would be a whole kingdom relying on them to rule justly and with wisdom guiding them, wisdom Belle felt she did not possess.

Seeming to sense the turmoil Belle was fighting against, Lio spoke. "If you'll excuse us, gentlemen, there is much left for my wife and me to discuss."

Cogsworth leapt to his feet as if his chair was on fire. "If you'll follow me, messieurs, we must begin arrangements for the coronations right away."

Everyone trickled out of the room, even Bastien, until Belle and Lio were the only ones left.

"I never got a chance to say yes." She spoke to the table.

"Yes to what?" Lio's voice was soft.

"Your request that I join your advisory." She smoothed the wrinkles in her skirt. "We went right from 'Will you be on my advisory?' to 'Will you be queen of Aveyon?' without much build-up." Lio began to speak, perhaps to convince her that it was the right thing to do, but she interrupted him. "I know it's what's best for Aveyon. I just don't know if it's what's best for *me*." She took a deep breath. "I can't do it, Lio." She hadn't known she would say it until the words had left her mouth. She wanted to regret them, to take them back and assure her husband she could do what she must for her kingdom. But now that they had been said, she found she couldn't pretend she didn't mean them.

Belle knew that Aveyon needed Lio to be king, just as much as she knew she could never be queen of a country she spent most of her life longing to leave.

She waited for him to brush away what she had just said, to assure her that she would make a wonderful queen. "I know" was his exhausted reply instead.

"You know?" She was incredulous.

"I'm not going to pretend that I don't wish with every fibre of my being that you would simply take the title to make everything easier, but I will never force you to do something you don't want to do, Belle." Left unsaid was the fact that he had done so before, when he took Belle as his captive in place of her father, and they had lived with the consequences of that decision, both good and bad.

"So where does that leave us?"

"I expect Cogsworth will be apoplectic, but that hasn't stopped us before. I suppose we just take it one step at a time." He reached across the table for her hand. "I'll be king" – he grimaced at the thought – "and you'll be Belle."

That she didn't have to fight with Lio about her refusal made all the difference. "You'll make a great king."

Lio tore the black cord that held his long hair and let it fall in disarray around his face. "Truth be told, you and Bastien are the only ones who are making me feel like I can do this."

She had just promised not to keep things from him any

more, but she couldn't find the words to explain her gut feeling about Bastien. He had saved her that day in the alley, and yet still she didn't trust him. But the duc was the only family Lio had left, and Belle refused to plant seeds of doubt in him when she had no cause for how she felt.

Cogsworth poked his head back into the room. "Terribly sorry to interrupt, sire, but—"

"We have a lot of planning to do," Lio finished for his majordomo. He stood up and let Belle tie his hair neatly back. She pressed a kiss to his neck when she finished, and he pulled her into his arms, kissing her forehead.

"I know you haven't eaten," he said into her hair. "And I suspect you'll need a full stomach to deal with Cogsworth."

"Thank you," she sighed.

"Come find us when you're done." His smile was small, and Belle knew how much her refusal was hurting him, but she couldn't bring herself to consider the alternative. Lio left, and all at once, Belle was alone in the throne room. It was a space meant for hundreds, not just one person. The stone walls draped with thick tapestries muffled all sound, leaving it eerily quiet. She watched, lost in thought, as motes of dust swirled, suspended in beams of sunlight. She wished she was strong enough to support Lio in whatever way necessary, but Belle couldn't put aside her fears.

Even if she wanted the crown, she doubted she would have made a good queen, and she thought that was reason enough to avoid the matter entirely.

CHAPTER TEN

Lio knelt before his throne, waiting for the crown he never wanted.

He was resplendent in his crisp ceremonial uniform and coronation cloak trimmed with ermine – Madame Garderobe had truly outdone herself in so little time. It had only been a few weeks since Lio's advisers agreed to secede from France and make Lio their king. Belle wouldn't have thought such progress would be possible, but Bastien had proven an efficient diplomat. The duc had overseen the drafting of the legal document severing ties between Aveyon and France, and had seen to it that it was delivered straight to King Louis's secretary of state to ensure that it was signed. They hadn't heard much from the king of France since, but then, he was busy attempting to suppress a revolution. In the eyes of Aveyon's legal scholars, the kingdom was free of its obligation to France, and Lio could be crowned king.

Belle stood in the audience, though Lio had tried to convince her to stand beside him on the dais. But she wanted the day to be about Aveyon's new king, not his reluctant wife.

She hoped her support would be evident in other ways, like the gown she wore, made to match her husband's – as crimson as his dress uniform, but hers as soft as velvet, with ermine cuffs. Her hair flowed loose down past her shoulders, brushed and pinned into submission by her attentive maids. She was grateful to have resisted Cogsworth's efforts to place a tiara on her head, though she thought he would likely never forgive the slight.

Having already understood that Belle would not be Aveyon's princess, it seemed that most of their people accepted she would likewise not be their queen. Her humble beginnings helped most people to understand why she might refuse a title so grand as queen, even if Cogsworth had threatened to resign over her decision.

At the end of the day, Lio's acceptance of her desire to remain a commoner was enough for everyone else, and the fervour and pageantry surrounding the coronation was a balm to soothe any hurt feelings. Lio would be monarch enough for a whole kingdom. She didn't need to be queen. She would serve her people better by simply being Belle.

"I swear to serve the kingdom of Aveyon and to govern its people in accordance with its laws and customs." Lio spoke the oath that he and Belle had written together. Cogsworth had speculated that she was likely the first commoner to help write a coronation oath, but Belle thought the history of the world was too long and varied to be certain.

"I swear to perform my duty faithfully and to execute justice and mercy in all of my judgements." The bishop dipped a golden spoon into the ampulla of oil and anointed Lio's forehead with a light flick of his wrist. The bishop began to murmur a prayer over Lio, and Belle's eyes flicked to the immense portrait of his father and grandfather that towered over the throne. They were dressed in military regalia and wore sashes across their chests that sagged under the weight of the medals and ribbons they won fighting for the French king in conflicts that had cost Aveyon many lives. Now Aveyon would be free of that obligation.

Attendants presented the crown on a red velvet pillow, and the bishop slowly lowered it to Lio's head, eliciting a rush of happy murmurs from the crowd.

"I swear my allegiance to Aveyon, above all else." Lio's voice echoed through the throne room as the crowd before him roared to life. He turned, newly crowned, to face his people.

"Vive le roi!" Bastien's voice was a clap of thunder that shook the throne room. When the crowd echoed his words, she found herself whispering them too, as if in prayer.

If Aveyon was going to resist the fever that was consuming France, Lio was going to have to put his new-found power to good use.

• • •

Belle wanted nothing more than to shrink away from the

scrutiny Lio's coronation placed them both under. She was not a girl who relished attention or finery. She seized a quiet moment and tried to sneak away for some fresh air, only to be apprehended by a militant Cogsworth before she'd even cleared the room.

"This is not how the wives of kings behave," he hissed out of the corner of his plastered smile as he guided her back into the fray.

"I'm not sure any of us know how the wives of kings behave," she countered.

He let his smile fall for a fraction of a second. "Today is not the day to test me, madame."

She believed him.

Plates piled with hors d'oeuvres made their way around the receiving hall, and the champagne flowed freely, but Belle was not allowed to indulge just yet. She had never attended an event so lavishly decorated and catered; not even Bastien's unwanted dinner came close to the opulence. Belle had baulked at the expense, but the duc had been insistent: the coronation was to be a message to the rest of Europe – Aveyon was strong, even with the turmoil in France.

She stood in the castle's immense receiving hall under bright velvet banners, greeting the guests Bastien had strategically invited. More than a few of them cast sidelong glances her way when they thought she wasn't looking. She could understand where their curiosity came from, not to mention their contempt. She was a commoner wed to a king. She watched as people tried to peg her motives for refusing the title as they curtsied before her like they would to a queen.

She knew well enough that they must appear strong. Belle had seen the worst of what was happening in Paris, and she feared for her kingdom. She also feared for Lio, who had taken a crown only to protect his people. Would that matter to those who would seek to call it vanity? Would the distinction be apparent? She knew that fear was keeping him up at night, so she did her best to stand a bit straighter and smile a bit wider each time he looked her way, and hoped her efforts were noticed by Cogsworth as well.

"Charles Frederick, margrave of Baden," the majordomo breathed in her ear as a gentleman with an ornately embroidered collar and voluminous wig approached. She racked her mind for some bit of information she may have recalled from her studies. He sighed as she faltered. "Outlawed torture in 1767—"

Belle nodded subtly as she remembered.

"My lord Charles, we are honoured by your presence," said Lio as Charles bowed.

"Deeply honoured," Belle added. "Thank you for coming all this way."

"Madame, I wouldn't have missed it," he replied. "It had been a great while since we had any word from Aveyon."

Lio's smile faded by a fraction, but Belle noticed. "Yes, well, my illness—"

The margrave interrupted as if he hadn't even heard Lio speak. "I have heard the most monstrous things from French nobles travelling through Baden on their way to more sympathetic climes. Ah" – he clapped Lio on the back as if he were a boy and not a king come of age – "in these tumultuous times, who can be faulted for favouring isolation over hospitality?"

Lio simply nodded, and Belle dipped in a shallow curtsy for lack of anything better to do. He had defeated the curse and come out stronger, but those who knew him seemed only to remember the spoiled prince he was before.

The margrave moved on, weaving between marble columns to the dining room. Belle and Lio had reached the end of the line at last. Cogsworth was gone, no doubt attending to some duty of utmost importance, or spreading word that Belle was as hopeless a conversationalist as he had predicted.

"That went better than I expected," Bastien remarked.

"How do you mean?" asked Lio.

"Only that your extended illness hardly arouses the most confidence in your abilities as king of Aveyon. I'm surprised it didn't come up more, though I suppose most people have other things on their mind."

Belle bit back her retort. Bastien still didn't know of the

curse that had held Aveyon in its grip for a decade. Lio had flirted with the idea of telling his cousin everything, if only to seek more informed counsel going forward, but Belle had strongly urged him to keep the curse a secret. Some gut feeling still prevented her from trusting the duc fully. She didn't know if he was as convinced of Lio's illness as he pretended to be. As for the guests, no one had brought up Aveyon's ten years of silence save for the margrave. France was an ever-shifting landscape, and it was at least a little plausible that a border realm could be overlooked for a stretch of years. Any gaps in their story were quickly filled in by Aveyon's nobles, who had lived for those ten years as if nothing were amiss.

Lio loosened his cravat. "I'll admit I expected it to go worse."

Belle tried to change the subject. "You know, I'm quite glad I'll never have to attend another coronation."

Lio adjusted his crown and gestured towards her. "Never say never, Belle."

She stuck her tongue out at the implication that she would one day be worn down. "Putting a crown on my head is not part of some great conquest."

"I know," he sighed. "You can't blame me for hoping, though. Ready?" He reached for her hand.

She took his hand and a deep breath all at once. "As I'll ever be."

"I'm sure Cogsworth would be thrilled by your lack of

confidence."

Bastien piped up from behind them. "Actually, etiquette dictates that a king enters alone and everyone else must wait until you've sat down."

Belle thought back to Cogsworth's exhaustive lessons and preparations for the day and could recall nothing of the sort. "Since when?"

Lio held her hand tighter. "Screw etiquette."

"While I would normally agree with the sentiment, in France you would only cause a sensation by walking in with your common wife. Hell, even if she was queen consort it would cause a stir."

Belle narrowed her eyes at the duc. "Yes, well, the entire point of the day is to prove that Aveyon is *not* France, is it not? And given that the crown now rests on Lio's head, is it not true that we get to decide how things are done in Aveyon going forward?"

Bastien peeked in through a crack in the doors. "You're trying to convince a roomful of nobles that you're now the king of what used to be a fledging principality of France, correct? That is the goal here?" He waited for Lio to nod. "Then don't ruffle their feathers for something as benign as walking into a room a slight bit before your wife."

Belle expected Lio to continue to rebuff Bastien, but instead, he let go of her hand and gave her a sympathetic smile. "Remember, we're doing this so that we can ensure

Aveyon is the kind of place revolution could never take hold in."

Belle was taken aback, but she nodded and watched him walk into the dining room. She didn't actually care about the order they walked in, but she did worry about Bastien's influence over her husband. She moved to follow him now that he had traversed the room, but Bastien stopped her.

"You must be announced."

"Lio wasn't."

He rolled his eyes. "Lio doesn't need to be announced, Belle. He's the king."

She shifted impatiently. "Can't you do it?"

He gave her a wink. "I outrank you, and etiquette dictates—"

"Don't finish that sentence." She held back the desire to tell him what he could do with his precious etiquette. "So am I to stand here for the duration of dinner? Will someone bring me a plate or am I to go hungry as well?" she asked sarcastically.

"Easy, now. I'll find Cogsworth."

As soon as he left, she cracked open the door, prepared to enter without a bloody announcement, but stopped short. What Bastien had said about the nobles and ruffling feathers rang true. She didn't want to give anyone a reason to doubt Lio's capabilities as king of Aveyon, knowing full well she was already doing so by refusing two titles. So she waited at the threshold.

The receiving hall behind her was deathly silent, allowing the fears she had buried for weeks to come to the surface of her mind. She didn't know if Lio was ready to be king of a whole country, or if she was ready to be married to one. When he was prince, Lio had been duty-bound to adhere to the treaty his ancestors had signed with France, but so had King Louis. Aveyon had been under the protection of the French crown, and if they had been invaded, they would have had the full force of the French army behind them.

Now they were alone, and all the scrutiny would rest squarely on Lio's shoulders. Even if he strove only to do good by his people, he could still fail. The thought terrified her — that they could do everything right but still hurt the people of Aveyon.

But she feared the spread of revolution even more. And ultimately, she feared inaction so much more than she feared Lio making a mistake.

As she heard Cogsworth announce her, she decided to take her fears and use them to push her forward.

She knew the worst was still ahead of them.

CHAPTER ELEVEN

The feast passed as unbearably slowly as she thought it would.

Belle met more people because of the coronation than she had in all of the rest of her life combined, and the fact that she mostly remembered everyone's names and titles was due entirely to Cogsworth's impatient schooling.

She despised the artifice of it all. Celebrating the crown on Lio's head with members of Europe's aristocracy did not feel like a step towards protecting her kingdom. Lio had wanted to have a simple coronation that ended with a feast on the castle grounds, open to all of Aveyon's citizens who would make the journey. Bastien had told him that while his heart was in the right place, the idea was too small.

And so the duc's vision for the coronations was realised, and Belle was left feeling empty and numb to it all. She only hoped that Lio would begin rebuilding his relationship with the commoners of Aveyon as quickly as he had assumed the crown. But that was a conversation for later.

When they had seen the last of their guests off to bed,

Lio and Bastien cracked open a bottle of cognac the duc had brought all the way from Paris and sat around a small table in the kitchens nursing their glasses. Belle opted for a particularly strong cup of tea brewed from the tin of leaves Mrs Potts kept aside for her.

"I'd say that was a success," offered Lio.

"And what exactly did we succeed at?" Belle asked through a haze of exhaustion not even the tea could help.

Lio shrugged. "Showing the world we aren't weak."

Bastien tipped the bottle toward his cousin in salute, but Belle was unconvinced. "I think the trouble is still ahead of us."

Lio rubbed his eyes. "Come, now, Belle. Our people do not suffer like the citizens of France. It is rare that anyone in Aveyon faces starvation."

She had seen the effects of hunger on Paris's peasants, but more than that, she had seen how quickly anger and fear could infect a crowd. She had seen how ineffective rule could harm those at the bottom long before those at the top felt the sting. "I think there is quite a bit more to the unrest than starvation."

Bastien put his glass down. "There isn't really, though. This year's drought and last year's destructive hailstorms ruined two seasons' worth of harvests. The grain price is unsustainable, and people are starving. If Louis were a good and capable king, he would have implemented strict austerity measures in an effort to ease the burden off the shoulders of

France's peasants. Instead, he tried to tax starving people further and pushed them to revolt. It's that simple."

But for Belle it was far from simple. She had seen the suffering first-hand. She wasn't able to dismiss it like the duc. "I heard the sans-culottes and bourgeoisie making speeches. I saw the pamphlets. It's about more than starvation. It's about giving commoners an equal voice. It's about representation, and holding the king accountable for the mistakes he made with the war in America, and with the États généraux."

"Those are fringe desires, Belle, put forth by opportunists. The people marching in the streets are doing so with empty bellies. The men that chopped off the marquis de Launay's head did so with minds clouded by starvation."

"I know what I saw."

Bastien sighed. "I infiltrated these groups for King Louis, Belle. I daresay I know a great deal more about the subject than you do."

Belle was shocked to hear of Bastien's undercover activities, but she was even more shocked to see that Lio was not. Anger bubbled up inside her. "So that is what you were doing by the Hôtel de Ville that day? I should have known you weren't searching for me out of a sense of obligation. You were rioting with the rest of them; it's why you were dressed so plainly."

He quirked a brow at her. "Harsh words from someone whose life was saved by my being there that day."

"I guess while I was in the wrong place at the wrong time,

you were in the right."

"Enough." Lio's voice brought them both back to the kitchens. "Fighting among ourselves achieves nothing."

"But—"

"Belle, I love you, and you're easily the smartest person in this room, but Bastien has been there. He knows so much more than we do about the specific tensions at play. His advice has been invaluable."

She leaned back and folded her hands over her chest in defiance. "He knows the noble perspective. He knows nothing of how France's peasants feel."

"And neither do you." Bastien's words cut right through her. The duc was making sure Belle remembered she wasn't a peasant any more, and that after marrying a prince turned king she had no right to claim that she spoke for them. She wanted to rage against him for it, but he had merely vocalised the same thoughts that cycled through her mind. She was made up of conflicted allegiances. She was someone who didn't belong anywhere.

• • •

As they undressed in the confines of their room later that night, Belle wondered if she should pester her husband about his plans for fixing Aveyon. But they were so exhausted by the events of the past two days, and the weeks leading up to the coronation, that she couldn't bring herself to do so just yet. As they fell asleep holding each other, she felt she had made the right decision.

When she awoke once more to an empty space beside her, she knew she had been wrong.

She was puzzled. Lio never rose earlier than she did – she often had to drag him out of bed. She supposed that now that he was king, his priorities may have shifted. If that was the case, she should be happy. But the gnawing in her gut told her that Bastien was behind the early mornings, and that the meetings were an effort to keep Belle out of the loop.

As she wandered over to her dressing table and attempted to fix last night's hair, Lio appeared at the door with a small bunch of lilacs in his hands.

"Oh, good, you're getting ready." He went over to the table and placed the flowers in an empty vase. A breeze brushed in through the open window and immediately filled the room with their scent.

She pulled what was evidently a structurally integral pin from the crown of her head, accidentally releasing a cascade of frizzy curls. Belle sighed and turned to him. "Ready for what?"

He gave her a look. "You didn't forget about breakfast with all our guests now, did you?"

But she had forgotten about it, or rather, pushed that particular horror far from her mind. "You mean the one Bastien forced us to include? You know, I think I got through the bulk of my farewells last night. I'm going to sit this tedious breakfast out." She rose from her dressing table and attempted to sink into the armchair by the window, but Lio scooped her up before she hit the cushion. She playfully thrashed in his arms, but he held her tight to him.

"Oh, no you don't. I will not be facing the margrave of Baden on my own. I'll carry you all the way down if I have to."

"You're making my hair worse," she lightly protested.

"I hardly think I can be blamed for this," said Lio as he surveyed the state of last night's limp curls. "It's one last stuffy event and then we're done," he reminded her.

"Pardon," a voice creaked from the direction of the door that Lio had left ajar. There stood Cogsworth, as red as a beetroot. "I... didn't mean to interrupt – that is to say I must be—"

Belle hopped down from Lio's arms and winked at the majordomo. "To what do we owe the pleasure, monsieur?" She walked back over to her dressing table and swept her hair from her face with a soft brush.

Cogsworth adjusted his lapels in a dignified manner. "I was sent by Mrs Potts to ensure you and the king did not tarry to join the breakfast being held in your honour."

Belle twisted her hair and pinned it down and thought it looked perfectly fine, given the circumstances.

"You know you don't have to use my title when it's just the three of us, right?" said Lio. Cogsworth looked at him blankly, not even daring to entertain the notion.

Belle sighed. "Thank you, Cogsworth."

He bowed so low he was at risk of losing his spectacles. "And may I say, madame, that you performed admirably yesterday, despite your persistent refusal to adopt the title that is now rightfully yours."

Belle knew this was the closest she was going to get to praise from the majordomo. "You weren't so abhorrent yourself."

If anything, his red cheeks went an even deeper crimson as Belle passed him through the doorway. It warmed her heart to see him so flustered. At least some things hadn't changed.

• • •

Everyone stood when Belle and Lio entered the room. She was sure she'd never get used to the deference people showed her now. She was finding that it didn't quite matter that she hadn't taken a title – people treated her as though she were queen regardless. It made her skin itch, but she couldn't exactly ask them not to. Cogsworth would surely combust if she even brought up disliking it.

She took her spot at one end of the table, and Lio took the other. She could smell the feast Mrs Potts had prepared, even if she couldn't see it yet. Garlands of flowers lined the centre of the table. Lilies, lilacs and tulips twined together with ivy leaves. Pots of sunflowers were dotted throughout the room, angled hungrily towards the sun shining in through the balcony doors.

Some fifty or so guests had deigned to stay for breakfast, including the margrave of Baden, who was evidently intent on making up for lost time in Aveyon. She searched the table for Bastien but couldn't find him. If he had declined to attend the breakfast he had fought so bitterly to include, she would strangle him.

This is the last of it, she reminded herself.

After some aimless chatting, Lio stood, and the rest of the table looked to him. "Belle and I would like to thank everyone for supporting us and Aveyon in this time of transition." He paused, still holding his drink aloft. His eyes met Belle's, and he was emboldened. "It wasn't too long ago that this kingdom experienced its own kind of darkness," he began. "In truth, it was a darkness of my own making, and Aveyon is indebted to my wife for pulling me out of it."

Belle thought he was coming dangerously close to revealing all too much about what had really happened in Aveyon, but her heart swelled at his words nonetheless.

"Now we are stronger than ever before, and our allies—"

A sudden commotion at the entrance stole everyone's attention. A red-faced Cogsworth bowed apologetically as a man in uniform stepped around him. "Forgive me, sire, he would not wait."

The man was pale and his uniform was splattered with mud, like he had ridden hard to get there. He dropped to one knee before Lio. "Sire, I carry word from Commandant Robinet. I must speak with you immediately."

The room burst into worried whispers. Belle had no experience with military matters, but even she knew that a sudden messenger could only mean something dire. Lio nodded at the man and turned to address their guests. "Please continue as you were." He signalled to some of the guards posted around the room. Lio walked the length of the table and took Belle's hand. They were ushered from the room by an agitated but concerned Cogsworth and quickly joined by an excitable Lumière.

Cogsworth gave him a look of utter disgust. "You could at least pretend not to be thrilled by the thought of bad news."

"Mon ami, I am far from thrilled. I am intrigued. My interest is piqued. My curiosity aroused." Lumière patted Cogsworth on the back. "I am a man of certain needs."

"Your needs are reprehensible."

"And you would rather be bored every day of your life."

Belle hid her laugh behind a forced cough. She was grateful for Lumière's lightness in a moment that could have descended to panic.

The group made their way down the eastern hallway to a small solar that Belle sometimes liked to take her morning tea in.

Lio held open the door for everyone. Belle whispered in his ear as she passed. "Commandant Robinet commands the garrison at Lavaudieu?"

He nodded. "I know him to be a man of great caution."

They all found places to sit around the room – Belle opting for a chaise by the fireplace. Lio stood next to her. Now that they sat across from him, Belle could see that the messenger was young, perhaps no more than twenty. The barest hint of scruff covered his cheeks. He had shaved yesterday. It would have taken the average man almost two days to ride from Lavaudieu to the capital. He had ridden through the night. The situation must be urgent indeed.

"What is your name, soldat?" asked Lio.

The soldier finished the cup of water he had been given and wiped his mouth on the back of his hand. "Claude Desroches," he replied. "I'm a gendarme based out of Lavaudieu." His rank explained his skill at riding.

Bastien burst into the room and bowed his head at Lio. "Apologies, I was delayed." He sat on the nearest chair.

Belle ignored him. "Are you hungry?" she asked Claude. "Can we get you something to eat?"

"Yes, thank you, madame, but first I must deliver my message." Lio nodded and gestured for him to continue. The soldier stood and cleared his throat. "Commandant Robinet has received word that a group of nobles may be planning a revolt."

Belle had not anticipated that. Most of Aveyon's nobility had been present at the coronation, a great many were currently enjoying Mrs Potts's excellent breakfast as they spoke. Belle hadn't sensed any threat from them. Was it possible she had missed the signs?

Lio did not react. "What proof does he have?"

Claude shrugged. "Only vague reports, sire, but he was concerned enough to send me."

Lio seemed to be weighing the messenger's words carefully. He looked over to Claude, who swayed in exhaustion. "Thank you. Lumière, please find the soldat suitable lodgings and a hot meal. Heaven knows we have plenty to go around."

The messenger saluted his new king before being ushered from the room.

Lio looked to both Belle and Bastien. "Before either of you speaks, know that I am moments away from calling a meeting of my advisers to discuss matters. Perhaps you should save whatever you have to say for then." Bastien visibly deflated.

Belle asked what felt like a stupid question. "How do you know it isn't one of your advisers planning to revolt?"

"I don't," he replied.

• • •

The throne room was still decorated for a coronation but devoid of people. There was something eerie about it – a crown had been placed on Lio's head only yesterday, but now the room was frozen in time. Belle shivered and made her way over to a seat at the table, choosing the one directly across from Lio, and by association, Bastien.

All six of Lio's original advisers had stayed for breakfast, so the meeting was gathered quite quickly. Once the ancient Montarly shuffled at last to his seat, Lio began.

"I had hoped to postpone our first meeting for at least a week while I settled into my new role, but circumstances prevent us from taking even a small sojourn from duty. A messenger arrived this morning, bringing unconfirmed reports of a nobleman planning to revolt."

"He described it as a group of noblemen," Bastien interjected.

Lio looked over to him and frowned. "The truth is, we don't know much. All we have to go on are vague reports. We don't have proof. We don't have names."

The room was silent. It wasn't every day treason was a topic of discussion. Belle was still gathering her thoughts but was pleased that Lio wasn't jumping to anything too quickly.

Bastien stood. "Cousin, you must fix this."

"And how would you suggest I do that? I don't even know who may be planning such a thing."

"I worried this would happen, that some of Aveyon's nobility would not take kindly to your becoming king so suddenly."

"You never made these worries known before this moment," said Belle.

Bastien glared at her. "I was too busy organising a secession from France and planning the coronation."

"Too quickly, it would seem."

"Enough," said Lio.

But Bastien was not finished. "Cousin, I urge you to embark on a tour of Aveyon's estates as soon as you can." Despite how little Belle cared for titles or formalities, she thought the duc wielded his lack of deference like a weapon. "If your nobles are flirting with revolt, it is because they feel slighted and view your coronation as a nail in the coffin. They see what is happening in France and they fear it. You must work to regain their confidence; you must show them that you mean to bring an end to the spread of revolution from Paris."

Lio did not react as he mulled over Bastien's proposal, though the feeling in Belle's gut returned, the one that said Bastien was wrong. The nobles should not be Lio's focus, not when it was France's peasants and middle class revolting against the king.

"Any insurrection must be quashed, sire," agreed Gamaches.

Montarly nodded. "Treasonous plots must be torn out at the root."

Belle felt her heartbeat quicken. Lio looked to her. "Please state your opinion; I know you're dying to." It was said without an ounce of annoyance.

She took a steadying breath. "I don't think vague reports are enough to go on. I think we should of course be kept abreast of the situation with the nobles, but I think your attention should be focused on enacting reforms for Aveyon's commoners."

"Madame, respectfully, it is not the time for reforms," said Montarly condescendingly.

Belle persisted, even though she felt Bastien had come to the meeting with his mind made up and quickly gathered everyone to his side with no more than vague allusions to what was happening in Paris. "Reforms for Aveyon's commoners will affect everyone, including our nobles. They needn't fear the spread of revolution if we make Aveyon a place in which revolution could never take hold." She was parroting Lio's own words back at him, urging him to see reason.

Geoffroy stood angrily. "Reforms will mean nothing if the king loses the confidence and support of his nobles. Reforms will mean nothing if civil war comes for Aveyon."

"If we lose Aveyon's nobles, we can say goodbye to mounting any real defence if the Holy Roman Empire chooses to test us, and test us they will. Keeping the noblemen happy will ensure the rest of the kingdom follows suit," Bastien explained as though Belle were a child. "True revolt, the kind that shapes kingdoms, is born in estates, not slums. Would you like to see your kingdom torn apart by protracted battles with enemies who are both well armed and well positioned?"

"Of course I don't wish to see that—"

"I have made my decision." He didn't shout, but Lio's words

cut through the room as if he had. "Belle isn't wrong. We must work towards improving the lives of Aveyon's commoners. But—" He looked away from her. "But we cannot do so with the threat of a war of succession looming on the horizon. I will go on an estate tour, if only to see for myself that the reports are false."

"Then I'll go with you." If she couldn't convince him of the importance of working with Aveyon's commoners first, then she would at least be with him while he tried to figure out which of his nobles were potentially working against him. She couldn't imagine staying behind while he toured the countryside. They had only been married a few months, and she feared what would occur if he had to face his nightmares alone.

Lio shook his head. "If I'm going on this tour because we've accepted that there is a threat against me, then we can't put you in danger, too. What would happen to Aveyon without both of us?"

The men in the room murmured their agreement, and Belle fell silent, feeling like it didn't matter what she might have said anyway. Bastien had got his way.

They eventually returned to their guests to see them off, now that breakfast was complete. Once the room had emptied, Belle and Lio took to the balcony to wave farewell.

She couldn't stop herself from speaking her mind. "You were quick to take Bastien's side."

Lio grimaced as he waved. "This isn't a matter of choosing sides. Bastien has more experience in matters such as this. He is knowledgeable, and it would be wrong to dismiss him simply because you don't like him."

"It's not that I don't like him, it's just that..." But she didn't know what to say.

"It's just what? You have to give me something, Belle."

She swallowed the words she wished to say: that she didn't trust the duc, that she suspected he harboured ulterior motives, that she questioned where his loyalties truly lay. None of it was proof of any wrongdoing and would only drive a bigger wedge between her and Lio. "Nothing," she finished. "It's nothing."

He looked back to the fading carriages. "Bastien is the only person in my advisory who has a certain expertise in dealing with matters of state. Without him, I'd be lost."

Belle nodded, trying not to feel the sting of his words. The carriages had all but disappeared on the horizon as she made a promise to herself.

The next time Lio sought opinions on matters, Belle would make sure she was the most prepared person in the room.

CHAPTER TWELVE

B elle hadn't thought a week could feel so long.

Her body was ready to collapse, but she reserved her swift decline for the confines of her chambers, where she left a trail of her clothing from the door all the way to her bed until she was clad in nothing more than her chemise. She lacked the energy to change into nightclothes, so she simply climbed under the thick covers and closed her eyes.

But sleep eluded her. Belle had gone to bed with a mind filled with the names and family trees of Aveyon's nobility for a few weeks in preparation for Lio's rushed coronation. She had readied herself for the event the only way she knew how – by immersing herself in books, fastidiously memorising everything she could get her hands on about the great royals of history, about the monarchies of the world and about the various philosophies of governance and social order. She had felt at least marginally prepared for the task ahead.

But now that it was over, the momentum that had kept her going was gone, and doubt came creeping in to take its place.

Lio had been Aveyon's king for all of a day, and already the country was at risk of descending into war over no more than an unsubstantiated rumour. Belle feared they were ignoring the more pressing threat – of revolutionary ideas taking hold in Aveyon and inviting violence to their peaceful kingdom – for one that didn't seem to her like a threat at all. Her mind drifted to the vision she had seen of Aveyon burning. She still didn't think it had been true, but having it play over and over in her mind while she worried about the state of her kingdom was not helping.

She worried that what was happening in France could happen in Aveyon, but Lio wouldn't see her point of view, especially not when he valued Bastien's counsel over hers. More than that, she didn't even have the benefit of certainty on her side. It would be easier to fight Bastien if she *knew* he was wrong, but she didn't. All she had to go on was a gut feeling that the duc was mistaken. It did not make for compelling evidence. But she did feel certain that Bastien didn't know Aveyon or her people, and for that reason his expertise should hold less weight.

She gave up on the idea of sleeping. Her unquiet mind needed a distraction, and she had the perfect one in mind. She sat up and looked to Lio, who was breathing evenly and snoring lightly. She got out of bed and put his discarded overcoat on over her chemise. The velvet sleeves trailed past her wrists, but the fabric smelled like him. She glanced back at his sleeping form one last time before leaving the room. She only planned on being gone for a few minutes.

The castle was completely dark as she travelled through it, tracing a path she took at least once every day. Light leaked out from the crack under the great doors at the end of the hall like a beacon. The fireplace was always lit, and Belle had spent more than one sleepless night curled up in front of the flames, surrounded by piles of books. She closed the doors softly behind her and paused as she always did to take it in. Of all the luxuries that came with her new life, Belle was certain she would never grow accustomed to the sheer vastness of knowledge available to her.

Her library.

She had plans to seek out a specific book, the one that had been gifted to her after she read it so many times it had imprinted in her mind. It had everything she loved in a book – an unfamiliar, faraway setting, magic spells and sword fights, and characters in disguise. She had brought it from home and added it to the library only a few weeks before, shelving it hastily before they left for Paris. Normally she would wander the stacks aimlessly, taking the time to pause and pull books from the shelves. But tonight she was on a mission.

She walked with purpose towards the back of the library, where the shelves were sparser. She found what she was looking for right away, taking the book in her hands and turning to leave now that her task was complete. But something behind where the book had rested caught her eye, glowing green in the pale light of the empty library. She reached between the books and pulled out a thing she had long thought destroyed.

It was the mirror Lio had given her so she could see her father, back when he was the Beast and she his captive. It was so hard for her to fathom now that the curse was broken and Lio was restored, but Belle had found happiness with the Beast. It wasn't love, that came later, but it was contentment. How long could she have lived with contentment, she wondered, if the Beast hadn't given her the mirror and thus a glimpse back to the life she had left behind?

She knew the moment she touched it that this was the one from the time of the curse, though it was the twin of the one she held in Paris. The engraved silver filigree was so similar it sent an involuntary shiver down her spine. It was curiously familiar in her hand, like the magic imbued in it recognised her as the person who broke the curse's hold on the kingdom. But all she could remember as she held it was how it had felt to use the magic, proving her father wasn't lying when he said she had been taken by the Beast. Even now, months later, her heartbeat raced when she thought of how quickly her neighbours had marched on the castle to kill the Beast, and how quickly thereafter she realised she loved him.

In a way, she knew that it was *because* he had given her the mirror and then let her go that she had been able to recognise the love she had for him. But the emotions were bittersweet. Belle didn't want to remember certain aspects of her past, or speculate as to why the mirror had survived the destruction of the curse. She didn't want to invite that magic back into her life.

Belle hesitated, wondering what to do. Should she destroy it? Hide it? She certainly couldn't show it to Lio, not with everything else going on. She decided to put it back where she found it and return for it once she had made up her mind.

But as she moved to hide the mirror once more, it glowed even brighter, casting green light across the spines of the books. Belle held the mirror before her, and her heart caught in her throat.

The reflection looking back at her wasn't her own.

She was looking into the eyes of the woman from the mirror shop.

Instinct told her to drop the mirror, to break it into a thousand pieces like the one she had held in Paris, but curiosity kept her hand gripped around the silver handle.

"Belle." The woman spoke with the same otherworldly tone she had used in the shop. "I know you don't trust me, but you must at least listen to what I have to say."

Belle's throat was bone dry. She had no reply for this woman, or for this magic she didn't understand.

The woman pressed on. "You must not wait for others to save Aveyon. You need to trust your instincts and become the queen you're capable of being."

The knowledge that the curse had lived on and followed her to, and from, Paris was far too much for Belle to bear. She looked away from the woman's eyes and hastily placed the mirror back where she had found it. She fled the library, and as she closed the door behind her, a frightening thought emerged. If the enchanted mirror *was* a part of the curse on Lio and Aveyon, the one they fought so hard to destroy, what did it mean for the kingdom that it was back?

Or that it had never fully left?

She knew she had to tell Lio about what she had seen, but she dreaded it. He was already labouring under the weight of the mistakes he had made in the past, and the nightmares that haunted him still. She didn't want to be the one to tell him that in some way, the curse remained. The smallest bit of hope blossomed in her heart that telling him might at least make him listen to her, but she wasn't sure it would be worth the cost.

She ran softly through the halls of the castle and tried to take stock of everything that had happened since they arrived in Paris. None of it made sense and none of it boded well for the future of her kingdom. Fears pressed in all around her. The woman from the mirror shop seemed to know so much about her reluctance to take the title of queen, and that suggested she was more than a simple peddler of trickery like Belle had convinced herself. This was a deeper kind of magic, the kind Belle thought they had eradicated from Aveyon. It was the kind that came with a heavy price.

She shuddered at the implications of it all.

If the worst happened, be it the noblemen revolting or the peasants rising up, or the return of the curse they had fought so hard to defeat, Aveyon would need her to be strong enough for a whole country.

Belle didn't know if she had that kind of strength in her.

• • •

As soon as she stepped back into her room, Belle sensed something was amiss. The air was tinged with the metallic scent of fear, and the bed was empty, the sheets and blankets in disarray.

It didn't take long to find Lio crouched in a dark corner, still in the grips of the nightmare that had taken him.

She rushed over and shook him, not caring in that moment that it was usually better to let him come out of the darkness gradually. "Lio, Lio, I'm here."

Her touch and her voice brought part of him back to her. He reached his shaking hands up the length of her arms all the way to her face. "Belle." There was anguish layered in the way he said her name. "You were gone."

"Shhh," she whispered. "I'm here."

"I was the Beast." She sat down on the carpet beside him and pulled him into her embrace. "I—I was him again, I felt his claws in my hands and his fangs in my mouth."

The admission startled Belle. Lio's nightmares had always been vague shadows of the fears he carried with him every day. To dream he was a monster again must have been torture.

"You aren't the Beast any more," she tried to assure him.

"But I am him, Belle, don't you understand?" His voice was frantic. "I lived as him for so long he will always be a part of me."

Belle couldn't help but think back to the vision she had been shown in Paris, of the people of Aveyon rising up against them. She had dismissed it as false, but a small part of her wondered what would happen if their people ever discovered the truth of Lio's ten years as a recluse. An even smaller part of her wondered if it could happen again, if some enchantress could decide that her husband wasn't doing enough for his kingdom and curse him like one had cursed a child so long ago.

But that sort of catastrophising was anathema to her. She refused to entertain it.

Belle knew there was nothing she could say to ease the nightmare from his mind and the feral panic from his bones. He had to come back to her on his own, bit by bit. She twined her fingers in his hair and waited for his pulse to stop beating so forcefully against her skin.

They sat in the silent dark, two people adrift in a storm, holding on to each other for dear life, but in time, the fear left him. She knew it was gone when he sat up straight, his spine no longer weighed down by darkness. His eyes weren't clouded any more, but the bruise-dark circles beneath them would take time to fade.

"You dreamed of the Beast?" she asked, probing as gently as she could manage.

He pushed his hair from his face. "Yes," he whispered, perhaps too frightened to lend the nightmare any more credence than it deserved. "I don't think it would have been so bad, but I woke up in the middle of it to find you missing."

She ran her fingers through the hair loose around his shoulders. "I was in the library. I couldn't sleep."

"I know, but logic has no place in my mind during a nightmare."

She tried for levity. "Did you think someone had kidnapped me from my bed and you'd managed to sleep through it?"

He cast his eyes down as his cheeks reddened with shame. "Is it worse to admit my first fear was that you had left of your own volition?"

Her chest tightened. Of course he would think the worst of her absence. She nestled close to him, finding a spot in the crook of his arm, desperate to find the closeness that came easily before. "One disagreement isn't going to make me want to leave you, Lio. I chose you and I'll keep choosing you, even when it's hard."

"I know," he breathed into her hair. "It's just, with the coronation and everything happening in France, and our earlier fight... it was harder to pull myself out of the nightmare. Usually I—" He hesitated.

"Tell me."

"Usually I can make it through the worst of it because I'm anchored to something." He paused. "To someone." Belle waited for what she knew was coming. Lio shifted slightly. "In every other nightmare, I've been anchored to you. I know it's a nightmare and that it will come to an end because of *you*. For some reason I didn't have that awareness this time."

Belle knew in that moment that she couldn't tell him about the mirror in the library, or the strange phantom woman with a disturbing vision who had haunted her from Paris all the way to Aveyon. It wouldn't do him any good to know that, in some way, the curse lingered. So she bottled up the words she had been prepared to tell him, burying them deep in the recesses of her mind. She would have to discover what it all meant without him.

"Losing you or losing my kingdom used to be my worst fear, but this nightmare gave me a new one," he admitted, his voice rough.

"And what is that?"

"Losing myself." He gripped her hand harder. "Losing myself to the past, losing myself to the Beast again or losing who I am because of some threat or villain I don't understand."

Belle could understand that fear, for it was one she shared with her husband. Belle didn't fear losing herself to her past but rather to her future. She feared life with Lio might require her to become someone she was never meant to be. So when she reassured him, in a way she was reassuring herself as well.

"You are much too strong a person to lose yourself like that, Lio."

She believed the words she spoke, but when her mind flickered to the mob killing the marquis de Launay, she remembered what fear and anger could do to people.

Belle had tried to make Lio see that the real threat lay with Aveyon's commoners. She wanted them to work together to enact reforms and make sure Aveyon was the kind of place revolution could never take hold in. But Lio had chosen to focus his efforts on his noblemen, and she couldn't fault him for it. That left Belle to figure out a way forward with Aveyon's commoners, and maybe with Lio and Bastien gone, she could truly devote herself to the cause.

Belle swore an oath to the darkness that night, one that promised she would do everything in her power to make sure Lio's greatest fears were never realised.

CHAPTER THIRTEEN

She woke just before the sun was up, feeling anxious and uneasy, vaguely recalling being tucked into bed by Lio at some point in the long night. The bed was empty now, but there was a note on Lio's pillow. He never could sleep much after a nightmare.

Up early to prepare for the tour. Get some sleep.

She tried, but her bed was so large without him in it, and all she could think of was how long he'd be gone.

She had sworn the night before that she wouldn't fight with him any more. He had to make his own decisions, and she didn't want their parting to be more difficult than it was already.

Lio was doing what he thought was best for his kingdom, and she had to accept that. She didn't want to see him torn between two possibilities again. His nightmares had roots in the past, but it seemed their fights could awaken old ghosts and pull bad memories to the surface.

She didn't want to be the reason Lio didn't sleep at night.

Belle felt like she was unravelling, so she left her too-big bed and wrapped herself in Lio's discarded overcoat once more. She didn't know her destination until she found herself in the kitchens, searching for something sweet to distract her from unhappy thoughts. She couldn't find a pastry but thought a leftover croissant would do.

"Good morning," called a warm voice from deeper in the kitchens, causing Belle to jump and drop her stale snack. Mrs Potts emerged from the depths of the kitchens with a healthy dusting of flour on her cheeks. "I didn't mean to scare you, love. Tea?" She gestured to the pot boiling over the kitchen fire.

"I'm sorry," Belle started as Mrs Potts poured the hot tea into a mug and plopped two lumps of sugar in after it. "Did I wake you?"

Mrs Potts handed her the mug and saucer. "Don't be silly. I've been up baking loaves for two hours already."

The lemony tea may as well have been a tonic for how much it revived Belle. "Thank you, and thank you again for all your hard work for the coronation feasts and the breakfast. I wish I hadn't been pulled away; I'm told it was a revelation."

Mrs Potts smiled at that. "Yes, I've received a number of tantalising offers from your guests wishing to purloin my services from you."

Belle raised an eyebrow. "None worth pursuing, I hope."

"Of course not." Mrs Potts patted her on the shoulder. "How could I ever leave you and Lio, love? And tell me who would keep Cogsworth and Lumière in line if I were gone?"

"Certainly not me," Belle replied, shuddering at the thought.

Mrs Potts offered her a pastry out of thin air. "Now tell me why you aren't in your bed."

Belle nibbled on the raspberry tart. "I'd rather wander than sleep most nights." She didn't feel like she had any right to tell her about how she doubted Lio's decision to tour his nobles' estates, or that he suffered from nightmares so long after the curse was broken.

But Mrs Potts was as persistent as she was observant. "Is he having nightmares?"

"How do you—"

She held up her hand. "I get them too, you know." She reached for Belle's empty teacup and began to refill it. "We were in that darkness with him, of course, but none of us had to live as a monster." She passed the teacup back to Belle. "I'm not saying we had it easy, but he had it the hardest."

The tea was so hot it burned Belle's tongue. "I worry that if he bottles it all up inside him he'll never heal."

Mrs Potts reached out and took Belle's hand in hers. Her skin was warm and soft as velvet. "I'm not sure any of us will ever fully heal, love. We've all got our cracks and tears, but we learn to live with them. I'd wager it's like that for anyone who has seen trauma." She got up from her chair and placed her hand on Belle's shoulder reassuringly. "You have to be strong,

Belle, especially now that this kingdom is crowding with voices, some of which are louder than others."

Belle raised her eyebrows. "Nothing gets past you, does it?"

Mrs Potts smiled serenely as she let go of Belle's hands. "Of course it doesn't." She put the teapot back on the hook over the fire.

"You don't seem worried," Belle remarked.

"Hasn't anyone ever told you not to borrow trouble?" Mrs Potts extended her arm for her empty teacup.

Belle handed it to her and nodded. "You're right."

Mrs Potts paused, deep in thought. "I spent a lot of my life worrying, Belle, but ever since you came to us, my worries haven't been such a burden." She straightened her apron absent-mindedly before clearing her throat. "I must get back to my loaves. And you should be getting ready for breakfast, dear."

She was gone before Belle could thank her properly.

• • •

The stone walls of the courtyard baked in the August sun and held on to the heat of it so efficiently it made the space feel like a furnace. It reminded Belle of how hot Paris could get, and how she hated the feeling of sweat dripping down her back.

She had barely seen Lio all morning as he prepared to embark on his tour. Cogsworth had never been more over bearing as he oversaw the packing of Lio's carriages and the inspection of the staff that would be accompanying the king. Cogsworth walked along the line of them in the courtyard, peering out over his spectacles and interrogating them at random.

"What is the name of Seigneur Montarly's eldest daughter?" he snapped at a junior coachman, who shrank under the majordomo's scrutiny.

"Félicité... Félicité Lucie Montarly?"

Cogsworth eyed him with disdain. "Wrong." He scratched something off the parchment he was holding. "Her name is Félicité *Lucille* Montarly. Are you attempting to sabotage this entire endeavour?" He moved to his next victim before Belle could step in. "You! What type of wine does Baron Boisselet like best?" Belle made her way over to the group and put a hand on Cogsworth's shoulders just as he shouted at the poor maid, "A Chablis from Bourgogne! It is not that difficult!"

"Come, now, Cogsworth," Belle said gently. "Don't you think you're being a bit harsh?"

He pulled himself up by his lapels and cleared his throat. "Not in the slightest. There is a great deal resting on the success of this venture, and I won't have anyone putting it in jeopardy."

"I hardly think knowing Baron Boisselet's favourite wine will make or break it all."

Cogsworth deflated a bit. "Perhaps you're right."

She patted him on the back. "I think we're all a little

stressed."

The majordomo nodded. "I have agendas and lists and accounts and research behind me, but nothing that advises what to do when you secede from your closest neighbour and former ally."

Belle understood that Cogsworth was helping in the only way he knew how, but she had also been on the receiving end of his efforts and knew how intense he could be. "Why don't you go find Lumière and shout at him for a bit? He can take it better than our poor staff."

He clicked his heels together and saluted her, happy to have been given a task he knew he could perform admirably. Belle watched him go as Lio sneaked up behind her and gripped her waist.

"Sacré, Lio, I nearly jumped out of my skin," she scolded, though she was happy to find herself in his arms before he left.

He pulled them over to a more private area. "Belle, I need to ask you something." He took her hands in his as she tried to read the curious expression on his face. Was it guilt? "Will you keep to the castle while I'm gone?"

She withdrew roughly. "You cannot be serious."

His face fell. "It isn't safe, Belle. With everything going on in France and word of possible insurrection here in Aveyon, I can't help but make this request of you, especially after what happened in Paris."

"So I am to be your prisoner once more?" She saw how it

hurt him, but she needed him to understand what it was he was asking of her.

"This is different," he whispered. "In my absence, you'll be ruling in my stead."

Belle couldn't fathom being locked away in a castle again, even if this time she was its ruler. She had lost her freedom once before, and it had taken all her strength to break the curse and get it back. But she recalled the oath she swore to the darkness the night before. She had promised herself she would not be the reason Lio's greatest fears came to life. She had meant the fear of losing his kingdom, but in his nightmares the two of them were torn apart as well. Mrs Potts had urged her to be strong, and she thought perhaps there was a strength in giving something up for the person you loved.

She couldn't say the words that were like the locking of a door, so she nodded.

Lio was relieved. "And while I'm gone, why don't you begin planning your salon? We could plan to have it coincide with my return. It would give me something to look forward to."

Belle knew he was merely attempting to placate her, and she was furious to discover it worked. She reached for something contrarian, if only to assert her will. "You don't think a salon would be a waste of time, especially now?"

His brow creased. "I think it's important to portray a sense of normalcy to our people and beyond. Yes, we've seceded from France, and yes, a prince is now a king, but in many ways things should go on as they usually would. A salon is a good way to show all is in order in Aveyon."

Belle was still angry, but she was not a fool. "I'll consider it."

"Wonderful. Shall we have it the day after I return, on the tenth of October?"

"I said I'll consider it; that doesn't mean I've agreed," she replied firmly, knowing she couldn't quite give herself over to the idea just yet. Her voice took on a softer tone when she spoke again. "I still can't believe you'll be gone so long."

He reached a hand out to her cheek. "I know, but with the salon to plan and the kingdom to run, you'll hardly notice my absence." She pretended not to hear his certainty with regard to the salon just as someone cleared their throat behind them.

Bastien had found them. "If you two are quite done wasting everyone's time, Cousin should be going."

"You're not going with him?" Belle was puzzled. The tour had been Bastien's idea; she would have thought he would be insistent on joining the party.

"I've asked Bastien to stay back and help you with the day-to-day running of things. Because of his background on King Louis's council, I've asked him to lead the meetings of my advisory." Belle looked over to the duc and tried to read his expression to see if that was truly Lio's idea or if Bastien had something up his sleeve, but his face was blank. She had no interest in running the advisory while Lio was gone, but she wasn't sure how she felt about Bastien taking up the mantle.

She tried not to give over to paranoia but found it difficult considering everything that had happened in such a short time. Lio continued, "You're both on my advisory and I trust the two of you implicitly, but, Belle, you are my voice."

Belle was assuaged by that, though she bristled at the thought of merely being Lio's voice. And yet she couldn't explain her reaction. She had rejected the titles that might have given her a voice of her own, but that didn't mean she was powerless. Her plan was to spend the time Lio was away focused on making the lives of Aveyon's commoners better, though now she would have to contend with Bastien as well. She hoped he wouldn't slow her down.

The trio walked back into the courtyard, where Cogsworth had calmed down considering he wasn't shouting at anyone. Everything seemed ready for the king's departure.

"I'll write letters as often as I'm able," Lio assured her. "Perhaps when you're not planning the salon you could start cataloguing the library. I know the lack of organisation has been eating away at you."

"Maybe," she agreed. But thinking about the library and the knowledge and history it contained inspired an idea. She could spend a good deal of her time researching which reforms had been successful elsewhere and how best to serve Aveyon's commoners. Perhaps if she had a plan already laid out by the time Lio returned, he wouldn't be able to refuse her, and nor would he want to.

"I left a detailed itinerary of the trip in our chambers so you'll always know where I am." He reached his hand out to her and pulled her close, touching her chin to tilt her head up at him. "If you need me, Belle, just send word and I'll come home." He spoke low, the words meant only for her.

"And if *you* need *me*, simply send word," she countered. "I will hurry to your side as quickly as Philippe can carry me."

He laughed at that and pressed a kiss to her lips. It felt like a goodbye, and Belle's heart tightened at the thought. Being forced apart for some months was not how she envisioned her first year as a married woman. But she and Lio had obligations towards a whole kingdom, not just each other. She hoped the parting would only make them stronger.

Lio climbed into his carriage, and Belle stepped back to where Bastien stood, waving her husband and his retinue away.

"It's good that you'll have something to focus on while Lio is gone," Bastien said teasingly, without looking away from the carriages as they rolled down the lane to the bridge that spanned the gorge between the castle and the forest beyond.

"What?"

"The library," he said. "I couldn't help but overhear. It's a worthy venture, to be sure." She didn't fail to note the sarcasm behind his words.

She decided to play along. "It will be nice to keep busy," she replied, also not looking away from the carriages.

"Yes, and then it will be just as nice to luxuriate in your thousands of books, knowing in your heart that each one has been accounted for, and that even if you lived a hundred lifetimes you'd never be able to read them all."

She looked over to him, her ruse falling away. "I wish to catalogue them so we can open the library to all of Aveyon, actually."

He paused to study her. "Truly?"

"Truly." She hated that her plans surprised him, but she hated how much it bothered her even more. "If you'll excuse me, I have to see to some things."

She left him standing there in the courtyard, dumbfounded, and it gave her a small bit of pleasure.

But she wasn't ready to let go of Lio just yet. She quickly climbed the West Tower and emerged on the balcony to watch the party as it entered the forest, feeling something in the pit of her stomach that resembled shame. She had promised Lio she would stay within the castle walls even if it meant giving up the freedom she had fought so hard for. She had done it to ease his mind, but what about hers?

Mrs Potts joined her at the lookout, having lived in the castle long enough to know where the best view was. "The faster we lose sight of him, the quicker he'll be home," she said, and though Belle knew it was just a platitude to make her feel better, she felt reassured. Mrs Potts had surmised that Belle was missing Lio already, but she didn't know the entirety of the complex emotions she was wrestling with.

"He's asked me to stay confined to the castle out of fear for my safety." The words tumbled out of her without much effort, because Belle knew Mrs Potts would understand why the request had stung so much.

Mrs Potts sighed and looked out to the barely visible carriages. "We do such foolhardy things in the name of love."

"That's why I said I would," Belle confessed. "I don't want to cause him any more stress."

"And what about your stress?" Mrs Potts asked, making a noise of pure exasperation. "We women are always twisting ourselves into knots for those we love without a care or consideration for how it might affect us." She reached for Belle's hand and shook it slightly. "You must always consider your own feelings as much as you consider his. More, even."

Belle hesitated. "I suppose you're right."

"I'm always right, dearie." But Mrs Potts could tell something was bothering Belle still. "I know this isn't how you envisioned your life with Lio. And right up until what happened in Paris, I almost believed you'd be able to hold on to the way things used to be."

"But now everything's different," Belle conceded.

Mrs Potts nodded. "But *you* don't have to be."

"What do you mean?"

Mrs Potts took a deep breath. "You're right: everything

is different. Everything has changed. Borders, titles, allegiances… My point is that amid all this upheaval, *you* can stay the same. You can be the constant the kingdom needs you to be." She looked out to the horizon. "The person you are now is the same person who saved our kingdom. Why should you ever want to change into someone else?"

It was a revelation for Belle to realise that Mrs Potts was right. She didn't have to change who she was just because she was married to a king, or because a whole country had its eyes on her, or because of the fear that had followed her all the way from the mirror shop in Paris. "Thank you, Mrs Potts."

Mrs Potts smiled at Belle. "I know you're going to do right by this kingdom and by Lio simply by being the girl who stood up to the Beast when he needed standing up to."

Mrs Potts squeezed Belle's arm and moved to leave the balcony.

"I meant to ask you," Belle called to Mrs Potts's retreating form. "Does Chip get nightmares too?"

Mrs Potts turned back and gave her a small smile. "No, he doesn't. Children seem more equipped to move past the bad things that happen to them."

"I envy them," Belle replied, remembering that the balcony she stood upon was the very spot where the Beast died.

"Don't. The bad things that happen in our lives serve to shape us just as much as the good."

Perhaps that was true, Belle thought. As she watched the last carriage fade into the forest, she remembered that the balcony was also where Lio came back to her.

CHAPTER FOURTEEN

The first day with Lio gone passed uneventfully.

Belle spent most of it walking barefoot through the castle gardens, collecting flowers and fruits and trying to distract herself from missing him. She knew she was being ridiculous. He had been gone less than a day, but they hadn't spent a night in separate dwellings since the very first time she had wandered into the castle searching for her father. It was strange to be without him in it. She preferred the open air of the gardens. She had fewer bad memories there.

The second day was just as uneventful.

Belle awoke to heavy rains, so she spent most of her day with Chip in the library, where they read aloud to each other before the fireplace and fed bites of his mother's pastries to a grateful Chou. The dramatic voices he did in a sweet attempt to cheer her up were a good distraction from her thoughts.

On the third day, she was restless. She hadn't seen Bastien since she had left him in the courtyard the day Lio departed. Bastien took most of his meals in his room, and Belle was left wondering why he had opted to stay at the castle if he was just going to avoid everyone else inside it.

Belle was wandering the halls aimlessly as rain battered the windows she passed. Chip and the other children who lived in the castle were being tutored in the library, and she didn't wish to disturb them. She knew she should get to work on her efforts towards reforms for Aveyon's commoners, or perhaps begin planning the salon like Lio had suggested, but she didn't know where to begin with either. She decided to let the ideas ruminate in her mind for a day or two, knowing her best plans came when she wasn't focusing too hard on a subject. Out of a desire to keep her body moving while allowing her brain to continue thinking about the work she had yet to do, she had decided to chart a course through the entirety of the castle and see how long it took her to go from one end to the other. She had barely begun when her path took her past the throne room, and she noted the door was shut tight.

She paused at the threshold, realising she could hear voices inside. Who could be in there, when the chief occupant of the throne was away, and Belle herself was standing on the other side of the door? She leaned close, straining to hear what was going on.

She realised in shock that the person speaking was Bastien. She couldn't hear what he was saying, but from the sound of it he wasn't alone.

She debated for a moment about interrupting whatever was going on, before reminding herself that she was married to the king of Aveyon and this was her throne room just as much as his. Whatever took place inside was every bit her business, especially in times such as these.

She pushed open the heavy door.

Bastien paused mid-sentence. "Belle," he said as though he had been expecting her. Her eyes swept the room. There was Baron Gamaches, Seigneur Geoffroy and most of the rest of Lio's advisory – *her* advisory – sitting around the table at which both she and the king were notably absent.

"What is this?" she asked, gesturing to the room of men. Evidently she had walked into an advisory meeting she hadn't been invited to.

Bastien smiled. He was almost unrecognisable without his painted face and powdered hair. If Belle hadn't spent an eventful carriage ride with him in that very state she might not have known him. "Just a dull meeting," he said in an offhand manner.

"I am on the advisory, and I wasn't informed of it."

"Don't be cross," he implored lightly. "It was done out of an effort to spare you a few hours of boredom."

She looked around the table at the men she knew didn't respect her one bit, and felt a blossom of defiance in her chest.

Bastien continued. "Honestly, Belle, it's hardly worth your time."

"Yes, madame, we are dealing with administrative tasks that you wouldn't wish to trouble yourself with," said Baron

Gamaches brusquely, despite having no earthly idea what she'd like to trouble herself with.

"I'll be the judge of that," she replied smartly, taking her seat at the table. The men around her sighed like they were indulging the whims of a child, but she would not be deterred. "Where is Montarly?"

"Entertaining your husband at his manor in Domard, I expect." Bastien pulled a parchment from his stack and passed it to her. "Are you not keeping abreast of the king's whereabouts? He was careful to make you a schedule to follow."

Belle didn't take the parchment he offered. "Of course I am." She just hadn't memorised it. She gritted her teeth. "Carry on, then."

Bastien made a show of returning to his parchments and seeking the correct one. "Right, where were we?" he muttered lightly. "Here we go." He frowned as he read the paper, which was creased from being folded tight, suggesting it was delivered by a messenger. "This one is actually not important; we can table it for another day."

"May I see it?" asked Belle, extending her arm.

Bastien looked torn between outright denying her and handing it over. Belle knew she didn't have any allies on the advisory, but she thought it would ruffle at least a few feathers if the duc refused her. She was still the king's wife after all, and though she hadn't taken a title, everyone knew what her rank would have been if she had.

"It's merely conjecture at this point," he told her while handing the creased parchment over by way of explanation. "Nothing to be too concerned about."

The script was small and tight, she had to bring it closer to her eyes to make it out. She read it aloud.

"Witnesses report three protests in the villages of Livrade, Foy and Plesance. Small in number, expressing pro-revolutionary sentiment. No reports of violence or destruction of property as of yet."

She looked up at Bastien. "This is not nothing." Plesance was where Belle had grown up, just a few short miles away from where she lived now, and under the jurisdiction of Seigneur Montarly. Her mind turned to speculating over who might have organised a protest in their sleepy village, though she had to concede it wasn't the unlikeliest place for revolt to bubble up. It had only been a few short months since the residents of Plesance had been worked into a frenzy by one man and formed an angry mob. Belle still shuddered when she remembered the crazed look in the eyes of her neighbours and friends as they marched on the castle, intent on killing the Beast with no cause other than hatred propelling them forward. She hadn't thought any of them capable of such anger, but they had proved more than competent. Belle could still hear their rhythmic chants echoing in her mind.

Kill the Beast!
Kill the Beast!

But they hadn't known him at all. Memories of their roles in the mob had been erased when the curse was destroyed, but Belle couldn't forget. It was why she hadn't been home since.

Bastien waved her away. "Three non-violent protests, if we can even classify them as such, *are* nothing. Are you going to suggest it is illegal to form a crowd in Aveyon? To discuss ideas freely in the open?"

She knew he was baiting her. "Of course not, but this is an indication of something bigger. If our commoners aren't happy, if their needs aren't being met, then we should be focusing on them and not our nobility."

"The king is *exactly* where he needs to be," said Bastien, his tone leaving no room for questioning.

"Madame," Geoffroy said, his voice dripping with contempt, "we received reports like this all throughout the king's illness and forwarded them diligently to him, and he never seemed overly concerned about them. It is a common thing, I think, to protest. Have any peasants ever truly been happy with their lot?"

Belle took a deep breath and tried hard not to lash out at Geoffroy, who was lying through his teeth, since everyone had been cursed to forget Lio's existence for those ten years. The likelier story was that he and the rest of Aveyon's nobility did what they could to quash the protests while also ignoring and refusing to fix the cause of them.

"The happenstance of someone's birth should not determine whether or not they are impoverished. It is up to those of us with power in whatever form to work to make the lives of everyone better, starting with those less fortunate than us," she said.

Geoffroy drew himself up. "You speak as though you would abolish the monarchy, madame."

"If I thought Aveyon's problems would be solved by doing so, I would hope that Lio would consider it, seigneur. But we are not America. Good can still come of our institutions, if they are not left to fester." She let the last word hang in the air so that the men who had indeed left Aveyon to fester while Lio was cursed would maybe consider their behaviour, knowing that was wishful thinking on her part.

Bastien surveyed her with his chin resting on his fist. "And how do you suggest we better the lives of Aveyon's peasants? What sweeping reforms do you suggest we implement? And on whose authority and with what money? Aveyon's coffers are hardly overflowing."

Belle knew that was true. They didn't have the money to simply throw at Aveyon's problems and hope they went away. Lio's time as the Beast had not been a prosperous period for Aveyon's fledgling industries of lumber and the like. But money wasn't required for the idea that had finally bloomed, fully formed, in Belle's mind.

"I'd like to hear from Aveyon's commoners by opening

the castle to petitioners who may tell us what they think of the state of our kingdom. I'd like to hear their ideas for how things can be done better." She paused and looked around at the blank faces of the advisory. "I'd like to give them a voice."

But Bastien had the same look of surprise on his face he had worn when she told him about her dream to open the library to all of Aveyon. It was like she had not lived up to his preconceived notions that she was just a flighty girl who had found herself married to a prince by some accident. She had been similarly surprised by him a few times, but they were rare moments and he almost always returned to the person she was fairly certain he had been all along – arrogant, selfish and insouciant when it came to matters not directly affecting him.

She could tell the advisers wanted to refuse her request, but how could they? All she wanted was access to the people of Aveyon. Monarchs had been receiving petitioners for hundreds of years, so it was hardly a radical idea. And it would cost them almost nothing but time. She couldn't believe she hadn't thought of it sooner. Through the information she collected from petitioners, Belle could begin to identify common problems and even form a hypothesis for how to fix them. She could be scientific about repairing Aveyon. And when Lio returned from his estate tour, she could present him with evidence and options.

"I suppose it's not the worst idea," admitted Bastien.

"Thank you for your ringing endorsement."

He ignored the sarcasm. "All in favour of opening the castle to petitioners once a week?"

"Twice a week," she corrected.

He pressed his lips together but conceded. "All in favour of opening the castle to petitioners twice a week?" The men around the table raised their hands as though they were made of lead, but Belle had her consensus. Bastien banged on the table. "It is done." He looked over to Belle. "I'll see to the arrangements. I hope you're ready to take on all the mundane ills of the kingdom."

She smiled serenely. "If I can help, I'd like to."

The duc looked back to the advisers. "I think that's enough for today."

The men rose, but Belle wasn't done yet. "I expect to be informed of all future meetings. It's what the king wanted, after all."

"Of course, madame," said Gamaches, bowing stiffly. They began to shuffle out, and Belle imagined a future where the decisions made for the good of Aveyon had nothing to do with old rich men.

She stopped Bastien from leaving with a light touch on his arm. "You've been missed at meals," she lied, knowing that Mrs Potts, Lumière, Cogsworth and the rest of her friends didn't mind the duc's absence at all.

Bastien squirmed a bit out of reach. "Yes, I've taken to dining in my room—"

"Join us in the dining room tonight. It does you no good to be shut up in your chambers." She made it clear it wasn't a request, but used a tone that made the demand come across lightly.

He nodded. "I will."

In truth, Belle didn't care if Bastien dined with them or didn't. She found his company to be grating at best. She had never quite trusted Bastien, and now that he was excluding her from meetings, she had reason not to. She wasn't sure she bought his explanation that he was trying to save her from something tedious, but then, she had no reason to suspect his motives were more sinister. Still, she wanted to be prepared for all possibilities. Her insistence that he join them for dinner had little to do with any desire to be near the duc and everything to do with wanting to keep an eye on him until Lio returned.

CHAPTER FIFTEEN

B elle would never admit it, but she was beginning to think Bastien might have been right about the mundane ills of the kingdom.

In the two times she had received petitioners, she had not come away from either session with a clear idea of what Aveyon's commoners were thinking. There had been the baker who complained about her rival in business setting up shop next door to her out of spite. Belle wasn't sure how to explain that she couldn't simply tell the other baker to vacate his legally occupied premises, as the petitioner seemed to wish she would.

Then there was the droguiste whose complaint boiled down to not being able to find a satisfactory amount of live snails for vulnerary applications, and Belle had to explain that she didn't think it was within her power or abilities to increase Aveyon's population of snails.

Not to mention the washerwoman who had used her petition time to simply gossip about the various scandals going on at her place of employment, of which there were many more than Belle had thought possible for a laundry. Mercifully, the woman didn't seem to require an answer or solution from Belle and was content to simply say her piece and leave.

Most petitions were of a similar ilk, and despite her earlier desire to hear from everyone who would petition her, Belle was coming close to suggesting a sort of vetting process, if only to weed out the truly actionable problems from the petty complaints.

Bastien, present for all petitioners, would look to Belle and shrug, or smirk knowingly, or laugh under his breath when she struggled to find a response for those who brought their problems to her. She had thought Aveyon's commoners would be lining up to tell her in great detail what was wrong with the kingdom and what they believed would help. She had not expected to come away more confused than ever.

After her third session was again filled with interpersonal conflict, petty disputes and neighbours informing on their neighbours over the smallest infractions, Belle was beginning to suspect she was being had. Word had gone out in the villages and shires of Aveyon that she was receiving petitioners in the castle, surely any number of the people who had protested in Livrade, Foy and Plesance would have had the opportunity to bring their grievances directly to her by then. Bastien's repeated reminders that Belle had *asked* for this and she should be *grateful* that so many of her people had answered her call for petitions were not helping. Something wasn't sitting right.

She hatched a plan and bribed Lumière into calling Bastien from the throne room to attend to a very important, very imaginary matter. Belle was listening to a young girl who claimed her neighbour was stealing herbs from her garden in the dead of night. When she paused to catch her breath, Belle jumped in.

"What is your neighbour's name?"

The girl faltered. "Her name?" Belle only smiled so as not to intimidate the girl further. After a long moment, she spoke again. "Emilde."

Belle shifted in her seat as though wrestling with a decision. "I'd say the only solution is to bring Emilde in and figure out a way forward together." The girl blanched. "That is, of course, if you're willing."

"Madame, that is a most generous offer, but I think I've overblown the situation." She curtsied and everything about her posture begged for dismissal.

"I'm going to ask you a question, and I want you to know that there is no wrong answer, nor will you be in trouble in any way based on your reply." The girl looked like she wished she would melt into the floor, but she nodded. "Is your quarrel with Emilde real?"

"Real, madame?" The girl fidgeted with her skirts.

Belle tried to give off a sense of calm. "By that I mean"

– she leaned closer and spoke softly – "is *Emilde* real?"

The girl looked to where Bastien had been sitting until only moments before. When she confirmed that he was still away from the room, she looked back at Belle and shook her head ever so lightly. Belle felt she had enough to go in for the kill, but she restrained herself.

"Did someone tell you to come here today?" The girl nodded. "Did someone tell you to fabricate a story to present to me?"

"He—he offered me twelve livres to come here."

"Who?" Belle didn't want to goad her into answering. She knew if she was going to get her facts in order, the girl would have to tell her voluntarily.

The girl looked down at her hands twisting together. "Madame, I cannot. I swore not to tell."

Belle nodded, trying her best not to appear annoyed by the girl's reluctance to identify the man. She rose from her chair and stepped closer to the girl. "If you hadn't been told to come here, would you have known about my taking petitioners?"

The girl shook her head. "No, madame."

"No announcement has been made about it?"

She swallowed. "None that I have seen or heard." Footsteps echoed in the hall beyond them, and the girl paled. "Please do not say anything, madame. My family needs the money."

Despite the rage coursing through her, Belle held up her hand to stop her. "I won't. I promise." The fact that the girl was more afraid of Bastien than she was of lying to the wife of the king of Aveyon spoke volumes. Belle's blood was boiling as the doors to the room opened once more and Bastien strolled back inside, giving the two girls a curious look.

"Thank you," Belle whispered. "For telling me the truth." She pressed another twelve-livre coin in the girl's hand, hoping she understood the need for discretion. The girl bobbed in an uneven curtsy and left.

Bastien came to stand beside her, watching the girl leave the room. "Everything all right?" he asked.

Belle sighed. "Just another mundane complaint that has almost nothing to do with the kingdom at large."

He gave her a sympathetic smile. "What did I tell you?"

"You were right," she agreed, making a show of it.

"Don't be too hard on yourself, Belle. You're doing your best."

He walked back over to where he sat during the petitions, and Belle bit her tongue. She couldn't be positive that it was Bastien who had put the petitioners up to lying to her. There was a chance it was another adviser, like Baron Gamaches or Seigneur Geoffroy, working diligently to undermine her. But despite how much she knew they disliked her, she didn't think they had it in them to make a move so overtly against her.

Either way, it was baffling. More work would have gone into finding commoners willing to lie to Belle and keep their mouths shut about it than simply announcing that she was taking petitioners. But there was something Bastien, or someone else, didn't want her to know, didn't want the people to tell her. What could it be? She was aware of the protests already, so it didn't make sense that anyone was trying to shield her from the unhappiness of her people.

She was going to have to be smart about her next move, smarter than the duc de Vincennes, who she suspected had been playing at deception all his life, having learned from the best at the court of Versailles. She knew if she were to confront him right away, he would have some excuse for his actions at the ready, and she wouldn't be able to decipher his true intent.

The question remained: now that Belle suspected Bastien was lying to her, what was she going to do about it?

• • •

The pain of missing her husband was Belle's constant, aching companion.

She did her best to keep busy to avoid losing herself to the yawning void of it, but if she paused long enough, it crept upon her like a chill.

It even rendered her favourite pastime, reading, difficult. Her mind was too idle, sitting in a sun-drenched parlour with only someone else's words to occupy her. She thought of Lio, alone when they should have been together, and sadness began to pool around her like a rising tide. She stood and tried to shake free of the melancholy, setting out from the room like she was running from something.

The halls were empty, and Belle needed a refuge from her thoughts. She tried to think of happier times with Lio, back before they had left for Paris, when everything seemed simple in the wake of destroying a curse, back before he took the crown, when it had felt like there was nothing that could come between them, and even if something tried, they would have been able to take it on together.

But she hadn't anticipated that the thing that would come between them was family.

As she walked the empty halls, Belle thought back to Bastien's desk full of revolutionary pamphlets. She wondered if they came from infiltrating the ranks of the sans-culottes or bourgeoisie on behalf of King Louis, or if perhaps Lio's cousin had secret revolutionary sympathies. It was hard to know which Bastien was real and which was an artifice. He painted his face and powdered his hair and threw parties infamous for their intemperance, and yet he defended the Third Estate to her.

And if he was a secret revolutionary, then what was he doing so far from Paris? And why was he doing his best to foil Belle's plans to improve the lives of Aveyon's commoners?

It didn't make any sense. She needed more information before she could accuse him or clear him of any wrongdoing.

She wandered all the way to the kitchens and was happy to find Mrs Potts inside with a sinkful of teatime dishes and soap up to her elbows.

"Do you mind if I dry?" Belle asked.

"Now tell me, why would I mind a bit of help?" Mrs Potts replied, gesturing for Belle to take a tea towel and get to work on the pile of dripping cutlery. "What's troubling you? Aside from Lio being gone."

Belle picked up a fork and got to drying. She trusted Mrs Potts more than almost anyone in the castle, but she didn't want to sully the cook's opinion of Bastien just yet. All Belle knew was that he, or admittedly someone else, was lying to her, which was egregious enough, but she needed more to go on before she pointed fingers. So she went with another thing that was bothering her. "Lio's advisers refuse to take me seriously. They act as if I am a child, not the wife of their king."

Mrs Potts raised her eyebrow. "You're more than someone's wife, dearie."

"You know what I mean."

She sighed. "I do." She glanced over at Belle. "I hope you don't take this the wrong way, but why on earth do you give a damn what those decrepit windbags think about you?"

Belle was so shocked to hear Mrs Potts curse that she dropped the cup she was holding. She had never heard Mrs Potts swear before. It was a shock, but a welcome one. "I suppose I don't care, but they still hold a lot of power here. Everything I do must pass through them first, and they don't think very highly of my desire to work with commoners."

"So stop seeking their approval."

She said it like it was the easiest thing in the world. "Then I'm no better than King Louis."

"We all know that isn't true. What I mean is, dear, you're not a queen, so stop acting like one."

Belle tried to grasp what she meant and failed.

Mrs Potts dropped the dish she was scrubbing back into the sink and wiped her hands on her apron. "A queen must answer to everyone: her staff, her advisers, her nobles, her people. Every move she makes is scrutinised, dissected and judged, because her decisions affect the entire kingdom, yes?"

Belle nodded, still unsure of where Mrs Potts was going with this argument.

"But you aren't a queen, nor do you wish to be. Your decisions will not be acted upon as though you are. You are free to associate and learn from who you wish. And you are free to give Lio wise counsel when he returns so that he can be the one to shoulder the responsibility, as he should."

"So you mean to say that I can do as I please."

"If Aveyon can't have you as their queen, being its people's advocate might be the next best thing."

Belle smiled but then remembered her promise. "I told Lio I'd stay in the castle."

"And did you ever really intend to? What Lio doesn't know won't hurt him. He was wrong to ask that of you, and I'll tell him that myself when he returns." Mrs Potts plunged her hands back into the soapy water but then paused again. "I'd keep all of this from the duc if I were you. There's something about him…"

Belle touched Mrs Potts's arm. "I know what you mean."

They had come to the end of the pile of dirty dishes. "Thank you for your help."

"Anytime," Belle replied.

"Now go make yourself useful."

Belle knew what she meant, and she left the kitchens feeling like she had a great deal more control over her life than she had an hour earlier. Now that she understood that she didn't need the advisory's approval for every step she took, they could stop butting heads so much. She would keep her activities and research to herself, and still attend meetings to remain aware of what was going on in the kingdom.

As she walked through the castle, a new plan for how she would gather ideas and research from the regular people was forming in her mind, one that would require a disguise.

She would have to be careful to keep it from Bastien, though. Knowing she wasn't the only one suspicious of the duc was reassuring. If there was anyone whose instincts Belle trusted even more than her own, it was Mrs Potts.

• • •

Belle meant to slip from the castle just after the sun

went down.

No one knew she was leaving, and she made sure there were no witnesses to her departure. She had feigned illness all day, steadily increasing the severity of her apparent ailment until Cogsworth sent her away from the dining room at dinner, begging that she retire to her chambers until her symptoms abated.

She faked a cough in Bastien's direction as she left the room, relishing the way he flinched from her.

In her chambers, she undressed quickly and donned her disguise – a simple rough-spun dress not unlike what a maid would wear, and a hooded cloak – and studied herself in the mirror. The outfit had the same effect as her plain gown in Paris. She would blend right into the streets of Aveyon. She would be invisible.

Belle opened the door and looked both ways down the empty hall. She shut it quietly behind her and slowly made her way to the stables, occasionally hiding around corners to avoid seeing anyone.

The stables were dark, but she knew where to find Philippe. She stepped up to his stall and whistled a familiar note to her dear Belgian draft horse. She hadn't had reason to ride him in months. He whinnied excitedly and pressed his velvet-soft coppery nose to her outstretched hand, searching for the treat he knew she'd brought him.

"Are you ready to go on a small adventure with me?" she

whispered into his ear while removing the apple from her pocket and holding it to his mouth. He made a noise that could have been an agreement and made quick work of the snack. She saddled him in the dark, working from memory since she couldn't quite see what she was doing. Philippe stood patiently still and waited for her to mount him.

Together they left the stables. Philippe seemed to understand the need for secrecy. Belle guided him through the gardens and out to the northernmost edge of the castle grounds, where there was a small breach in the wall no one had got round to repairing yet.

"Think you can make the jump?" she asked. Philippe grunted as though the question was an insult. He trotted over and made the jump with ease, earning a gracious scratch around his ears from Belle. "We're going to the village, Philippe."

He walked her dutifully down the winding hill and all the way into the village of Mauger, the only one that lay between the castle and Belle's home village of Plesance. Everyone in Plesance knew who she was, but in Mauger, she could be anyone.

Night had fallen in full by the time they reached the village. Belle rode Philippe all the way up to the busiest-looking tavern and dismounted. The streets were far from empty, but she didn't get a sense of unrest just yet. No one gave her a second look as she tied Philippe to the post and rewarded him with a second apple she had taken from the kitchens.

As she entered the establishment, Lio's voice echoed in her mind: *it isn't safe, Belle.* She wondered how he would react if he could see her in that moment, walking alone into a busy tavern.

But Belle wasn't a fool. She understood that she was taking a risk by being in the village unescorted. Even without the threat of revolution and unrest, it wasn't wise to be a woman out on her own. She had to keep her wits about her.

Belle pulled her hood tighter around her face and made for an empty table. She knew in her heart she would rather put herself at risk than be as out of touch as King Louis and Queen Marie Antoinette. And the only way she could get a sense of how the people of Aveyon were truly feeling was to walk among them. Especially since she thought Bastien was hiding something from her.

The barmaid came over to her and smiled. "What'll it be?"

Belle looked at the tables around her for clues but found none. "A tea?" she asked. She had long steered clear of the tavern in Plesance in an effort to avoid its most dedicated customer, Gaston, so she didn't know if the request was an odd one.

"One tea, coming right up." The barmaid turned on her heel, and Belle leaned back in her chair.

The room was large and filled with people of all sorts. She

saw labourers, spinners, weavers and farmers lined up at the bar ordering ales to ease a hard day's work out of their tired muscles. Huddled around tables drinking wine were men dressed in the finer clothes that marked them as merchants, traders or lawyers. And dancing between them all were three or four barmaids who moved with a practised efficiency.

The tavern was loud. Belle could hardly make out what anyone was saying, and if she couldn't hear anyone, her plan would be a failure.

The barmaid appeared and placed a steaming teapot on the table, followed by a chipped cup and saucer. A flash of pain flickered through Belle as she unwittingly thought back to the days of the curse, when a boy as vibrant as Chip had been wickedly confined to a form so delicate. The woman gave her a curious look. "That'll be a sou."

Belle pulled out the coin and handed it over. The barmaid gave her a small curtsy and was on her way. The gesture concerned Belle – she worried she stuck out in the tavern despite the roughness of her garment. But then the thought felt silly. She had spent the vast majority of her life belonging in places like the tavern. It was only recent events that would have marked her out as different from the rest of the crowd. She poured the hot tea into the cup and stirred some sugar into it for want of something to do with her hands.

"Are you alone?" asked a nice-enough-sounding voice.

Belle looked over to a girl in an apron and cap.

"Yes," she offered.

"Not sure I'd want to be a woman alone in a place like this. You can join us, if you like." The girl gestured to her table of women, all wearing similar caps and aprons. Belle didn't hesitate and dragged her chair over to the group. The girl who had invited her over spoke. "I'm Sidonie, and these are the ladies I work with. We're weavers over at Saint Madeleine's."

"I'm Delphine," Belle replied, using Lio's mother's name as an alias. "I'm... a maid."

"You're clothed like a castle maid," remarked one of the women.

Belle hesitated, but decided to stick as close to the truth as possible so as to avoid confusion. "I am."

Some of the table looked at her with renewed interest. "That's a plum position. What's it like?"

"Being a maid?" Belle asked.

The woman rolled her eyes. "No, working in the castle. I hear the king and his wife are kind employers."

A man who had been eavesdropping nearby scoffed. "What does it matter if they're kind?"

Sidonie rolled her eyes. "Oh, tais-toi, Guillaume." It seemed they knew each other. Guillaume came over and wrapped an arm around her shoulder and looked over at Belle. "Tell me, is the king truly touring his noblemen's estates?"

Belle swallowed. "Yes, but—"

Guillaume tipped his mug of ale back and slammed it on

the table. "Of *course* he is."

Another man joined in. "He didn't give a damn about us for ten years – why would he start now?"

Sidonie rolled her eyes. "It's not as though he's done nothing. We've seceded from France."

"And now we don't have to take part in the corvée," offered another woman, referring to the unpaid labour Aveyon's peasants had long been subject to at the behest of the French crown.

Guillaume gave her a pitying look. "You don't think our good king is plotting his own version of the blasted corvée with his nobles as we speak? Forced labour is far too lucrative a thing for him to give up. Besides, working twelve-hour shifts at the mill in order to afford rent and taxes and food is hardly better."

Belle spoke before thinking. "The king believes in equality."

Guillaume waved at a barmaid and gestured for another round. Then he leaned in close to Belle. "Tell me, if he believes in equality, why are the classes taxed differently? Why does Aveyon still operate under discriminatory French law, the same law, might I add, that pushed the people of France to revolution? Why has he changed nothing save for who wears the crown?" Belle was silent, and Guillaume nodded as if he had expected it. "Until the peasants of Aveyon can advance in society without barriers, the king has earned only my disdain."

"His wife was a peasant," offered another man with a smile.

Guillaume threw back his ale and belched. "Yes, well, sadly we can't all marry the king."

Sidonie folded her arms across her chest. "I still think it's too early to judge him. He's been king for less than a month."

"And look at where his priorities lie," said Guillaume with a shrug. "I remain sceptical."

Belle wanted so badly to defend Lio, and by extension, herself, but it would not be prudent. She decided to be grateful to have a peek into the minds of everyday people, which was all she had wanted when she opened the castle to petitioners. She studied Guillaume and Sidonie, feeling something like a kinship with them. Though Guillaume's complaints would not be easy to address, they were things she knew Lio would be quick to correct. At least they weren't marching in the streets or pushing for more violent tactics. Lio would have to earn back the trust of his people, who were concerned about unequal taxation and eager for their king to establish an Aveyonian code of law, separate from French law. She felt somewhat more capable now that she had a clear direction to move in. Perhaps when Lio returned and Belle presented him with a way forward, Aveyon could begin to heal.

Sidonie shuffled closer to her, pressing her hands into the grain of the table. "You never told us what it's like up in the castle, what the king and his wife Belle are like." She spoke with an awe in her voice Belle was sure she didn't deserve.

She looked at the weaver's hands, battered by the work that she did. Sidonie's cheeks were hollow, and she looked like she didn't often get a restful night's sleep. Belle knew Aveyon was nothing like France, but that didn't mean the kingdom couldn't improve.

"They're far from perfect," she admitted. "But they care a lot about this kingdom."

That seemed to confirm Sidonie's suspicions. "I only wish they'd listen to us, you know?"

"Me too," Belle replied. And she meant it.

CHAPTER SIXTEEN

By the time Belle and Philippe made it back to the castle that night, her mind was bursting with ideas. Instead of doing research and circling around the idea of planning a salon, Belle wondered if she could combine them. She imagined herself hosting a salon like Lio had urged her to, only instead of a typical salon spent discussing literature and the like, the goal of Belle's salon would be to establish reforms that would improve the lives of everyone in Aveyon. She would gather the brightest minds to the castle – philosophers, economists, scientists and the like – to debate governance and politics in order to establish the best way forward.

The thought of it filled her with hope. She wanted to get to work straight away, starting with a visit to the bookshop in Plesance in order to brush up on Aveyon's tax and labour laws so she could establish a baseline to work off. She briefly considered riding all the way to Plesance and knocking on Monsieur Renaud's door until she woke him up and he let her into his shop, but decided she would seem a great deal less mad if she waited until morning.

She brought Philippe back to the stables and took her time brushing out his glorious blonde mane. He was one of the last reminders she had of Plesance and the small cottage she shared with her father there, and she was happy to have brought the best parts of her old life with her to her new home in the castle. She kissed his nose and made to leave, but someone else entered the stable first. Belle ducked into an empty stall and pressed herself into a shadowy corner to avoid detection.

It was a stable boy seeing to the last of his nightly duties. Suddenly a horse and rider clattered in, nearly scaring him out of his skin.

"I didn't know you had left, monsieur," said the stable boy, speaking to the ground in a low bow.

"I had business in the village."

Belle almost revealed herself by the noise she made when she heard Bastien's dismissive tone. She moved her body so she could see into the rest of the stable. Bastien tossed the reins at the boy and peeled his gloves off. "Make sure she has enough to eat; I rode her hard tonight." Belle thought that contradictory to his earlier claim that he had simply had business in the village.

"Yes, my lord."

"And speak of this to no one." His voice did not leave room for lightness. Belle didn't often hear Bastien speak so plainly, without an ounce of warmth or a customary witty barb.

"Y-yes, monsieur."

The duc left the stable in a rush, leaving the poor boy to tend to his horse well after he should have been sleeping. Belle waited until he walked the horse to her stall before hurrying away unseen. As she made her way to her chambers, she was left to contend with a troubling thought: She hadn't been the only one to sneak away from the castle that night.

• • •

When she walked into the book shop in Plesance the next morning, it felt a bit like coming home.

She had left Lumière – who had insisted on coming – at the bakery next door, but only after making him promise not to pester the baker too intensely. The shop wasn't as well stocked as the grand bookshops of Paris, but what it lacked in inventory it made up for in warmth. She could have drawn the shop from memory – the threadbare carpet, the worn-out shelves, even the books that rarely changed. She had read most of them at least once.

"Belle!" cried Monsieur Renaud, an ancient yet ageless man Belle had known her whole life. "I've been wondering when you'd show up." It was said kindly, for hardly a week had gone by in at least ten years without Belle visiting at least once. "I've been saving a pile of your adventure books for you," he told her while making his way over to the desk he worked behind most of the day.

"That's very kind of you, monsieur, but I am here for a

different kind of book."

He paused, bent over and raised a quizzical brow. "Oh?"

"Do you have any books pertaining to Aveyon's tax laws or labour laws?"

He drew up straighter. "I'm sure we can find something." He shuffled over to a shelf she would have usually avoided. "Did you see Madame Tailler on your way here? She's been asking about you."

Belle had predicted as much, and had left the castle as early as possible in order to avoid most of her old neighbours. They didn't care for her much when she lived there with her father, and she couldn't bear the thought of them playing nice with her now, acting as though they hadn't whispered unkindly about her every time they had crossed paths. "No, I didn't have a chance."

"Next time, perhaps," he muttered while scanning the shelf. "Are you still hoping to catalogue your library?"

She had confided in him the last time she visited the bookshop, well before they left for Paris. "It's a dream, to be sure, but perhaps a distant one. I wouldn't even know where to begin."

"Why, at the beginning, of course." He gave her a wink before looking back at the shelf. "Ah, here we are." He pulled a dusty tome down and handed it to her. "This covers everything from the reign of Louis XIV onwards, though now that we've seceded I imagine this book will soon be obsolete."

He looked at her expectantly over his half-moon spectacles, but she didn't indulge him. Belle didn't want to make any promises she couldn't keep. He noted her slight frown and patted the back of her hand. "It was the right decision."

She cleared her throat, suddenly aware of how small the bookshop really was and how much she had needed to hear him say that. "Merci, Monsieur Renaud. How much do I owe you?"

"Don't you worry about that, madame."

"I insist." Belle had benefited from the shopkeeper's generosity before, when she had almost nothing to give him. Now that she was able, she'd make sure he was properly compensated.

He blushed a bit. "An écu would do."

She handed him a silver coin just as the door behind her rang out a new arrival. Monsieur Renaud looked over her shoulder and smiled. "Ah, Mademoiselle de Lambriquet," he called out.

Belle turned and was shocked to see Marguerite de Lambriquet strolling into the shop, as striking as the first time she saw her at Bastien's fête. She wore an emerald-green dress that wouldn't have looked out of place in Paris but certainly did in Plesance.

"Bonjour, monsieur!" she called jovially before noticing who stood next to the shopkeeper. Heat rose to her brown cheeks as she made her way over.

"Come, Marguerite, you must meet our dear Belle." It was a possessive way to refer to her, but Belle didn't mind. A part of her would always belong to this provincial town and the people she had grown up beside.

Monsieur Renaud gestured to her until the two of them stood face-to-face. Belle had forgotten that Marguerite had several inches on her. Someone at the door caught Monsieur Renaud's attention, and he gave them a quick bow before turning away.

"Oh, but we've already met, monsieur, back in Paris," called Marguerite to the back of the shopkeeper, giving Belle a conspiratorial smile.

Belle could hardly believe she was standing right in front of her. "What are you doing in Aveyon?"

Marguerite's smile turned bashful. "Is it horrible of me to admit that I may have taken your vague invitation to visit Aveyon a little too seriously? I meant to be here for your husband's coronation, but travel within France has been somewhat hampered of late."

"You came all this way for Lio's coronation?" Belle could hardly believe it.

Marguerite's brow creased. "It was foolish of me to come. You must be so preoccupied with everything happening with the secession." She began to back away from Belle as if ashamed. "I am so sorry to have burdened you further."

Belle reached out a hand to stop her. "Burden me? Don't be

ridiculous, this is the happiest I've been in days."

"Truly?"

"Truly," Belle assured her. "That dress alone has brightened up my day."

Marguerite looked down at the dress and fanned her skirts out to admire the way the satin shone in the light pouring in from the window. "Yes, it is quite fine, isn't it? I normally prefer a more subdued type of gown, but I couldn't resist when I caught sight of it in Rose Bertin's shop for practically nothing. I'm told it was made especially for Marie Antoinette just before she suddenly decided she abhorred the colour. Her loss is my gain."

Belle grinned. "She wouldn't have been able to do it justice like you." She pulled Marguerite to a corner of the shop and spoke at a lower volume. "How did you get here? Where is your escort?"

Marguerite blanched, her big smile fading. "I am on my own," she admitted.

"What of your father and brother?"

She sighed. "My father grew tired of the whole charade and has absconded to America with what little remained of his money, and my brother, the rogue, has sensed the shifting tide and taken up with the ever-progressive Philippe, the duc d'Orléans, suddenly and suspiciously uninterested in his birthright." She rolled her eyes.

"Your father just left you?" Belle thought of her own father, and how she worried every time he travelled far from Plesance. She knew he hated being away from her too.

Marguerite waved away Belle's concern. "My father and I were not particularly close. After my mother died, Aurelian and I were mostly raised by governesses. My father informed me he was selling our manor via a letter written by his valet, whom I liked a great deal more, if I'm being honest." She looked out the window absently. "I know I should miss my father, but I think perhaps I miss my mother more, though I barely knew her." She paused and heat rose to her cheeks as she seemed to remember whom she was speaking to. "I apologise, I forget myself."

"Don't apologise," Belle assured her. "I lost my mother when I was quite young as well. It is a pain that never leaves you."

Marguerite smiled a sad smile. "Yes, well, my mother had the sense to leave me a small inheritance my father could not touch, and since I have no interest in moving to America and even less interest in staying in Paris, I thought I'd take inspiration from you and begin a tour of the Continent myself. I had made it as far as my great-aunt's home in Arlon when I heard about Aveyon's secession and subsequent coronation and found I couldn't resist. I've always been someone who is drawn to the action and the drama, no offence. And now that I'm here, I've fallen in love with the countryside and can't seem to pull away from it just yet."

Jealousy washed over Belle, making her skin itch. She had never known a woman so free, so independent. She found she envied and admired Marguerite in equal measure. More than anything she wished to know her better, and having her appear in Aveyon was a welcome distraction.

"See, I've always found Aveyon to be painfully dull. I spent my childhood longing to leave this kingdom." Belle snapped her mouth shut, realising she had just disparaged the kingdom to someone who may as well have been a stranger. But it was so easy to converse with Marguerite. Something about her put Belle at ease.

Marguerite touched Belle's forearm. "I know what you mean. It would seem we always want what we don't have. I longed for stability, for a slower pace. Paris is balls and salons and the theatre and opera night after night after night. It's exhausting and expensive keeping up with the latest trends, but here I feel like I can breathe."

Belle looked out the back window that faced the rolling fields and mountainous horizon and felt like she could understand that, especially after her small taste of Paris. "I liked Aveyon a great deal more once I returned to it," she conceded.

Marguerite began to circle the room, pausing before the sparse shelves of books. "I'll admit I was tantalised by stories of how magnificent your library is."

Pride rushed through her. "It's been my dream to catalogue

it so I can open it to everyone in Aveyon." The words poured from her lips easily, despite the fact that aside from Monsieur Renaud and Lio and Bastien, she hadn't revealed her desire to anyone.

Marguerite looked over her shoulder back at Belle. "What's preventing you?"

Belle looked down to the heavy book in her hands. "I have other duties I must see to first."

"Surely a queen can delegate tasks?" Marguerite scoffed.

"I'm not—"

"Not a queen, I know. I remember how much you abhor titles, so I cannot pretend I was surprised to hear you rejected the grandest one of all. But, madame, you are a queen in all but name."

Belle stopped herself from revealing just how much she chafed at the idea of being queen of Aveyon. There were some things she'd never reveal to anyone, no matter how obvious they were. "There are things I need to do first. The people of Aveyon need egalitarian reforms before I get round to the library."

Marguerite snapped a book shut and returned it to the shelf. "What could be more egalitarian than access to literature for all people of Aveyon?"

Belle knew she had a point, but she was beginning to get overwhelmed by all the things she wished to do. It was true that if she had some assistance, then perhaps her plans would seem more achievable. She looked over to Marguerite, a woman who could come and go as she pleased, who could follow a whim to a whole new life if she wished. Instead of envy, Belle felt a glimmer of possibility. "How long are you planning to stay in Aveyon?"

Marguerite frowned. "Sadly my lodgings are short-term only. I should be returning to my grand tour quicker than I'd like."

Belle thought it was sudden, and that she hardly knew this captivating woman who had done and seen all the things Belle had longed to do her whole life. But the more the idea formed in her mind, the more right it felt in her bones. "And you said you've been to many salons?"

"Madame, I've been to and *hosted* plenty."

Belle's mind was made up. "Perhaps I should begin work on the library," she conceded.

"Perhaps you should," Marguerite countered.

"And perhaps I should host a salon while I'm at it."

"I can't see why not."

"And perhaps," Belle added in summation, "you could help me with both."

Marguerite was stunned. "Me?"

"You said it yourself; you're exhausted and wish to extend your stay. Why not do so in the castle? You can help me begin the work of opening the library and teach me how to host a salon."

Marguerite shook her head. "Belle, I couldn't."

"It's not glamorous work, especially for one used to King Louis's court, but you can take up residence in the castle, and I'd pay you a wage of course."

She could see how the offer was enticing Marguerite, a girl adrift in a world that would be increasingly unkind to her. "You'd really offer me all that?"

"I know it's not Paris, but—"

"It's perfect," Marguerite interjected, as if afraid Belle would talk herself out of offering the position.

Belle laughed. "Truly?"

"Truly!" Marguerite clapped her hands together.

"It won't be easy," Belle warned. "There are many thousands of books, most of which haven't been touched in decades. I hope you don't mind dust. And I'm planning something different for the salon, something I don't believe has been done before."

Marguerite raised an eyebrow. "I must say you've piqued my interest, though I'll warn you, I was in attendance at Pauline Lemaure's infamous bacchanal of a salon, so I truly have seen *everything*."

Having seen Bastien's guests behave like utter boors at a simple dinner, Belle shuddered to think what was meant by *infamous bacchanal*, but she decided it best to leave that a mystery. More than anything, she was thrilled to have someone as sharp as the Mademoiselle de Lambriquet by her side as Belle navigated her new role. When she recalled how swiftly Marguerite had handled the comte de Chamfort when he derided her status, she knew she had at last found an ally against Bastien.

CHAPTER SEVENTEEN

I n the span of a day, the course of Belle's happiness shifted dramatically. Suddenly, she had tasks and duties as well as a trusted friend. She spent her mornings with Marguerite, cataloguing the books and learning everything there was to know about hosting a salon. It was a great deal more than she had anticipated, and Marguerite more than proved her worth the moment she explained the guiding notions of a salon: politesse, civilité, et honnêteté and the subsequent dismissal of such notions at a truly *good* salon. Belle would have been in well over her head without her.

Some of her afternoons were reserved for receiving petitioners. Despite how ineffectual the sessions were, and her lingering suspicion that Bastien was at the root of it, she knew it wouldn't look good to Bastien and the rest of the advisers if she were to cancel what she had fought so hard to win. Belle had no desire to give them any ammunition against her. Bastien for his part had not failed to invite her to an advisory meeting again. Otherwise, every spare moment was dedicated to brushing up on the celebrated thinkers of the day so she could hold her own in a debate. It had been months since Belle had devoted so much time to reading; she had begun to feel rusty.

For the first time since Lio left, each night she practically crawled into her bed and slept like the dead all the way until morning.

When Belle had spoken to Cogsworth about establishing rooms and a salary for Marguerite, he hadn't even protested like she thought he would.

He had tutted after she expressed her surprise. "It is customary for the wife of a king to establish a staff of her own."

And so Marguerite moved into the castle, to a set of rooms in the West Wing. Belle thought the furnishings and linens were fine enough for the daughter of a duc, but she didn't have much to base that on. At the very least, she thought, Marguerite was not the type to complain if she were off the mark entirely.

Belle was happy to have a companion now that Lio was away, and even happier when she got to show Marguerite the library for the first time a few days later. The Mademoiselle de Lambriquet had seen the legendary galleries of Versailles, had dined with King Louis's court, and frequented the most lavish manors in France, but Belle was quite sure she had never seen a library quite like hers.

"Sacré, Belle!" Marguerite had exclaimed upon entering,

and though the grandeur of the room had never dulled for Belle, it was a treat to see it through Marguerite's eyes, and only made Belle more certain that opening it to the public was the right decision.

"I know. It's magnificent, isn't it?" Belle replied dreamily.

Marguerite ran her hands along the gilded banisters encircling the spiral staircase. "I've never seen so many books in all my life." She turned back to Belle and gave her a wry grin. "Is it true that your husband simply *gave* it to you during your courtship?"

A blush crept up her neck. She had thought of her time in the castle as many things, but a *courtship* was never one of them. "Something like that," she admitted. She wondered if she would ever feel close enough to Marguerite to tell her the truth.

Marguerite let out an appraising whistle. "No wonder you married him."

Belle blushed as she pulled her through the stacks, pointing out favourite books along the way. She ushered Marguerite to her favourite chaise nestled in her favourite alcove.

"This spot is best for a gloomy afternoon," Belle told her, pointing to a red velvet settee next to a small fireplace, framed by a window almost as tall as the room itself. "The patter of raindrops on the glass mixed with the warmth of the fire..."

"It must be heavenly," said Marguerite.

"It is."

Marguerite spun back around, head tilted to the ceiling, before collapsing in a heap on the plush carpet and motioning for Belle to join her on the floor. Belle acquiesced, lying down beside her friend and noting the view was even more remarkable from that new vantage.

"I'm beginning to think roping me into this venture before I'd actually seen the size of the library was something of a calculated decision." Marguerite held up her hands, framing one of the massive lion statues that sat sentry on the second level.

Belle laughed. "I am sorry to have tricked you."

"Don't be mistaken, madame. There's nothing I love more than sifting through centuries of dust."

They made quick work of recording entire sections of books, but the hardest task was ahead of them. In Belle's limited time spent living at the castle, she had yet to visit the books at the uppermost reaches of the towering shelves, but she suspected the books up there hadn't been touched or seen by anyone in decades, perhaps even a century.

They climbed the gleaming spiral staircase up to the balcony that marked the midway point, shifting then to rickety ladders in order to reach the top of the shelves. They both paused halfway up to catch their breaths.

"Couldn't we just… close off this part?" asked Marguerite. "Who in their right mind is going to climb this deathtrap of a ladder for no promise of reward? We don't even know what's up here."

"We'll certainly be improving the infrastructure of the library before inviting anyone else in," Belle replied. "Now gather what remains of your courage and follow me."

At the top, they found shelves deeply caked in inches of dust. On them were books so old they had begun to rot in earnest, and Belle feared if they touched them the books would disintegrate. The titles were illegible, and Marguerite was taken by a fit of sneezes.

"Perhaps we deal with these ones last," Belle choked out, the dust in the air swirling around her mouth.

"Good idea," replied Marguerite, already descending the ladder.

When they reached the bottom, the clock chimed noon, and Belle was due at a meeting of the advisory. "Time to be condescended to for a few hours."

"*Another* meeting? Why even attend if they're just going to ignore you?"

Belle brushed off the dust that coated her hem. "Better to be ignored but aware of what's happening than to be ignorant of the goings-on in my own kingdom. Lio asked me to be his representative, so go I must. Besides, Bastien shouldn't be left unchecked."

"It's been five days. I'm surprised he hasn't come to see me yet."

Belle and Marguerite had been taking their dinners in

Belle's chambers since the Mademoiselle de Lambriquet's arrival at the castle. Belle hadn't wanted to push her to meet everyone all at once, understanding that moving into a castle was perhaps an overwhelming experience for most anyone. But she had been sure to tell Bastien that his friend Aurelian's sister had been hired to assist her. The matter seemed of little import to him, but Belle thought he would have at least greeted her upon arrival. His failure to do so only added to Belle's mounting suspicions.

"Shall we make plans to dine with everyone tonight?"

"Yes, I think it's time. I can't keep hiding away forever; a wardrobe as fine as mine deserves to be appreciated widely." Marguerite spun in a tight circle, in part to show off her indigo dress and also to rid it of the dust that had collected on the fabric. A cloud enveloped her.

Belle coughed and waved her arms to clear the air. "Mrs Potts will be thrilled."

The dust settled, and Marguerite sank into a chair. "It will be nice to eat her food in a room more befitting of her talent, and with easier access to second helpings."

• • •

Belle was exhausted spending a great deal of time among endless piles of dusty books, so she was happy to be distracted. Ruling in Lio's stead was not as simple as she had predicted it would be. The advisers were as dismissive of her as ever, but she was used to that. What was worse was knowing that Bastien had very likely lied to her and would continue to do so without intervention. At the very least, Belle knew he was sneaking about under the cloak of darkness and did not wish to be seen. And yet, without Lio to take her side, she was outnumbered. At best, the men on the advisory wouldn't much care for Bastien's alleged lies, and at worst, they were active participants in them. Belle decided that the only way forward was to pretend not to know a thing about what Bastien was up to in the hopes that he wouldn't pay too close attention to what she was doing, and the effort took all her patience.

She entered the throne room to find the meeting already under way. Bastien was speaking, as usual, reading from a pile of papers. He was paint- and powder-free, but his clothes were still opulent. He looked younger, more vulnerable. She didn't know if it was the real him or if the absence of the trappings of Versailles was just another mask he donned.

He looked up and made a great show of annoyance at being interrupted. Belle had the sneaking impression that he had started the meeting early with every intention of making her look bad.

He eyed her before continuing.

"Baron Prejean has reported an increase in French nationals crossing through his province on their way to safe havens in the rest of Europe and beyond. Many are carrying goods to trade or sell with them, and Prejean would like permission to impose a tax upon them for Aveyon's coffers, not to mention his retention of a healthy percentage as a fee." He grinned as the advisers sniggered knowingly. "All in favour?"

All of the room gave their assent save for Belle. "I thought the plan was to maintain the status quo in all matters until the king's return?"

Bastien sighed. "Yes, but this can only be good for Aveyon. The coffers are dwindling; this is an easy source of income for the kingdom."

Logically, Belle understood this, but still she chafed at the ease with which a large-scale change was being accepted by the advisers after her ideas had been so roundly rebuffed. "I think it's only fair that we treat this in the same way we've treated any change – by staying the course until the king returns. We can revisit this initiative when he's back in the capital."

She could see the wheels turning in the duc's mind. "I think it would be prudent to allow this," he said. "It has no lasting implications for the kingdom. Right now, we're allowing goods worth thousands upon thousands of livres to pass through Aveyon untaxed. It would be logical to impose a tax on them, like every other sovereign nation they pass through."

Belle was torn. She knew that there was sense in what he was proposing, but she couldn't help but have her guard up. She was almost certain Bastien had been lying to her for weeks, and when he wasn't lying, he was explaining to her in excruciating detail that nothing could be done for Aveyon's commoners until their nobles were dealt with. Still, she hesitated. She didn't wish to do anything that would harm her kingdom, but she likewise feared a dangerous precedent would be set if she acquiesced.

She tried for compromise. "And what of other changes?"

Bastien's face was blank. "What of them?"

"If we can bend here, surely we can bend elsewhere."

Bastien was smug. "Now is your opportunity to present your proposal." He clearly thought she hadn't been doing anything useful with her time.

Belle hadn't been planning to seek the approval of the advisory for her salon, but she wanted to wipe the look of condescension off the duc's face. "I will be hosting a salon, the purpose of which is to gather and share information that will benefit the commoners of Aveyon." She gave Bastien a pointed look. "I do believe this will prove more fruitful than listening to people simply air their petty grievances. This will be a forum for discussion and meaningful change."

More silence elapsed. Finally, Geoffroy's pinched expression turned sour as he deigned to respond. "Have you ever been to a salon, madame?"

A muscle in her jaw twitched. "As I have only been in a position to do so for some short months, I haven't yet had the pleasure. But I have done a good deal of research and understand that at their core, salons are meant to facilitate the exchanging of ideas. The subject of my salon will be governance, and more specifically, I will be fielding ideas from philosophers and economists on how best to serve all the people of Aveyon via reforms and initiatives."

The room was utterly silent. Every man seated around the table wore an expression of distaste, as though Belle had presented them with a rotting carcass instead of a workable idea.

"And just how do you expect to plan a salon if you've never attended one?" asked Gamaches, going in for what he thought was the kill.

Belle smiled. "Wonderful question, Baron. My assistant, Marguerite, has attended many and will be an asset in the planning of mine." She looked to Bastien, expecting him to deride her idea as foolish.

But then Bastien spoke. "I think that is a brilliant idea."

And all at once, it was as if his praise broke a dam.

"Our economy could certainly use whatever bolstering it could get from tourists," said Geoffroy, as if he hadn't been personally offended by the idea until Bastien voiced his approval of it.

"And with the upheaval in France, you'd be sure to secure the attendance of many famous intellectuals who have fled Paris, raising the prestige of the event and subsequently the kingdom," added Gamaches.

Montarly was beaming. "And perhaps the rest of Europe would begin to see Aveyon as more than a French backwater. The kingdom can be a power its own right!"

"A truly wonderful idea, Belle," praised Bastien. "Have you asked the king?"

"Asked him what? For permission? That is not how our partnership works."

Bastien looked at her contemplatively. "Well. Please let us know if there is anything we can do to help in the planning of it. And now for the matter of Baron Prejean's tax scheme." So there it was. She had fallen into his trap. Belle knew his praise could not have been genuine. Bastien sensed his victory and pressed on. "Are you in favour of this one small, beneficial change for the kingdom? It is, of course, up to you as the king's representative on the advisory."

Belle knew she had to give in after Bastien had supported her. "I am in favour, yes."

"Then it is done." He marked something on a piece of parchment and set it down, picking up another. "Lastly we have an update from Paris." He began to read with utter disinterest, but Belle hung on every word. "It would seem the National Assembly has crafted something they are calling the Declaration of the Rights of Man, article one of which posits that 'Men are born and remain free and equal in rights', and they are pressing for King Louis to ratify it, though he has refused so far. He is being somewhat supported by a contingent of moderates calling themselves the Monarchiens, who believe that France should always have a strong king, and they in turn are being opposed by the revolutionaries of the so-called Club Breton, who want to strip the king of his absolute power and deny him veto power over the National Assembly." He took a deep breath and looked around the table. "Essentially, France is going to start a civil war over whether or not their sovereignty lies with the king or with the nation itself." He sat back down in his chair as though exhausted and bored by what he had just described. No one else spoke up, but Belle was burning to know more about it. "That was all we had to discuss today. Thank you, messieurs." He looked over to Belle and bowed his head apologetically. "And madame."

The room emptied until only the two of them remained. Belle didn't know where she stood with Bastien. She didn't trust him one bit, but he had supported her salon from the start. Perhaps he had only done so to force her hand in support of Prejean's scheme, but she wondered if there was more to it than that. Could he have actually thought her idea was good after weeks of dismissing all her others?

He surprised her again by speaking. "I know that concession wasn't easy for you, Belle."

It was a curious thing to say and only served to make her more suspicious of him. "It's not Prejean's request that bothers me, Bastien; it's your vacillation in regard to my ideas."

He waved his hand lazily. "I put the needs of the kingdom first, and I won't apologise for it."

"And yet you are not open to helping Aveyon's commoners. The health of the kingdom is not measured in taxation schemes. It is measured in the quality of life for those at the bottom."

He frowned. "Of course I can see that. But it is because they are vulnerable that I am cautious. I have seen what empty promises can do." Belle was surprised to find that what he was saying rang true. She had expected more lies, more arrogance. He continued. "I am not trying to sabotage you; I'm trying to ensure the decisions you make are ones weighted in reality."

"And what do you know of reality? Besides, a lot of the time that reads as an attempt to undermine me completely."

Belle was struck to see that he looked hurt by the accusation. "Then I apologise. I would never want to do such a thing. In my own way, I was trying to support you. But obviously it didn't come across as such. I promise I will do better."

Despite her suspicions of Bastien's involvement with the petitioners, Belle couldn't help but sense that what he was saying was sincere, and sincerity was not something she had come to expect from the duc de Vincennes. She had seen so many sides of him in such a short amount of time: the out-of-touch noble, the duc with revolutionary sympathies, the subject loyal to his king and the man willing to abandon him.

She gritted her teeth. "You can understand why it's been hard to trust you, Bastien."

He nodded. "I can swear to you my allegiance lies with Aveyon."

Despite everything, Belle sensed that the duc did not make oaths he did not intend to keep. Perhaps that was a symptom of someone who lied as easily as they breathed – those rare times he actually made promises, he kept them, and the rest of the time he simply didn't promise anything at all.

CHAPTER EIGHTEEN

Belle was relieved to find that almost everyone else liked Marguerite as much as she did, including the priggish Cogsworth, who took to her quicker than Belle had ever seen him take to anything. And yet, though he knew her from Paris, Bastien didn't seem inclined towards friendship. Privately, Marguerite explained that she and Bastien had never been close, but it struck Belle as odd that the duc de Vincennes wouldn't be warmer to someone from his past.

Despite all that, Belle couldn't wait for Lio to meet her again. Their encounter at Bastien's dinner had been brief, but she knew they would be fast friends, and she had told him as much in their correspondence.

The group dined on Mrs Potts's enviable spread and laughed and sang – quite poorly – late into the night. Cogsworth disapproved from a distance, regardless of how much he clearly liked the Mademoiselle de Lambriquet. He never could abide much joviality, not even when Lumière gave a rousing, operatic performance of "Vive la rose".

"Mon amant me délaisse,
Ô gai, vive la rose,
Je ne sais pas pourquoi,
Vive la rose et le lilas."

The room clapped along with him as he wailed the lyrics, and held their collective breaths when he fell to his knees before Cogsworth and gave him a dramatic solo performance. The majordomo's disapproval was not infectious, and for the first time since Paris, Belle didn't quite feel like the current of fear she had been treading against was going to pull her under. She had let herself feel hopeful, knowing that Lio would return soon and all her hard work would pay off.

One by one, the room began to empty as everyone retired to their chambers, until only Belle and Marguerite remained, sitting across from each other at the long table in the dim light. Belle still felt a rush from revealing her salon plans to the advisory and having them approve it; she was in no hurry to return to her empty bed.

"We have outlasted the lesser mortals." Marguerite lobbed a grape at her. "You never told me how it went."

"How what went?"

"The advisory meeting. I assumed since you hadn't murdered Bastien that it may have gone well for once?"

Belle popped the grape into her mouth. "I told them about the salon, actually."

"And?"

"Well, at first they acted like I hadn't said anything at all, such was their disgust, but then Bastien said it was a brilliant idea, so now everyone is on board."

"Oh," she said, as surprised as Belle had been. "That *is* unexpected."

"Yes, but I've spent weeks being suspicious of everything the duc does; it's nice to relax for once."

Marguerite laughed. "You know, if you had told me a few weeks ago that I'd be dining with a queen, sipping on lukewarm champagne, wearing a gown positively coated in dust... I would have thought you were mad."

"I think I have you beat in the 'How on earth did I get here?' department." Belle didn't need to elaborate. A peasant marrying a prince was unheard of. A peasant married to a king was impossible. And yet she was.

Marguerite smiled wickedly. "Yes, that is a story I've been dying to hear."

Belle had been bracing for the question, even if she wasn't aware of it. "It's a simple enough story," she started. "We met under the unlikeliest circumstances, and somehow we fell in love." She wanted to make it sound as exciting as living it had been, but not being able to mention the curse hampered the telling of it.

"It's not every day that a prince—"

"Marries a commoner, I know." Belle picked up a grape and

popped it into her mouth. "I suppose love is one of the rare things that trumps protocol."

"Do you think that's true? That every monarch in the world could discard protocol and marry for love if they so desired?"

"Of course not. It helped that Lio didn't care much for political considerations, and that his parents were no longer around to forbid it." Belle didn't know how to explain it to Marguerite, how they fell in love in such constrained circumstances that couldn't be replicated elsewhere. "It was a bit like falling in love in a place out of time. It didn't matter that we didn't make sense together; it didn't matter who he was or who I was. We just... fell."

Marguerite had been hanging on to her every word but was a bit deflated when Belle didn't reveal any specific salacious details. "I suppose that's romantic," she offered.

"It was for us." Belle pulled a pin from her hair and let it tumble around her shoulders. "I wouldn't change anything."

Marguerite considered that. "And being married to him means you're married to his kingdom as well."

"Yes, and that's not something I ever dreamed of."

Marguerite brought her knees up, resting her feet on her chair and wrapping her arms around her legs. "What did you dream of?"

Belle took a deep breath. "Travelling, having adventures, never settling in one place."

"So, the opposite of your life now."

"Essentially." Belle took a sip of her champagne. She didn't like to think of it that way, but it was hard to ignore that it was the truth. "I didn't expect to fall in love. I chose Lio over adventure, and I'll never regret it, but it is true that this is a life I never envisioned for myself. I never thought I would be someone's wife, let alone that of a king." She paused, noting the champagne had loosened her tongue. This was the most honest she had ever been with anyone – perhaps even herself. "I don't mean to sound ungrateful or unhappy."

"I think I can understand that." Marguerite swung her legs up onto the table. Belle's eyes widened as she imagined Cogsworth's reaction to Marguerite's shoes perched atop the white linen tablecloth. "I know my life must seem terribly exciting – getting to go where I wish and do as I please – but it is a result of me losing my home and my family. I am anchorless. I might as well be an orphan, and I am very aware that the small sum of money my mother left me is the only thing keeping me from a far worse fate. So in a way, I have everything most girls would ever wish for – some semblance of autonomy, nice gowns, invitations to the most desirable parties – but it came at a cost I would never willingly choose to pay." She leaned her head back to gaze at the ceiling. "Oh, look at me, feeling sorry for myself. Is there anything worse than a rich person who feels bad for themselves?"

Belle shrugged, sensing that Marguerite was not interested

in her pity. "I'd take that over a rich person who feels nothing at all."

"True, those are the worst of us." Marguerite put her feet back on the ground and leaned over the table. "You know, I think your salon is a brilliant idea, but I'm not the duc de Vincennes."

Belle allowed herself a small bit of doubt. "You don't think it's a bit self-indulgent of me?"

Marguerite scoffed. "I have been to self-indulgent salons that are little more than celebrations of the host's purported brilliance. I have suffered through ideological debates that only serve one side of the argument." She sat back down. "Rich people are very good at confirming each other's biases, but you have the added benefit of growing up, well, poor." She said it like she was worried about insulting Belle. "I think you'll make an excellent host, and this will be good for all of Aveyon."

Belle was heartened by her enthusiasm. "Well, there's no turning back, now that I've told the advisory about it, so let's hope you're right."

• • •

The next morning, Belle passed Seigneur Montarly on her way to breakfast. The advisers taking up residence in the castle was one of Belle's least favourite traditions. She thought it even further removed the idea that men like the seigneur should be attending to the needs of the people who lived on his lands, and gave him a convenient excuse to ignore their plight. They were walking in opposite directions through the great hall. He pretended not to notice her, and normally she would have done the same, but he had information she needed.

"Seigneur!" she called out to his retreating form, her voice echoing off the marble pillars. He paused, as if debating whether or not to ignore her fully, but eventually turned her way.

"Madame," he said, bowing ever so slightly. "What can I do for you?"

She stepped closer to him. "I only wish to know how my husband is, seigneur. I know he recently left your estate."

He looked around at the people passing them by, perhaps seeking rescue, but found no one. He sighed. "He is the picture of stability and strength, madame," he droned. "He and my daughter, the Mademoiselle Félicité Montarly, got on very well. I always thought a match should have been made there." He shook his head like an opportunity had been missed.

The insult stung, but someone behind Montarly caught her eye. "You know, perhaps a match could be made instead with the duc de Vincennes. I know he'd make an excellent husband to any noble lady." She watched Bastien nearly choke just behind Montarly's shoulder.

Montarly considered it. "Perhaps you're right, madame." She watched wheels turn in his head. "Perhaps you're right," he muttered under his breath, leaving her there without so much as a goodbye, to say nothing of wishing her well.

Bastien rushed over to her. "Merde, Belle. What was that about?"

"I only thought you'd be looking to Aveyonian ladies for your future wife, since you have such a vested interest in the kingdom," she replied innocently.

He grimaced and leaned in closer to Belle. "I'd ask that you not act as my matchmaker in the future since I am more than capable of finding a wife on my own."

"I only want to see you happy, Bastien."

"Yes, well." He pulled at his collar. "Thank you." It was said hesitantly, as if he couldn't pinpoint where exactly the insult lay, or if it was meant sincerely.

"And thank *you* for supporting my salon," she replied.

He smiled and clapped her on the back. "Ah, I'm nothing if not well-connected, so if you're looking to off-load some of your duties, you can simply leave the guest list to me if you wish."

She ducked out of his reach. "I think not, Bastien. You can send me a list of who you'd like to invite, and we'll take it from there."

"You don't trust in my abilities to assemble a guest list?"

"I've been to one of your parties, Bastien. The salon will not be an excuse to descend into immoderation."

He clutched at his chest in mock betrayal. "You wound

me, madame."

She folded her arms. "You may submit guests for approval, but if they aren't bringing expertise or specific knowledge to the salon, they won't be invited."

He pulled on the lapels of his waistcoat. "You don't have to worry about that, Belle. My friends come armed only with good ideas," he replied with a wink.

She hadn't understood why Bastien had been so supportive of the salon at first, but as he spun away from her, the reason became clear – the duc was intending to use it as a way to prop himself up, to look good in front of his aristocratic friends. Her instinct was to reject all his empty-headed guests, but then she thought better of it. If Bastien had people to impress, it might guarantee that he would be on his best behaviour.

CHAPTER NINETEEN

Many days passed, full of planning and logistics and readying the castle for hundreds of guests. With days so full, Belle's nights felt empty. She longed for the warmth of her husband beside her. Marguerite liked to visit friends she had made in the village most evenings and would return to the castle flushed and brimming with stories of the people she met, whom she insisted Belle must meet as well. Marguerite had issued an open invitation for her to join them, but Belle thought she was just being polite. They both knew it wasn't proper for Belle to go to taverns and cafés in the village now she was the king's wife. Marguerite would often joke that Belle was on her way to becoming a recluse, and Belle had to pretend that the playful jab didn't sting as much as it did. It was at times like these that Belle felt a divide between them. Marguerite was free to come and go as she pleased without a consideration for her propriety or safety. Belle would have been a burden to her.

She was torn between two worlds, as always.

On those nights when Marguerite went out, Belle felt the

pain of missing Lio all the more acutely. She lay in bed feeling it like a brand on her skin and a fist curled around her heart. She missed the sound of him breathing evenly beside her, and the contentment she felt knowing his sleep was undisturbed. Lio had told her she was his anchor, his safe passage through the worst of his nightmares. How would he fare without her to pull him back from the darkness?

In his latest letter, Lio spoke of distrusting, sceptical nobles who had been content to be left to their own devices for ten years. Now that he had made his triumphant return, these men were resistant to any changes he may have brought with him, including the crown he now bore, however reluctantly.

They view my absence as a mark against me, and in all truthfulness, how could I blame them for thinking so? My explanation only goes so far in winning back their allegiance, and the threat of spreading revolution carries little meaning to these men, who consider themselves safe behind the walls of their impregnable estates.

I thought I'd easily sniff out which of my noblemen plot against me, but in truth, it could be any of them, such is their pessimism and suspicion in regard to my rule.

Reading the pain behind Lio's words almost tore her apart. She knew that for however much he was willing to admit in a letter, the truth of the situation must be far worse. She thought back to Montarly's assessment of Lio's visit and hated the seigneur for it. Of course Montarly would hold no enmity towards her husband – he held a position of great power on Lio's advisory. The same could not be said for the rest of Aveyon's nobles.

She wanted to be by Lio's side as he struggled with the realities of ruling a kingdom in order to protect it, not shut up in a castle far away from him, unable to do any good. She was powerless, impotent and ineffectual. Belle wanted more than anything to know that Lio was not being tortured by nightmares without her there to help him through it. Not knowing ate away at her, breaking apart her resolve, bit by bit, until nothing remained but the sharp certainty that Lio was in pain.

And then she remembered the mirror.

Long before she had seen a stranger's face staring out of it, Belle had used the mirror to see her father and again to see the Beast in a moment of great need. Surely after all she had been through with the curse and the magic following her to Paris, she deserved to use the mirror for something good? In her desperation, she thought it was worth trying. She left her chambers before good sense could convince her otherwise.

For once, the hearth was unlit, as if those who would normally tend to the fire were aware that she had been deliberately avoiding the library at night since her last encounter with the mirror. Belle was used to its liveliness in the daytime now, when she and Marguerite would work and talk and laugh for hours, their days punctuated by visits from Chip and Lumière. Now, however, it was as quiet as a tomb. She could sense the mirror that called to her like a beacon. A lump formed in her throat, and her palms were damp. She didn't like the idea of inviting magic back into her life, but it was the only way to see if Lio was truly all right.

She wound her way to the shelf where she had hidden it and reached a tremulous hand behind the books. Her fingers touched the metal, and a shock of cold spiked up her arm. Instinct urged her to leave, but her feet were rooted in place. She needed to see for herself.

Belle pulled the mirror out and held it at eye level, but now that she studied it more closely, she could see cracks at the edges. Just like the very first time she held it, and when she had held its twin in the shop in Paris, the mirror began to glow with tendrils of rippling green light. It warmed her hands like the light was spreading to her skin. Every fibre of her being wanted to drop it to the floor and flee. But something stronger pressed her to stay, staring into the glowing green swirls in the glass.

Nothing happened, and Belle realised the mirror was waiting for her to speak the words that would give it a purpose. She stood on a precipice. On one side was her unwillingness to accept that the mirror had continued to work long after the curse had been purged from Aveyon, like poison drawn from a wound. On the other side was the peace of mind that would come from seeing her husband's face, and knowing he was well. It felt like her decision carried weight far beyond that small moment. If she were to let the magic take hold, who knew how far it could go? She had spent so long keeping the secret of the curse. Accessing this strange magic felt like the start of a slippery slope to her secret – the castle's secret – being revealed. Inviting in magic was a dangerous idea.

But still, as if compelled by some power outside herself, she spoke the words as though they were an incantation. Perhaps, she thought, they were.

"I wish to see Lio."

The mirror came to life as Lio's tortured face filled it. He was lying in a bed in an unfamiliar room, gripped by a nightmare like she had feared. She watched helplessly as the dream played her husband like a marionette in some twisted show. The vision pulled back, giving her a view of the room. She could see that Lio had barred the doors, perhaps in an effort to keep himself confined to the room should the nightmare spread to waking.

She pushed away tears as she watched her husband fight against invisible monsters. His body alternated between painful rigidity and tormented writhing. Belle's heart pounded against her chest, but she couldn't, she wouldn't, look away.

Mercifully, as time went on, the nightmare left him. Lio's muscles went limp, his face softened, and his hands released the blanket he had been tearing at. He didn't wake, but it was a gift to watch him sink slowly back into restful slumber.

She watched him sleep peacefully until she was sure the last of the darkness had left him for good, and then she pulled herself from the mirror with great effort. The green tendrils of magic stuck to her skin like honey even after she had put the mirror down, fading slowly. She stepped back from the shelf and looked up. It took a moment for the dark library to come back into focus, and even longer for Belle to feel present in the space. Watching Lio through the mirror had transported her, like she had been there with him, a ghost hovering over his bed. To find herself back in the library was disorienting.

She found her way to the nearest chair and sat down, hoping the feeling of nausea would leave her quickly. She thought of Lio, who had felt so close to her but was in reality hundreds of miles away. It was a curious thing, to see him right in front of her yet to be separated by an impossible distance. Belle had banished the magic from her mind as soon as the curse was destroyed, but it had emerged in Paris, and again in Aveyon, like it was haunting her. When the Beast gave the mirror to her so she could see her father again, she had perceived it as a gift, and when she used it out of desperation to prove to the villagers of Plesance that the Beast was no monster, it had felt like a weapon against their hate. But when she beheld the vision in Paris of Aveyon burning, when the woman who knew too much spoke to her through it, and when she used it to see Lio, the magic had not been a gift or a weapon. It was a curse, as it always had been. The vision was a trick, the woman was a charlatan, and Lio was too far away to be helped, so the knowledge that he suffered was not useful to her.

The only thing she had to cling to while watching him struggle was that she was working hard to make sure Aveyon changed for the better. With that change, stability would come and Lio would sleep peacefully for the rest of his life. She would make sure of it.

By the time she got back to her room, Belle was close to collapse. She tucked herself in and pulled Lio's pillow to her chest, breathing in the now-fading scent of him.

She thought of Sidonie and her friends at the tavern in the village and what they had said about Lio. She thought of the nobles who didn't trust him. Surely there was a way to show them how Lio was different than King Louis. Surely there was a way to unite the commoners and the nobility, to make everyone's lives better, including her husband's.

But Belle could hardly keep her eyes open; she would have to sleep on it.

CHAPTER TWENTY

Belle awoke with a kernel of an idea and a heart full of hope. The problem of uniting the disparate groups of Aveyon had come to her overnight, perhaps in a dream she had now forgotten. It almost made her grateful for the mirror that had shown her Lio at his worst. Perhaps that had spurred her subconscious mind to action.

She dressed quickly and raced all the way down to the library, hoping her instincts were correct and that Marguerite was already getting to work.

She pulled the great doors open and saw that she was right. Marguerite was hunched over the ledger they had been using to record the many thousands of book titles they had been cataloguing. A pile of books towered over her. She held up a finger, not wanting to look up from her work.

"Whatever it is, it's going to have to wait. We're almost done with this section, and I simply will not abide any distractions until I can cross it off my list."

Belle deflated. "You're beginning to sound a lot like Cogsworth."

"I will take that as the compliment you surely meant it to be." She patted the spot next to her. "Now come, read aloud to me so I don't strain my poor eyes."

Belle hurried over and took the book from the top of the pile. The leather was worn smooth where hands would have held it, marking it as a favourite of someone who lived in the castle before Belle did.

"*The History of Rasselas, Prince of Abissinia*, by Samuel Johnson," she read out to Marguerite. She pictured Lio's mother, Delphine, reading it by the fire, utterly engrossed. Lio was always telling her how well the two of them would have got along. His mother was a voracious reader and had spent a great deal of time filling the library shelves.

Marguerite dipped her quill in the inkpot and bent over the ledger. "These long titles will be the death of me, or at least my eyesight."

"Would you like to switch?"

Marguerite cast Belle a sidelong glance. "No offence, but your penmanship is genuinely atrocious."

"You know, not all of us were taught by strict Swiss governesses."

"Yes, well, we can thank Madame Pierrefeu for her rigid instruction at a later date." Marguerite paused, nibbling on the end of her quill. "You know, she might genuinely expect a thank-you letter. I cannot be certain; etiquette was not my strongest subject. Next."

They continued on that way until Belle reached for the last book in the pile.

"*Evelina, or the History of a Young Lady's Entrance into the World,* by Anonymous." Belle turned the book over, noting that it was in near-perfect condition. "This book was written by Frances Burney, only that wasn't revealed until just after it had been published."

"So shall I write the real author?"

Belle opened the book to find the date of publication. "Published in 1778," she remarked, realising that the book may have been one of the last that Delphine bought for her library.

"An auspicious year, to be sure. Good old King Louis signed the Treaty of Alliance with America and declared war on Britain. Also the Battle of Monmouth took place."

Belle gave her a look. "You were what, seven years old while all of that was going on?"

Marguerite grinned. "What I lacked as a student of etiquette I more than made up for as a student of politics. Now tell me, am I to record dear Fanny as the true author?"

"Yes, to do otherwise would only bother me."

Marguerite scratched the last entry into the ledger and drew a line in the row below it. "Done." She leaned back in her chair and let out a breath. "Well, that section. Lord knows we have many thousands of books left."

"Still, it's nice to have made progress."

"What should we do to celebrate? Or— Wait…" Marguerite looked at Belle with renewed interest. "You came in here like there was a fire in you. What was that about?"

Belle had almost forgotten. "I've had an idea."

Marguerite leaned forward. "Let's hear it, then."

Belle rested her palms on the table. "I know the planning is well under way, and invitations have already been extended to our guests, but what if the salon wasn't just for intellectuals and scientists and economists? What if it was for Aveyon's commoners too?"

Marguerite looked at her thoughtfully. "That way they could take an active role in deciding the best way forward." She stood and started pacing as she thought. "We could even have them submit proposals to weed out the serious ideas from the more… shall we say, esoteric ones."

Belle's heartbeat had quickened at the thought of a more democratic salon, an event not just for intellectual posturing or debates for the sake of debating, but one that could craft a way forward for a kingdom in flux. If everyone in Aveyon felt represented, then the ideas born at the salon could be implemented with the express consent of the governed. It was the goal of the revolution in France, but perhaps in Aveyon the outcome could be achieved without bloodshed.

It could be what the États généraux had tried to be and failed.

"Can you see to the proposals? I imagine we'd have to act

quickly."

Marguerite nodded. "Of course. Has anyone ever told you how brilliant you are?"

Belle thought back to her childhood, when she was known as an odd girl more than anything else. "Not in so many words," she replied.

Marguerite grinned. "Well, I'm telling you you're brilliant."

Belle smiled too, relishing the feeling of having an idea to present not just to Lio, but to Aveyon's commoners as well. She imagined that Sidonie and the others she had met in the tavern might even attend and have their voices heard.

"Do you think the advisers will have any qualms?"

Belle shook her head. "No, they were very enthusiastically on board with the salon once Bastien said it was a good idea. I can't imagine that this will be reason enough for any of them to protest. Even with the inclusion of commoners, all the things they liked about it remain. The economy is still bolstered, the prestige of the kingdom will still increase, they'll still get to lord around the castle feeling very important."

"Well, what are you waiting for? Call a meeting."

• • •

Entering Cogsworth's office was like glimpsing the depths of the majordomo's mind. It was a spartan room, so neurotically organised that it made Belle wary of touching even a quill lest she invite his wrath down upon her.

"What is it you need?" he asked, not bothering to look up from what he was reading.

"Could you please call a meeting of the advisers?"

He paused and looked at her over his spectacles. "Would you consider this to be an emergency?"

"Of a sort," she offered.

He sighed a predictable sigh. "Well, luckily for you the duc de Vincennes has organised a hunt and most of the advisers are currently present. I'll have to call them back perhaps sooner than they would have liked, but if you insist…"

"A hunt? Since when do we host hunts at the castle?" It had never been discussed outright, but all residents of the castle knew that Lio felt the same way about hunting as he did about roses.

"I am not given to questioning the motives or habits of the duc. Should he wish to host a hunt, I am duty-bound to make it happen. I am similarly duty-bound to call together last-minute meetings of the advisers should *someone* decide matters simply cannot wait another few days."

She did not give in to his chastising. "Well, thank you very much, Cogsworth. I know you're a very busy man."

"Indeed I am, madame," he continued on in his nasal tone, not realising Belle was being facetious and that she had already left his office.

• • •

The meeting was not off to a great start. The advisers were unhappy to have been called away from the hunt, even though Belle assured them it would only take a few moments of their time. She wanted to inform them of the changes to her salon to get it out of the way of her planning. She would have happily kept the details from them if she thought they wouldn't perceive it as a slight against them.

"Where is the duc de Vincennes?" she asked them.

Montarly shuffled, incensed to find that the duty to respond had fallen to him. "We lost track of the duc at some point during the hunt."

"How do you lose track of someone? Isn't the point to stay together while you chase your quarry?"

Gamaches frowned. "And what would a woman know of the hunt?"

She opened her mouth to reply, but the door swung open and Bastien strode in, his cheeks red and his hair in disarray. He glanced around the room. It was the most unkempt Belle had ever seen him. "Sorry to keep you waiting."

Belle stood. "Gentlemen, I am sorry to have taken you from the hunt for even a short time, but I assure you this meeting will be a quick one."

Bastien interrupted. "Actually, your meeting comes at a good time. I have an update about the goings-on in Paris, if you don't mind?"

Belle normally would have minded an interruption, but

an update from Paris was not something she wished to push aside. "Of course not."

He stood and pulled a parchment from the inner pocket of his hunting jacket. "The National Assembly has voted against the two-chamber system put forth by the Monarchiens, and they have rejected the motion to allow Louis any veto power. It would seem that they thought the king would meet them halfway, but he refused to ratify either decision and has recalled the Regiment of Flanders to Versailles, which was, perhaps, not the best move. The people of Paris are on the verge of civil war due to the increase in unemployment and the subsequent food shortage. New voices are emerging in the public sphere. A barrister by the name of Camille Desmoulins is going around, stirring up the crowds of Parisians, writing incendiary pamphlets. A lawyer by the name of Maximilien Robespierre wrote a scathing rejection of the king's reply to the National Assembly; basically the chaos is such that new leaders are emerging from the unlikeliest places." He cleared his throat, allowing the rest of the advisers a moment to react to the idea of a simple lawyer having the gall to criticise the king of France. "The people of Paris do not trust King Louis. Rumours are spreading that he plans to use force against the National Assembly or flee Versailles altogether. His silence speaks volumes."

He sat back down and looked to Belle expectantly. "Is that all you have to report?" she asked.

"Indeed. The situation is fraught in France. It will be interesting to see how it all plays out. But please, continue with what you wished to talk about."

She felt flattened by his report. Belle had woken up with a heart full of hope, but news of the continued unrest in Paris only made her fear that all her efforts would be for naught. Despite her attempts to banish the false vision she had seen in the mirror in Paris of her kingdom burning, set aflame by its own people, in that moment she wondered if it could come true. Could the people of Aveyon be as driven to revolution as their neighbours in France? Belle had tried to gauge their anger and their thirst for change, but what if it didn't matter? What if revolution was an inevitable part of Aveyon's trajectory? She looked around at the table of privileged men and decided they could not dictate the future of her kingdom. She had to do what she could for Aveyon. There had to be a way out.

"I've come to you with a new proposal." The group made their displeasure evident in their posture and expressions. Belle soldiered on. "In regard to the salon, I've had an idea." Their scepticism radiated off them like a bad scent. "Instead of inviting only intellectuals, academics, philosophers and the like, I'd extend an invitation to Aveyon's farmers, merchants, factory workers, bankers, maids, lawyers, physicians, et cetera. I see it as an opportunity to take measure of what the kingdom truly needs, instead of allowing our institutions to decide for them." She looked over to Bastien, expecting his immediate and enthusiastic approval, considering the revolutionary sympathies he had revealed to her after rescuing her from the mob back in Paris.

He was, to her surprise, frowning. "I'm not sure you've really thought this through, Belle."

She stiffened. "I can assure you that I have."

"Have you considered the logistics of inviting commoners into the palace? I mean" – he scoffed a bit – "were you listening to the report I just made to the advisory? Have you any consideration at all for your *safety*?" He looked around to his fellow advisers as though Belle were being ridiculous. It made her blood boil.

"I thought the only threat against us came from the rogue noblemen who are plotting a revolt under our very noses. Not the Aveyonian commoners you've spent weeks assuring us are content, happy even."

Bastien eyed her as though seeing her in a new light. "Threats can take many forms, madame. It would not be prudent in times like these to invite them into your home."

"If we are willing to open our doors to the rich, then we must also be willing to open our doors to the poor. You speak as though wealth precludes someone from committing a crime, and that has not been true in my experience."

"I think I speak for everyone, the king included, when I say you are perhaps not thinking clearly."

"And I speak for myself alone when I say you're wrong. Do you forget that I *am* a commoner? That I grew up in a poor village with the very people you seek to malign? I do not fear them in the same way I fear a rich man who believes justice is a fluid concept and that innocence can be bought." She let them sit with what she had said for a few moments before continuing. "I called this meeting as a courtesy. This is how I envision the salon, and I believe it will be beneficial for all the people of our kingdom. You still get the prestige-raising, economy-boosting aspects, only now the doors are open for everyone. If you cannot abide by that, then I suggest you remain in your estates for the duration." If she had ruffled the feathers of the advisers before, it was nothing compared to how they viewed her now. "All in favour of the amendment to the salon?" They mutely assented with barely raised hands, but it was enough. In a way, it seemed they almost feared her. No one protested or voiced any concerns, and the meeting ended in near silence. She would take their unease over their disdain. She thought perhaps it was time for men like them to fear what a woman could do.

Bastien, of course, stayed back after the rest of them had left. "That was quite the display."

She didn't have time for false niceties. "Do you have something you wish to discuss with me? I have a salon to plan."

"I only wanted to know if you were aware that the Mademoiselle de Lambriquet often leaves the castle for large stretches of time."

She searched her mind for a reason he would bring something so mundane to her attention. "Of course I'm aware. I'm not her keeper, Bastien. She is free to come and go as she pleases."

"I ask because I've seen her in the village a few times, boasting about her access to you." He presented it to her like it was a gift, but Belle didn't see it as such. She tried to imagine Marguerite doing what he claimed to have witnessed and found she couldn't. "You know," he continued, "revolutionary agitators come in all shapes and sizes, often disguised as friends." He let the thought linger. "If you're worried about the messiness of it, I could have her removed from her position right away; you need only say the word."

"What?" she exclaimed. "Nothing you've told me suggests Marguerite needs to be removed."

"I think you need to be cautious, Belle. You don't even know the girl."

"I *am* cautious, Bastien. You forget that I met her in your own home. If you think so poorly of your friends, then I have to question your judgement."

He grinned smugly. "I was friendly with her brother, but Marguerite has always been something of a loose cannon. She caused quite a stir last year when she had a, shall we say, *dramatic* falling-out with the comtesse d'Armagnac and her coterie and is prone to raging fits if anyone asks her about the matter."

"That sounds like her business, Bastien."

"Oh, I can assure you that her tantrums were the talk of Paris." He looked at her expectantly. "She is just the type of girl to take advantage of your kindness and use you as leverage. You would be wise not to trust her. Everyone knows she is flighty and hot-tempered and only ever thinks of herself."

Belle stared at him blankly. "I can make my own decisions."

He paused, as if waiting for her to change her mind. When she didn't, he frowned and cleared his throat. "If you're sure you don't want her dealt with…"

She shook her head. "I'm more than capable of dealing with things on my own."

If Belle was sure of anything, it was that Marguerite de Lambriquet would not lie to her. The same could not be said for Bastien, duc de Vincennes, who had his own agenda in the castle. If anyone was not to be trusted, it was him.

CHAPTER TWENTY-ONE

Belle spent the bulk of what remained of the day in the library with Marguerite and Chip, recording titles in the ledger and making progress on the notice they would be posting in the town squares of the villages of Aveyon, requesting proposals for subjects to be presented at the salon. Chip was doing his best to distract them by building himself a throne out of any objects he could find in the library and subsequently carry.

"Which is the more kingly colour?" he asked, holding two pillows aloft as Chou jumped to bite them.

"The purple one, to be sure," replied Marguerite.

"Perfect," he muttered to himself while grabbing every purple cushion in the room. Marguerite and Belle had no sooner returned to their tasks, when a voice interrupted them from across the library. "Would a king carry a sword?"

Marguerite grinned at her. "I fear the implications of our answer."

"Not answering is always worse, though," replied Belle. She craned her neck to see if she could spot the boy. "A king would exercise *caution above all else!*" she shouted. "He would not be reckless with sharp objects!" But Chip was nowhere to be seen.

"A valiant effort, Belle." Marguerite laughed and bent back to her work.

"At least we can say we tried." Belle laughed, too, and tried to shake the feeling that she had wronged her friend in some way when she allowed Bastien to tell her something personal, something Marguerite hadn't chosen to tell Belle herself. And it was so small a thing, to have a fight with someone that ends a friendship, that Belle felt even worse for thinking it was something she should be ashamed to know about Marguerite.

"Is everything all right?"

Belle looked up from the rows of titles and dates to see Marguerite looking down at her with a concerned expression. Belle prayed she wasn't that easy to read. "Nothing, I'm just tired."

"That's a word for 'heartsick' I haven't heard before."

"Sorry?"

"I know you're missing Lio, Belle. You don't have to hide it from me."

"You're right." Belle felt a pang of guilt for the lie. She looked at the piles of books and pages of work they had got through that day, and an idea struck her. "Why don't we finish early for the day?"

Marguerite looked at her like she had suggested they set the ledger on fire. "Are you sure?"

Belle cringed inwardly, wanting so much to be the kind of person who would abandon work on a whim to go have fun. She wondered why she was intent on punishing herself. "Yes, of course I'm sure."

"You mean we're done already?" Chip asked, crestfallen, his arms full of cushions pilfered from the various chaises around the room. He had jammed a poker from the fireplace through his belt like a scabbard.

Marguerite's eyes widened. "Yes, I'm afraid you'll have to build your throne another day, mon ami."

"I was done with the throne," he muttered.

"Oh, yes?" replied Belle, looking over at the mess of cushions in the centre of the room. "What were you working on now?"

"My dungeon," he replied, as though the answer were obvious.

"Of course," agreed Marguerite, looking at the same ill-defined pile of pillows that Belle was. "I can see the moat and everything."

Chip looked at her with pure adoration, and Belle had to suppress a laugh.

"Shall we clean this up?" Marguerite asked the boy, and he agreed, happily setting off to clean his mess, such was her gift.

"Wait," Belle called out to her before she joined him. "What are you doing tonight?" She was done with worrying about what kind of burden she might be to her friend.

"Same as usual," replied Marguerite, a bit too casually. "Visiting some friends in Plesance."

Belle was a bit surprised she hadn't been offered an invitation right away. "I'm getting so tired of the castle," she said, laying the hint on thickly.

"Oh?" Marguerite stalled. "Well, I think I'll go give Chip a hand—"

"You know, I wouldn't mind joining you this time." Belle felt like a fool for needing the excursion as much as she did. "All those recluse comments have really got to me," she teased.

Marguerite's smile faltered. "I'm not sure that would be such a good idea."

Belle was taken aback. "No? You've asked me plenty of times before."

"It's just that this friend in particular isn't one for unexpected guests. I'd feel awfully rude." Marguerite gave Belle a weak smile. "I'm sorry, but I promise you can come next time?"

Her heart sank, but she plastered a smile onto her face and feigned lightness. "Of course. I'm sorry for my imposition."

"It's not an imposition, Belle. I'd like very much for you to join me if it were any other night."

Belle continued smiling her false smile and nodded. "I understand."

"Well, I'd better get going. See you tomorrow morning? I'll make sure the notice is sent to the press, and we should have more copies than we know what to do with by then."

"Bright and early," Belle replied.

She watched Marguerite pass Chip as he tidied without stopping to help him and commanded herself to remain calm. Belle had dismissed Bastien's accusations against Marguerite so easily because she could not fathom her friend lying to her, but Belle had a sinking suspicion that she just had.

As much as she liked her, Belle had to consider that since she had only known her for a short time, Marguerite's motives being impure was at least within the realm of possibility. But she also thought that her reluctance to include Belle didn't have to mean that Bastien was right about her. The truth could be what she said it was, or Belle's new friend could be betraying her.

There was only one way she could be certain, and it meant donning a disguise once more.

● ● ●

She left the castle a few hours later, wearing the same disguise she had worn when she sneaked to the tavern in Mauger, only this time, she was heading towards the village of Plesance.

There were enough travellers and merchants on the road for Belle to blend in while she followed her friend. Every step felt foolish, but Belle was convinced she needed to see for herself that Marguerite was not an agitator and was in fact exactly who she claimed to be in order to ease her mind and prove Bastien wrong.

As they got closer to Plesance, a crowd began to form. Almost as soon as they stepped through the gates of the village, Belle lost sight of Marguerite entirely. Belle paused at the fountain in the square and scanned around for the bright yellow gown Marguerite had been wearing, but she came up empty. The sun was setting in earnest now, and Belle thought it was a sign that the entire endeavour had been ill thought out. She didn't need proof that Marguerite was who she said she was. She had enough faith in her friend and in her own judgement to know that was true. She cursed Bastien for casting doubts upon her friend needlessly. Belle had just decided to sneak back into the castle and pretend none of it had ever happened, when she overheard something suspicious.

"Did you hear about the meeting at the atelier d'ébénisterie?" a woman asked her companion.

"They say a revolutionary has come all the way from Paris," replied the other. "To Plesance, of all places!"

Belle froze as the terrible feeling that the revolutionary might in fact be Marguerite washed over her. She wanted to be certain of her friend's innocence, but times were such that it was impossible to be certain of anything. She found herself following the two women all the way across the river to where the guild of furniture-making menuisiers plied their trade. It was not a place she had frequented as a child. This part of Plesance catered to Europe's upper class, who came to their sleepy village to buy fine furniture and porcelain, things the peasants couldn't dream of affording.

By the time the crowd reached the atelier, the sun had sunk beyond the horizon. Belle appreciated the dark, hoping it would do more to conceal her than her shoddy disguise could manage. It was foolish to walk into the building alone, but her curiosity could not be sated by mere speculation. Belle had to know what she was up against and if her trust had been misplaced so severely. She was propelled by the same conviction that had pushed her to explore the West Wing of the castle back when it had been forbidden to her – she refused to be kept in the dark, especially when the truth was so easily accessible.

A healthy crowd had formed inside. The air was thick with the scent of sawdust and ale. Belle stayed close to the walls, trying very hard not to catch anyone's notice. She was not in Mauger, where no one knew her. She was in the village where she had grown up, and she would be lucky if she escaped unnoticed. Her spine tingled as she made her way through the building, the villagers casting long shadows in her path, their bodies silhouetted by dim, flickering candlelight.

There was an undercurrent of darkness in the room. She recognised it as the same unease she had felt in Paris before the crowd became a mob. In the streets beneath the Hôtel de Ville, Parisians had been tipped towards murder as easily as a match caught flame. It had felt unbelievable and inevitable all at once. Belle couldn't help but peek at the gathered crowd, searching for some mark of madness in the faces of her former neighbours, but the room was intolerably dark.

Her heart cast a steady drumbeat against her ribs. Her mind protested each step that brought her farther into the hall. She tried to suppress her fears by reminding herself that it was perfectly legal for everyone to gather together, and that until she heard otherwise, she had no reason to suspect the people of Plesance were anything like the ones she had encountered in Paris. Though, it struck her that such a large amount of people were willing to at least listen to someone with ties to the French Revolution. Bastien's reports hadn't mentioned these clandestine meetings, or he had suppressed them, or worse, he knew nothing of them.

The thrum in the air reached a feverish pitch when the agitator took the stage. Belle was immediately relieved to see it was a man. But in the next moment, her chest tightened again as she realised it was someone she knew.

Someone she hadn't seen since the night she broke the curse.

She froze completely as LeFou took to the makeshift pulpit. He was thinner than she remembered, angrier too. Gone was any spark of mischief he used to carry. This version of LeFou had been hollowed out and scraped bare by the life he had lived since that fateful night.

"Sisters and brothers, I come to you tonight with a simple

message, carried in the hearts and minds of our compatriots in France all the way to our village and beyond. It is a message of change and hope. It is a message of revolution."

Belle expected silence, or perhaps laughter, since LeFou had been the butt of many jokes all her life, but the room roared to life as if by command. LeFou fed off their energy. She hadn't thought him capable of rousing a crowd the way Gaston had done. Belle had always pictured LeFou as the harmless sidekick to Gaston's villainy. When the dust settled after the curse had been broken, she had wanted justice for her father, for Lio, and for herself, but it was not to be. The mob that had been led by the now-dead Gaston couldn't remember marching on the castle, calling for the Beast's head. They couldn't remember standing idly by as Gaston and LeFou attempted to have her father committed to an asylum. They couldn't remember any of the things they had done.

But Belle would always remember.

Lio let go of the pain long before she could. She wasn't sure if she ever would. It wasn't as if justice could be served to those who could not recall the crimes they had committed, and reminding them of their sins would mean revealing what else they had forgotten – that their prince had been a beast, and they had wanted him dead.

She had done her best to put the darkness behind her and tried to bury her anger and her desire for vengeance, knowing nothing could be done about it, and for the most part she had succeeded.

Until she saw LeFou, and all of those feelings came rushing back, threatening to fill her heart once more. The people of Plesance had been spurred to action by one man. Gaston was dead – Belle had watched his body fall from the tower and disappear into darkness. But LeFou could very well be his successor, and she feared what he would say next far more than she feared for her own safety.

"It is up to us to spread the message of revolution further. Our king thinks he knows what's best for us, but since when does he care for his people? If he gave a damn about us, he wouldn't be holed up in his noblemen's estates, hiding from the truth: Aveyon hasn't had a king in centuries, and Aveyon doesn't need one now!"

The crowd roared once more, angrier than before, and Belle knew it was time to leave. Nothing would be gained from staying. She had confirmed Marguerite's innocence. That was what she had come here to do. This was not listening to petitioners, or even sneaking into taverns to hear what her people really have to say. This was a glimpse into something darker, something that wouldn't help her, something she couldn't fix. She needed to leave before she was noticed.

She pulled her hood tighter around her head and made for the door. She was almost free of the room when a man stepped into her path and her hood fell before she could stop it. The man looked at her, ready to apologise, but then recognition lit in his eyes.

It was the baker she had gone to for bread and rolls all her life. The one she had greeted every morning as she passed him in the square.

"Jean," she choked out before she could gather enough sense to flee.

He looked at her as if he couldn't believe she was real. "Belle," he exclaimed, much like he used to when she would step into his shop for a baguette. But then he seemed to remember all that separated them. She wasn't a villager any longer. She was married to the king. His face darkened. "You shouldn't be here."

His eyes darted past her and she sensed he was caught between wanting to let her go unnoticed and wanting to reveal her to the crowd, to whatever end. She watched the discord play out in the line of his mouth. She was frozen, waiting for him to decide her fate. Just as he opened his mouth to speak once more or shout her presence, she couldn't tell which, he was hit on the side of the head with a piece of wood, knocking him unconscious instantly. The wall broke his fall and before he could slip to the ground and make a great deal of noise, Marguerite stepped out of the shadows and braced the baker against her body, letting him come to the ground gently.

She looked up to an astonished Belle. "What are you doing here, mon amie?"

"I could ask the same of you!" Belle gasped.

Marguerite let go of Jean and pulled her hood back up over her head. "Come on, someone is going to notice this lump soon enough." She grabbed Belle's hand and half dragged her from the workshop. They were across the river before Belle managed to wrest free of her grip.

She stopped at the edge of the bridge. "You need to tell me what you were doing there. Now."

"*Pardon*?" Marguerite rounded on her. "That's an interesting way of thanking me for saving you from having to explain to a roomful of your own people why the queen of Aveyon was there spying on them in just about the sorriest excuse for a disguise I've ever seen." She laughed darkly. "You know, I may not be well versed in the finer aspects of ruling a kingdom, but I cannot imagine your infiltration would have been joyously received."

But Belle was firm. "You haven't answered my question."

Marguerite made an incredulous noise. "I was minding my own business when I heard there was someone making revolutionary speeches in the atelier d'ébénisterie. With all we are planning, I knew I had to go investigate the situation. I was going to make a full report of my findings to you tomorrow morning, or perhaps tonight had I thought the man worth the attention. I didn't expect to find you there in the middle of a tussle with the baker."

"You weren't going simply to hear what the revolutionary had to say?"

Marguerite glared at her. "If I wished to hear what every brainless sans-culottes had to say about the bloody revolution, I would have stayed in Paris. Look, do I think they have a point from time to time? Of course. But the moment they beheaded the marquis de Launay, I knew their methods would be far too radical."

Belle could tell the veiled accusation had wounded Marguerite, but she wasn't done with her questions yet. "Why did you lie to me earlier when you said I couldn't join you?"

For the first time, Marguerite was at a loss for words. "It's... complicated."

"I can handle complicated."

Voices broke out from the atelier, and Marguerite looked past her, concern lining her features. "Come, this is not the place for this discussion." She took Belle's hand and began to lead her away. "We need to leave before everyone realises the queen of Aveyon is among them."

Belle didn't bother correcting her. She knew that her lack of a title wouldn't matter much to an angry mob.

CHAPTER TWENTY-TWO

Belle let Marguerite bring her to a quiet, dark alley in the marchand-mercier district. It was deserted, but Marguerite still looked around for anyone who might overhear them. She was on edge, and Belle felt at least partially responsible.

Marguerite took a deep breath. "There's something about me I haven't told you. I suppose I was ashamed, or at least afraid that if I did, you would look at me differently."

"Is this about your quarrel with the comtesse d'Armagnac?"

"What? No." She scoffed. "Well, I suppose in a way it is, but that's beside the point. Who told you about our quarrel?" She paused and then laughed unkindly. "Never mind, I see what has happened. This whole thing has Bastien written all over it. Was he attempting to warn you about me?" She didn't wait long enough for Belle to reply. "Listen, Bastien is a snake for going behind my back with a story he only knows a fraction of. Yes, I had a quarrel with the comtesse, but it had nothing to do with some petty nonsense or whatever Bastien claimed. Did he tell you I threw tantrums all over Paris?"

Belle was beginning to feel like she was intruding on something her friend didn't want to divulge. "You don't have to explain yourself to me—"

"No, I need to now that the duc de Vincennes has besmirched my already-tarnished name." Marguerite twisted her hands together and swallowed thickly. "Sophie – the comtesse – and I were in love, or at least, I believed our feelings to be mutual. We talked and dreamed and made grand plans the way lovers do, but then she betrayed me, and even worse, lied to others about the source of our enmity when she could have said nothing, as I had chosen to do. She started making up outlandish claims about me, and I became an outcast, which, as you can imagine, was inconvenient in Paris. It's a part of the reason I left."

Belle's heart hurt for her friend. "Marguerite, I'm so sorry—"

But Marguerite continued. "The reason I didn't invite you to join me tonight was because I was meeting with a woman, one I like very much, and I wasn't ready to show you that part of myself."

"I'm sorry I forced you into telling me. I had no right—"

"No, you didn't."

Belle let the silence between them stretch, unsure of how to mend things. She had betrayed her closest friend and forced her hand for nothing. "I hope you know that this doesn't change anything about our friendship, at least on my end.

I understand why you feared telling me, but all I want is for you to be happy."

Marguerite sighed. "Honestly, Belle, I should have told you sooner, but that doesn't mean I'm happy to have been forced into telling you now." Belle opened her mouth to speak, perhaps to defend herself or beg for forgiveness, she wasn't even sure, but Marguerite interrupted her. "I think we should leave the village before that man wakes up and tells everyone who he saw prior to my rendering him unconscious."

She set off in the direction of the castle before Belle could say anything. Marguerite was silent all the way back, and guilt weighed heavy on Belle's shoulders.

She was a fool for thinking even for a moment that her friend was a secret revolutionary who had tricked her way into Belle's confidence, but she was an even bigger fool for allowing Bastien's vague warning to sway her in the first place. If there was anyone in Aveyon she shouldn't trust, it was the duc de Vincennes, who had already lied to her on more than one occasion.

She half expected her friend to retire to her chambers without speaking on the matter further, but Marguerite led them both to the library, which had long since emptied for the night. Chip's mess from earlier was still strewn about the room.

Her friend turned, hands placed firmly on her hips. "What exactly did Bastien say to you?"

Belle swallowed thickly, ashamed of her behaviour. "He told me he's seen you in the village, boasting about your access to me. He told me revolutionary agitators come in many forms. He offered to have you removed from the castle." Marguerite reddened with anger. "I refused, of course. My first instinct was to dismiss everything he said. And then, when you didn't invite me to accompany you, it served as proof of what he had told me. I should have trusted my gut." As she said it, the face of the woman from the mirror shop filled her mind. *You must not wait for others to save Aveyon. You need to trust your instincts and become the queen you're capable of being.* It was the best advice she'd received since they came back to Aveyon, and it had come from a ghost. "I'm so sorry I let his trickery come between us."

"He's an absolute weasel of a man, Belle. Versailles runs deep in that pautonier's blood." Belle had to agree with that particular insult – Bastien was proving to be something of a practised liar. Marguerite let out all the air in her lungs and continued. "But his biggest sin would be driving a wedge between us, and I'm not going to let that happen."

Relief flooded through Belle. She reached for Marguerite's hand, and her friend allowed herself to be pulled into an embrace. "I'll never listen to the weasel ever again," Belle muttered into her hair.

Marguerite pulled away and smiled. "You owe me, though. I can't believe I hit the baker over the head."

"He's known to be a bit of a drinker," Belle admitted. "There's a decent chance he won't remember a thing."

"Are you going to confront him?"

"Jean? Certainly not. I'd rather not know if the man I've been buying pastries from for over a decade was about to sell me out to the crowd."

"No, I mean Bastien."

"And risk having him shut me out of the advisory altogether? I wouldn't put it past him to start hosting the meetings exclusively on hunts just to keep me from them." She rubbed her temples. "I have to be smart about it and wait until Lio returns. The advisers are looking for a reason to discredit me or ignore me, and I can't let that happen until after the salon." Belle had done a good job of compartmentalising the events of the night, but all at once, the memory of LeFou working the crowd into a frenzy came rushing back. "Though after what we witnessed tonight, can I even pretend that hosting a salon will fix Aveyon's ills?"

"Don't be ridiculous. Aveyon needs the salon now more than ever."

Belle squinted. "Wouldn't it be a bit like wrapping a bandage over a gushing wound and hoping it will heal itself?"

"How do you mean?"

"Back there at the atelier, the crowd was frothing at the prospect of revolution. Is it even possible to stop it now?"

Marguerite frowned. "That room was filled with

suggestible drunks pulled from the taverns and alleys of Plesance. They would have crowned a goat king if someone shouted about it on a pile of crates." She sat down beside Belle. "Who was that connard, anyway?"

Belle choked at Marguerite's fitting choice of words. "That was LeFou. He has been my enemy for some time."

Marguerite raised her brows. "His name speaks volumes. But you don't need to worry about the crowd. They'll all wake up tomorrow with barely a memory from their time in the atelier listening to a loud fool making a speech. And in a few days' time, some of them will be in this very library, armed with their best ideas, and ready to exchange them with scientists and philosophers. Instead of being shouted at, they will be *heard*." She paused, but the silence was companionable. When she spoke again, her voice had taken on a dreamlike quality. "It will be a magical thing, I think, to watch a kingdom come together to rebuild itself."

• • •

Belle and Marguerite talked well into the night about the proposals they hoped to receive from Aveyon's commoners. They needed a wealth of ideas from all corners of the kingdom and beyond to really ignite a healthy debate. Belle was beginning to wonder if one day would be enough. She made a mental note to discuss the logistics of extending the event with Cogsworth, but only when he was in a rare good mood.

By the time they left the library, thoughts of LeFou were far behind her.

She stumbled into her bed and was asleep before she could decide to take off her dress.

She awoke in a room that was not her own.

Belle lay in the same bed she had fallen asleep in, but beyond that the room was featureless, a blank canvas. *I am dreaming,* she thought. She swung her legs over the side of the bed and stepped into white nothingness. As she stood, her bed disappeared like a wisp of smoke. She couldn't feel the ground she stood upon, or see any walls or borders, like the space went on forever.

"Is anyone there?" she called out, unsure what she wished the answer to be. She thought she should feel more afraid, but there was a sense of calm in her she couldn't quite account for. Her first thought was that the feeling was familiar – it was the same unnatural calm she had felt in the shop in Paris.

As if on cue, a figure emerged in the distance, blurry at first until she stepped into focus. Belle was not surprised to find it was the woman from the mirror shop, the one who had haunted her steps since Paris.

"This is a dream," Belle assured herself aloud. "I will wake up and none of this will have been real."

The woman stopped some distance away from her and tilted her head. "I suppose you could call this a dream, but in truth it is something else entirely."

"Who are you?"

"A friend" was all the woman offered.

"Why should I believe you?"

The woman stepped closer, arms outstretched like a plea. "You are entitled to believe what you will, Belle. But I ask that you at least listen before you decide I am your enemy."

In this strange dreamland, it didn't seem like an unreasonable request. "Go on."

The woman lowered her hands to her sides. "I am here to warn you of what's coming. There is a fire burning through France, and if Aveyon succumbs to its flames, nothing will stop it from spreading across the world."

The fire she spoke of was the revolution brewing in Paris and Versailles, that much was obvious. But Belle didn't know why it should matter so desperately to this woman that Belle be informed of the inevitable. Belle didn't want to reveal how afraid she really was, not even in this bizarre dream space. She shrugged as non-committally as she could manage. "There are kingdoms and empires in the world that should be forced to change."

The woman frowned. "Terror marches in the wake of this fire. Thousands will die, people will turn on one another, kingdoms will betray their allies. The instability will have far-reaching consequences. Aveyon will cease to exist as you know it. It is up to you to stop the fire from spreading."

Belle thought that believing the woman meant believing

the worst was coming for them, and there was nothing she could do to prevent it. She didn't understand why the responsibility to ensure it didn't ruin Aveyon fell on her shoulders, but she feared her own mistakes more than she feared the possibility that this mysterious, magical woman was lying to her. "What am I supposed to do?"

"I told you once before to trust your instincts. You've suppressed them for so long you no longer recognise them for what they are – a warning."

The room began to shake; Belle tried to ignore it. "You speak in riddles. Can't you just tell me plainly?"

"My foresight is limited, Belle; I only know what I have seen in vague visions – you wearing a crown, your kingdom burning, Europe crumbling under the weight of the violence this revolution brings. All I can do is wait and watch as each step you take on this path either obscures or enhances what I can make of the future. I cannot tell you what to do or whom to trust – those are decisions you must make for yourself," she admitted. "But one thing has been clear from the start: any vision I have of healing, of avoiding this fire, begins with you."

The ground began to shake, and Belle lost her footing. "What's happening?"

The woman was as composed as ever. "You're waking up."

In the distance, Belle could hear someone calling her name. She looked back to the woman. Belle wanted to demand answers of her, but her grip on the dream was failing. "Why can't you come to me in Aveyon as you did in Paris?"

The woman cast her eyes downwards, as if in sadness. "I should not think myself welcome there."

The dream began to break down entirely. The whiteness of the space crumbled into blackness, and Belle lurched to her side, hanging on to an edge she couldn't see.

"What if I need you again?" She had so much more she wanted to ask her, but one final earth-shattering crack sent Belle into the abyss. And then she was awake in her room, with a frantic Mrs Potts standing over her.

"Sacré, Belle, you sleep like the dead."

Belle sat up, knowing in her gut something wasn't right. "What's wrong? What's happened?"

"You need to come quickly, madame. Bastien is banishing Marguerite from the castle, on your orders, he says. I knew you'd never do such a thing, so I came straight here."

Belle was on her feet already, relieved to find she was still dressed from the day before. "Take me to them."

The two of them hurried through the dark castle. Belle heard the ruckus long before they came upon it. Shouts echoed through the empty halls, amplifying the angry voices.

"I must make sure Chip is in bed where he belongs. I'll come back as quick as I can," whispered Mrs Potts.

"Go." Belle urged her away from the messy scene.

Belle came at last to the entrance hall, where guards were attempting to forcibly remove a distressed Marguerite as a calm Bastien watched on. He turned and noticed Belle's arrival, shock alighting his features. Bastien had not anticipated that someone would come to find Belle, but he recovered quickly.

"Oh, good, now you can explain to the Mademoiselle de Lambriquet that I am only acting on your wishes."

"Stand down," Belle ordered. The guards hesitated for a second before obeying. Marguerite fell to her knees as soon as they removed their hands. Belle wanted to make sure she was all right, but she had bigger problems to tend to. "What is this, Bastien?"

He held up his hands in mock surrender. "I am only doing what you asked me to do, madame."

"I never once asked you to banish Marguerite from the castle."

"Perhaps not in so many words... You wanted her dealt with, and so I am dealing with her."

"That's preposterous. When have I *ever* asked—"

Bastien began to realise he had lost his grip on the situation entirely. "It would seem my reading of the situation was incorrect." He looked over to Marguerite and offered a tight smile. "Apologies, mademoiselle, this has all been a big misunderstanding."

Marguerite was shaken but still looked as though she could have murdered him with her bare hands, and Belle felt the same way. She was tired of the duc wielding his influence like a weapon against her. Piled atop one another, his sins could reach the top of the highest tower in the castle. There was no reason to trust him ever again, or to keep him around. How was she only just realising it now?

She looked to the guards. "You are never to take an order from the duc de Vincennes ever again, do you understand?" She was relieved to see they nodded without hesitation this time.

"Belle, be reasonable."

"You are not to address me unless it is to apologise for being a duplicitous ass." For once, Bastien had nothing to say. "Your days on the advisory are over, Bastien. You never belonged on it in the first place. I don't know what you're playing at, or what your goal is – perhaps you only wish to sow chaos, perhaps this is all a game to you, but it doesn't matter. You're done playing games with the people of Aveyon."

He opened and shut his mouth several times. She had never seen the duc at a loss for words.

"You are a guest in this castle, nothing more. You do not speak for me and you most certainly do not speak for the king, do you understand me?"

He swallowed and gave her a blank stare. "I was only doing what I thought was best for the kingdom."

"You have no idea what's best for Aveyon. You have never known. For all of your supposed wisdom, you have never once walked through our villages and towns; you have never spoken with the people who are the backbone of Aveyon, or the peasants, as you so blithely and exclusively refer to them. One might even think you had forgotten I too was a peasant once — if you were not continually reminding me."

By then, a curious crowd had formed behind her. Cogsworth stepped up to where she was standing, and she winced in anticipation. Surely he was about to chastise her for so roundly insulting the duc.

"I suggest you retire to your chambers, monsieur." It was as harsh a rebuke as the majordomo had ever delivered to an aristocrat. He turned to the rest of the assemblage. "The same goes for the rest of you. The night is late, and we all have work to attend to in the morning."

Slowly the crowd dissipated. Bastien lingered with a look of sarcastic bewilderment on his face, like he both couldn't believe what had happened and had anticipated it. "Belle, if you'll just let me speak—"

"Go to bed, Bastien. You've done enough harm for one night."

As he eyed her, she saw a spark of the rage that simmered beneath his carefully crafted facade. It frightened her, but she stood firm. He turned and left the entryway, his steps echoing all the way down the hall.

When they couldn't hear him any longer, Belle sank to her knees. The confrontation had left her reeling. "What on earth have I done?"

Marguerite stared down the hall Bastien had disappeared into. "What you should have done weeks ago." She looked over to Belle sprawled on the tile. "If he had managed to get me out of the castle, you can be sure he would have spun the story for your ears. *Marguerite was called away in the night; she asked that you not worry yourself over her departure.* The snake. He thought I'd believe that you wanted me removed, as if I hadn't just rescued you from a workshop full of angry drunk men."

"Pardon?" Cogsworth squeaked.

Belle ignored the enquiry. "Cogsworth, can you get a tea for Marguerite? She's had a rough night." For once, he didn't protest being assigned a menial task. She looked back at her friend. "What made him move against you now, of all times?"

Marguerite blushed. "I may have visited his rooms on the way to mine with a mind to confront him about the lies he told about me." She paused and looked to Belle, wincing as she did. "I hadn't even got a word in edgewise before he insisted he had an urgent letter for me from Aurelian down in his office. Can you believe I bought that load of nonsense. It was all a ruse, of course." She adjusted her rumpled gown. "The frightening thing is that it likely would have worked if not for your interference. I certainly wouldn't have been able to get back into the castle, let alone get a letter to you. He has entirely too much control here. Or rather, he *had*. You did the right thing, Belle."

Belle sighed. "It was, perhaps, a bad idea to ambush him in

his rooms, though."

"Oh, of course. But it galls me because we know each other, he and I. For all our enmity, Bastien and my brother have been lifelong friends. I don't know why he'd do something so cruel to me over my quarrel with the comtesse." She drew herself up and shook her head. "He's a snake, and now everyone knows it."

"Do they?" Belle asked. Marguerite didn't have an answer. "I don't regret doing it so much as I fear his retaliation."

"What could he do? You're the wife of the king of Aveyon, it's not as though he can bar you from your own damn castle." Marguerite reached a hand down and pulled Belle to her feet. "He's shown his true colours at last, and that is your defence should anyone question your decision. He tried to speak for you; he overstepped. You should have banished *him*."

"He's the only family Lio has left. I think it was enough to neuter his influence."

"I hope you're right." Marguerite tucked her unruly hair behind her ears. "I can't promise I won't strangle him the next time I see him, though."

"Such is your right," Belle replied. "I'm sorry that happened to you. I feel like everything is falling apart and there's nothing I can do to prevent it."

Marguerite squeezed her shoulder. "Firstly, your salon

is going to be a massive success, and secondly, I don't think you could cancel it now even if you wanted to." Marguerite grinned. "The wheels are in motion, Belle."

CHAPTER TWENTY-THREE

T he courtyard was fuller than Belle had ever seen before. Streams of carts laden with extra butter, eggs and flour, which Mrs Potts had ordered to accommodate the salon's guests, trickled in without end. Workers built temporary stalls around the edges for the merchants who had been permitted to sell goods in the makeshift market that would be open simultaneously, both to ease the burden on the castle kitchens and to provide attendees with a place to go that wasn't the library. The rest of the castle would be off-limits. If there was any piece of advice that Belle was willing to take from Bastien, it was that the safety of those who resided within should be paramount.

She hadn't seen the duc since the scene in the entrance hall two days before, save for glances of the back of him leaving rooms as she entered. She understood he was nursing his wounds. Belle had effectively ended whatever influence he had wielded in the castle and had half expected him to leave Aveyon entirely out of embarrassment, but it seemed for the time being he would remain, sulking and skulking around like a petulant child. She wondered if he was planning to tell Lio what had happened in hopes that his cousin would take his side. She had done her best to trust Bastien, but he had proven himself a liar time and time again. Lio would have done the same as she had in similar circumstances. Being family wasn't reason enough to forgive someone after they betray your confidence.

Cogsworth appeared at her shoulder. "Everything is in order, madame."

"Please, Cogsworth. Just call me Belle."

"Of course, Belle." He seemed to choke on her name like it was a bitter piece of fruit. "Does the king know you've opened the castle to commoners as well?"

"No," Belle admitted. "I didn't wish to burden him with anything more to deal with or worry about. It will be a surprise to him, unless, of course, he's seen the notices in the villages. Marguerite and I haven't slept since we received the proposals."

"Have you made your selections?"

"Yes, though it was difficult. We had to reject some very sound ideas simply because we won't have enough time to hear them all."

"Well, I normally abhor surprises, but I can't imagine that the king will have any reason to dislike this one. Had he been here, I suspect he would have been an enthusiastic participant in the planning."

Belle smiled at him as Lumière popped up behind them.

"Is that praise, mon ami?" Lumière came up from behind and grasped Cogsworth's shoulders. "Come, now. You can do better than that. Look around." He gestured to the courtyard. "Have you ever seen the castle so lively? It was what we spent ten long years dreaming of."

Belle perked up. The further they got from the curse, the less anyone who had lived under its yoke wished to discuss it. Save for Mrs Potts, she hadn't heard any of her friends mention it in months, and she wasn't interested in pushing them towards the subject.

Cogsworth shook free of the maître d'hôtel. "Yes, well, we have two days before us in which everything can go horribly wrong." His discomfort was obvious.

"Ah, that's the Cogsworth I know and love." Lumière departed for a group of maids he spotted across the courtyard before the majordomo could admonish him further.

Cogsworth sighed. "It's not as if I believe anything will go horribly wrong, I just cannot abide his constant optimism."

Belle laughed. "I rely on his optimism and your pessimism both. You balance each other out."

He wrinkled his nose at the thought. "Yes, well, there is only one day left until the king is scheduled to return. Are you ready to explain *everything* to him?"

She knew he meant was she ready to tell him of everything that had happened with Bastien in addition to the inclusion of

Aveyon's commoners. "Yes."

He nodded and didn't prod for more confirmation. "Then I will consider that item complete." He crossed something off his list. "I must see to the kitchens. Last I checked, Mrs Potts was not well enough prepared for the worst-case scenario I presented her with."

"Which was what?"

"That the attendees prefer the food that can be purchased in the courtyard over her prepared dishes."

"I don't think you'll have to worry about that, Cogsworth."

"Yes, well, we need a contingency plan for the fifty pounds of butter she ordered, should the worst happen."

He bowed at a ninety-degree angle and walked away, careful not to turn his back on her until he was out of sight. Belle hated that he was unable to let go of the etiquette she had tried very hard to banish.

Hoofbeats clattered over the cobblestones. Belle turned, wondering who of the notable guests would be the first to arrive, and why it was they seemed in such a hurry. Her heart was not prepared to soar when she saw it was Lio riding in, a whole day early. If he was surprised to see the courtyard full of people and stalls, it didn't register. His eyes found hers at once. His hair fell loose around his shoulders, longer than she remembered.

"Belle."

The distance between them was great, but she heard the

way he said her name nevertheless, like it was a secret only he knew.

He dismounted, and they rushed towards each other, meeting in the middle of the courtyard. Belle expected him to have questions and to launch into them right away. She did not expect him to take her in his arms in front of the crowd and press a rough kiss against her lips. His mouth tasted like the fresh mint he chewed on long journeys. Everything she had missed about him was condensed into one gesture. Standing there in Lio's arms felt more like home than the castle ever could.

When they pulled apart, Belle saw that he looked frightened. Only then did Lio seem to realise the bustle of unusual activity in the courtyard.

He smiled congenially at his people, but Belle felt overwhelmed by his sudden appearance and uneasy demeanour. Cogsworth had been expecting word from him when he reached Livrade, which would have given Belle time to ride into Plesance to greet him and explain why the castle was full of visitors when he had been expecting a staid salon. He wasn't supposed to arrive without warning.

Something was wrong.

He eyed the crowd that had gathered around them, cheering at the display. "What on earth is happening here? I take it this is not a welcome party?"

But Belle couldn't find the words to explain. "Why are you

back early? What's happened?"

He pressed his mouth into a thin line. "Let's go talk inside."

• • •

Cogsworth almost had a stroke when he caught sight of Lio striding in through the castle doors. Belle watched a vein nearly pop out of his skull as he did his best to act naturally.

"Your Majesty, what an absolutely unexpected surprise," he said, a current of barely controlled panic lurking beneath his duty-at-all-times manner. He looked over Lio's shoulder to the courtyard beyond. "May I ask where your retinue can be found? There is much to attend to."

Lio peeled his gloves off and stuffed them in his pocket. "I rode ahead; they'll be arriving tomorrow."

Cogsworth looked both unhinged and entirely calm, a special talent of his. "May I ask why?"

Lio touched Cogsworth's shoulder. "Listen, we don't have time to tell the story again and again. Could you please inform Bastien of my arrival and ask that he meet us in the throne room?"

Belle and Cogsworth froze, neither of them entirely sure how to inform Lio that Belle had all but banished his cousin from discussing matters pertaining to the kingdom. She looked over to her husband and saw hints of the fear that had kept him up at night—his skin was sallower than usual, his frame thinner. Whatever happened to make him ride all the way to Aveyon a day early couldn't have been good. All at once, she decided she couldn't burden him with another problem.

Cogsworth was looking between the two of them, begging for some sort of direction. Lio was distracted and didn't notice his majordomo's reluctance.

Belle cleared her throat. "Yes, please do, Cogsworth. And will you alert Marguerite as well?"

The name seemed to pull Lio away from his thoughts. He watched Cogsworth hurry away from them and spoke. "I don't mean to imply—"

Belle interrupted him. "I'd trust her with my life, Lio."

"All right." He pulled her into an embrace that felt desperate. "I've missed this so much."

She wanted to ask him a thousand questions, but questions could wait. For now she just held him in return, delighting in the feeling of having him back with her. It didn't matter what he had to tell them, so long as they were together. They could have stood there forever, twined together and perfectly still in the midst of the chaos that had engulfed the castle, and she would have been happy.

But reality set in. "We need to go," Lio whispered in her ear.

She nodded into his chest and let him guide her away from the sanctuary they had made for themselves. Perhaps one day it would last for longer than a few moments stolen from their real lives.

...

It was an advisory meeting unlike any other, with only one adviser in attendance. Belle looked around at her friends — Cogsworth, Marguerite and Lumière — at Lio's generals and at Bastien, the man she had banished from that room only two days before. He seemed unwilling to meet her eye, and she wasn't about to complain. At the very least, the two of them were ignoring their animosity for the time being. It was all she could have hoped for.

Lio stood. "I'll get right to it. King Louis and Marie Antoinette have been removed from Versailles by force."

The room was stunned save for the generals and Bastien, who Belle noticed were unsurprised. "How?" she asked.

"You know of the king recalling the Regiment of Flanders back to Versailles?" He paused as everyone nodded. "And of the general agitation in Paris? The unemployment, the price of bread increasing?" He waited again, but they knew all of that thanks to Bastien. "It would seem once the regiment arrived at Versailles a banquet was held, during which numerous toasts to the royal family were made and none to the nation of France. In times as fraught as these, that did not go unnoticed, nor did the fact that a lavish banquet was held in Versailles while the people of Paris starve."

Bastien piped up. "Claims have been made that Marie Antoinette cares very little for the suffering of her people.

When she was told of the price of bread reaching unattainable heights, she is said to have exclaimed that the starving peasants of Paris should eat cake instead."

Lio nodded. "Whether that is true or not, the people of Paris furiously marched on Versailles. They were some seven thousand strong by the time they reached the palace, and led mostly by women. Commandant Lafayette followed them with his command of Gardes nationales. Louis had no choice but to accept the decrees of the National Assembly, and offered the crowd all the bread, flour and wheat in Versailles to keep them happy."

Belle was confused. "After all his fighting and refusal to capitulate, he just accepted the constitution?"

"Under duress, but yes. There's more, though. Lafayette asked Louis to return with him to Paris the next day, and Louis agreed. That night, the marchers stayed in Versailles and drank into the early hours of the morning. Eventually, some of them invaded the palace and killed two of Louis's bodyguards and lifted their heads onto pikes. Lafayette managed to restore order by bringing the king, queen and dauphin onto a balcony to present to the rabid crowd. Some called for Marie Antoinette to be shot, but she stood firm. Louis promised the crowd that he and his family would go to Paris, and they did so in a procession some sixty thousand strong. They have been installed at Tuileries, but they are little more than prisoners."

"Prisoners? But what do they intend to do with them?" Belle asked.

"Who can say? There are many competing desires in the National Assembly. I'm not sure anyone knows what will happen, especially with mobs of Parisians calling for blood. Nobles are fleeing the capital; Marie Antoinette even sent her ladies away before the royal family left Versailles. It is chaos in Paris. I made for home as soon as I heard." He paused to take a breath. "Which reminds me... the castle seems rather busier than usual, Belle?"

Heat rose to Belle's cheeks as the whole table looked her way. She didn't fail to notice the smug expression on Bastien's face. "It's the salon—" she started.

"I'd forgotten all about that," Lio admitted, before continuing. "That's a lot more people than required for a simple salon."

"Our vision for it expanded," she explained, but all her reasons for inviting hundreds of people into the castle left her mind entirely.

Marguerite spoke up. "It's not just a salon, Your Majesty, but a step towards something democratic for Aveyon. It is to be a way to hear from *all* the people of your kingdom instead of just one group."

Belle found her voice. "We received reports of protests while you were gone. People were becoming restless."

"Reports but no evidence," Bastien added with a tone that

suggested Belle was being dramatic.

"I saw the evidence myself when I talked to commoners in a tavern in Mauger, many of whom criticised Lio for valuing his noblemen over the rest of his people." She left out that she had also witnessed the villagers of Plesance gather to listen to a revolutionary agitator, knowing it would only beget more questions.

Lio looked askance at Belle. "You did *what*?"

"I took precautions," she said defensively, knowing her choice to keep LeFou's rabble-rousing to herself for the time being was the right one. Lio didn't need to hear more bad news after his long journey. "I had to see for myself if the reports were true." She could tell Lio was thinking of all the ways she could have been killed between the castle and Mauger. "I'm *fine*, as you can see. And I got insight into how our people are feeling, which was invaluable."

Cogsworth cleared his throat. "The salon has been well received by all, Your Majesty." Belle could have kissed him for his support.

Lio frowned. "Nevertheless, I think we should call it off."

It was a knife to Belle's gut. "But everything is well under way, Lio. Guests have begun to arrive."

"King Louis and Marie Antoinette are *prisoners* in their own castle, Belle. Their people turned on them."

Bastien piped up. "Some would say rightfully so."

Lio looked over to his cousin. "And what of our people?

Who is to say that they don't think the same of us?"

Belle needed him to see the difference. "Lio, we are not Louis and Marie."

"You said yourself that our people have been criticising me, and you wish to invite them into our castle?"

"Criticising the king is not a crime here, Lio. Nor should it be." He opened his mouth to argue, but she wouldn't let him. "This is what we are hosting the salon for. We are giving everyone in Aveyon a voice. And by the end of it, presumably we will have some solid plans we can enact with the approval and consent of our people. We can change the kingdom for the better, and it won't just be our vision. It's a chance to fix the problems that became a crisis in France," she implored. "A chance to ensure the seeds of revolution could never be sown in our kingdom."

Lio shook his head. "I worry about putting us in danger needlessly. Surely there is another way forward."

"We don't need to be protected from our people, we need to listen to them. Of course there will be other ways forward and of course the salon is not the only solution. But it is the quickest way to show we are willing to hear everyone, including Aveyon's nobles. It's scheduled for two days from now, and everything has gone according to plan. To cancel it now would be a stain upon your return to the capital."

It was clear that Lio was torn. She knew his nightmares had followed him from estate to estate, never allowing him a moment's peace. And then the news from Paris had only intensified the fears he had learned to live with, making them unbearable.

"Cousin, it is a good plan." The room stilled. No one had expected Bastien to defend the salon, Belle least of all. "I understand your fears, but I think you need to put them aside and think of the good that will come of this."

As much as it annoyed her to see Lio take Bastien's words to heart, Belle was relieved the duc had spoken up. Lio contemplated his words and arrived at a decision.

"The salon will go on as planned." Belle and Marguerite looked at each other, unable to contain the joy that coursed through them. "But," he continued, "security is our paramount concern. No one comes into this castle without being thoroughly searched and vetted, and if we get any word or hint whatsoever of a plot against us, the salon will be over."

Belle wanted to assure him that no such plots existed, but after what she had seen in the atelier d'ébénisterie in Plesance, she wasn't so sure they didn't.

CHAPTER TWENTY-FOUR

Belle needed to speak to her husband alone.

There was so much she needed to tell him about what had happened while he was gone, but most of all, she wanted him to know about the incident between her and Bastien. She was once again unsure of where she stood with the duc – he had defended the salon to Lio, which had seemed like support for Belle, but she knew better. He must have wanted the salon to continue for his own personal gain. Perhaps he had made promises he needed to keep. Belle didn't have any desire to see the duc castigated for how he had gone against her, but she at least wanted Lio to know the truth of the matter before Bastien told some twisted version of events.

But she had barely had five minutes alone with her husband since he returned. Everyone wanted a piece of the king now that he was home. If Cogsworth wasn't at his ear, it was his generals. Noblemen had appeared at the castle throughout the day, either for the salon they had been invited to or to see their king returned to the capital. The advisory was present in its entirety, and they were showing Belle a great deal more respect than they had the last few months. She wouldn't forget how they had treated her while Lio was gone, but they could be dealt with long after the salon. For now, she just sat with Marguerite and stewed.

"You're making quite the sour face at Commandant Vasseur," her friend remarked through a mouthful of pastry. Mrs Potts had the kitchens in a controlled frenzy, producing vast amounts of food to feed the guests who had arrived early.

"What?" Belle realised she had been glaring at the man who held Lio's attention. "It's nothing."

"You just wish everyone in this room would go to hell and leave the two of you alone?"

Belle gave her a look. "Of course not. It's just… there's a lot we haven't been able to say to each other."

"I'm sure you'll be able to *say* it all later," Marguerite replied with a wink. Belle pinched her.

"I'm being serious. He knows nothing of Bastien's lies, or that I saw LeFou make a speech against him in the very village I grew up in." She pressed her hands to her eyes and made an anguished noise. "This was not how I expected his homecoming would go."

Marguerite gave her a sympathetic smile. "You'll have him all to yourself soon enough."

Belle could only hope that she was right.

A servant appeared beside them, bowed low at Belle, and then spoke to Marguerite. "Mademoiselle, I have been sent to inform you of your brother Aurelian's arrival."

Marguerite choked on a bit of tart. "Aurelian is *here*?" Her skin was pale.

The servant looked at her apprehensively. "Yes, mademoiselle. He arrived only a few moments ago. I was sent to fetch you at once."

"But I wasn't even aware that he was coming," Marguerite blurted. "We haven't spoken in months. How does he even know I'm here?"

Belle tried to nudge her out of her shock. "I am sure Bastien invited him for the salon," she said. "He probably mentioned that you were here as well."

Marguerite swallowed the rest of her tart and pressed her hands to her hair. "And he wishes to see me?"

The servant nodded, evidently afraid of speaking. Belle patted Marguerite on the back and dismissed the grateful servant. "You should go to him."

She shook her head. "He wasn't there for me when I needed him most. He did *nothing* to defend me when I was at my lowest. Belle, I can't."

"Perhaps he wishes to apologise and make amends." Belle knew a thing or two about a person's capacity for change. "Avoiding him means you'll never know."

Marguerite was lost in her thoughts. Not knowing the extent of Aurelian's betrayal, Belle didn't wish to push her. She didn't have any siblings of her own, but Belle knew if

Marguerite were her sister, she would never have abandoned her over someone she loved. But she remembered how Marguerite described her brother when they first met as a man concerned first and foremost with how others perceived him. Belle hoped that his time in a changing Paris, far away from his sister, had shifted his priorities.

After a time, Marguerite nodded. "I suppose you're right."

"And if he isn't here to do either of those things, then I shall have him thrown out of the castle." Belle took a sip of her lukewarm tea. "This also gives you a chance to tell him how monstrous Bastien has been to you. He should know who his friends are."

"Remember, he barely tolerates Bastien. I can't imagine he came all this way just to see someone he hates."

"All the more reason to speak with him."

• • •

Belle waited up for Lio, but he didn't join her in their chambers until well after midnight. She was all but asleep when he crawled into bed beside her, pulling her into his arms.

"I've missed you. I've missed this." His heartbeat drummed softly against her cheek, lulling her into a calmness she had been without since he left. Belle wanted their first night together to be just for them, but she had to say something.

She twisted his shirt in her hand. "We need to talk about what happened while you were gone. Our commoners are not happy. I was able to—"

He pulled away slightly. "I've been gone some months and the first thing you want to do when we're alone together is talk politics?" He raised himself up on his elbows. "I've got a whole advisory for that, of which you are a member. Right now I just want you. I don't want to hear about the plight of our commoners, who are treated a hell of a lot better than their French counterparts."

She wanted him too, but there was a part of her that refused to let go of the things she needed to tell him. "It's not just Aveyon's commoners, Lio. Bastien behaved—"

Lio was exasperated. "I know you two don't get along, and I'm not surprised to hear that didn't change in my absence."

"Well, there's more to it than simply not getting along—"

"Belle, truly, can this not wait until morning? I'm exhausted. I rode hard today to get back to you. I don't wish to talk about our people or least of all Bastien now that I have you in my arms." He caressed her cheek. "You cannot know how much I missed you."

But she did know. Belle had watched him fight his demons through the mirror, but she would never tell him so. As much as she had needed to do it, Belle also understood that it was a breach of the trust between them, and revealing that would mean she would have to explain the existence of the mirror, and the woman who had spoken to her through it, and she wasn't quite ready to do so just yet.

"I missed you too," she whispered. "I missed having a partner. I don't much like having everything fall on me. I never wanted to be queen."

"I know." He kissed her forehead. "I wasn't exactly having the time of my life on my tour."

"Things didn't improve?" she asked, though she knew the answer.

Lio sighed, and she worried he would tell her he didn't wish to talk about it. "There were bright spots – I met a few noblemen and women who had progressive leanings, which was encouraging, but mostly I met people who believed they had got along very well without me. They seemed to be expecting some sort of bribe in return for their loyalty. I could just hear my father's voice in my head calling them traitors, but my father never had to go through what I did." He pulled her closer. "I know we have things to discuss, but please tell me they can wait until morning? Right now I just want to fall asleep with you in my arms and forget all the worries that have haunted me since I left." When she was silent, he seemed to consider something. "But if it's something you think I need to know about, then I will listen and try to help." She didn't know what to say to him. After a few moments of silence, he was concerned. "Belle, is there something you need to tell me?"

Her mind went to the mirror, that last vestige of the curse they thought they had destroyed, and the mysterious woman who spoke to her through it. Lio was giving her a chance to tell him about it, but she found she couldn't. No good would come of revealing that the curse lived on in some form. She would hold that knowledge inside herself and hope it didn't break her.

"No, nothing important," she replied. Her voice sounded false to her ears, but Lio didn't notice.

"Then we shall talk in the morning." He kissed her forehead and fell almost immediately into a deep sleep, still holding her tight. Belle wanted desperately to feel at peace in his arms after so long spent sleeping alone and fretfully. But that peace eluded her. With so much happening around them, Belle couldn't let go of her fears. Some part of her she couldn't control or dismiss told her that this small moment of quiet with Lio was simply the calm before the storm.

• • •

She awoke out of Lio's arms.

He was fast asleep next to her, and Belle was heartened to see the early morning sunrise peeking in through their curtains. Lio had made it through the night without falling victim to a nightmare.

She didn't wish to wake him but was well aware that she wouldn't be able to lie there quietly. She decided to get up and pay a quick visit to the library to ensure their preparations were where they should be. Marguerite was very likely there already.

She dressed silently but knew it would take a lot more to wake up Lio. His sleep was deep and even, so different from what she had seen through the mirror. She prayed that the worst of his nightmares was behind him.

The halls were empty and cooled by the morning air. The hour was earlier than she had guessed. She walked to the library, and her heart nearly stopped upon entering. She hadn't expected it to be so transformed, but the room matched what Belle had hoped for in her wildest dreams. Once the fires were lit and the room was full of her guests, she knew she would hardly recognise it. Two long tables ran the length of the room, already straining under the weight of numerous inventions covered with thick white cloths. Belle couldn't wait to see what lay under them. Circular tables were scattered through the rest of the room, ready for people to gather around to debate or challenge one another. Belle imagined herself travelling between the tables, searching for the snippets of conversations that would turn first to debate and eventually to reforms for her kingdom. She flexed her writing hand and prayed she could keep up with the pace.

Belle felt calm. Despite the litany of things that made her nervous, at the very least the library was ready to receive their guests the next day. Only one hurdle remained: the welcome ball Bastien had insisted they host that evening for their more aristocratic guests. Belle tried not to catastrophise the upcoming event, opting instead to attempt to see the good in it. Bastien had told her the most successful salons in Paris were always opened by a ball, and when she had asked Marguerite if that was true, she had confirmed it. Not wanting to doom her salon before it even started, Belle had decided to go along with the plan. If all went as she thought it would, the salon would be a turning point for their kingdom. Perhaps, she thought, it could be that for her and Lio as well.

But only honesty could pave the way forward for them.

Maybe it was time to be honest with Lio about everything she had done and seen in his absence. Maybe she was ready to tell him about the woman in Paris and the mirror, about LeFou reemerging and calling for revolution as close as Plesance. Maybe she was ready to ease the burden from her shoulders so they could share it, as they had shared everything else. It wasn't right to assume he couldn't handle it. Lio had handled much worse, and together they had defeated the curse once before.

She left the library with purpose. It was time to tell Lio everything.

The halls were so empty and still that Belle stopped in her tracks when she heard a muffled conversation beyond a door to her left as loudly as if they were shouting. She tried to continue on, but as always, her curiosity got the better of her.

She pressed her ear to the door and strained to listen to the voices behind it.

"—sure we have a way out?" It was a man's voice, rough

and low.

"Once the deed is done, our path is clear," another man replied, his voice slightly higher, and his accent hard to place.

"How can he guarantee that?"

"You don't trust him?"

"Of course I trust him; I just can't imagine we'll have a clear path out of the castle once we've killed the bloody king."

Belle's heart stopped as a certainty almost drowned her: the men behind the door were talking about assassinating Lio. She didn't know what to do – should she continue to listen to get proof? Or should she run and find someone to tell? Indecision rooted her in place.

"If he says we'll have a way out, we've got no choice but to trust him."

"You're right, but I don't have to like it."

Damn waiting for proof, she thought. It was time to find help. But she spun away from the door straight into the arms of someone much larger than her. A face loomed over her.

"Going somewhere?" The man was wearing the uniform of the castle guard, but Belle had never seen him before in her life.

She opened her mouth to scream, but his hand clamped over it roughly. He carried her through the door while she fought as viciously as she could, biting his palm and gripping onto anything within reach for purchase, but it was no use. He was a great deal stronger than her.

"Caught her eavesdropping," he grunted to the men she had been listening to. The room was dark, but she could just make them out enough to see she didn't recognise them. They wore the same uniform as the man who had found her. He slammed her down into a chair, and one of the others stepped up and pressed a dagger to her throat, effectively silencing her.

"Merde," one of them muttered. "What do we do with her?"

"Who are you?" the thinnest of the three men demanded.

"I'm a maid," she whispered as the dagger pressed harder into her skin. She felt hot blood drip down her neck, but she was too afraid to register the pain of it. She knew she wasn't dressed like a maid, but she had to hope they wouldn't notice that.

"We should just kill her and get it over with."

"No," she pleaded. "Just let me go. I didn't hear anything. I need to get to the kitchens; they'll be missing me soon."

A noise at the door indicated someone else had arrived, but Belle couldn't see, and the knife at her throat prevented her from turning her head.

"Cover her mouth and eyes," said the new arrival. "That's the queen of Aveyon."

The pressure at her throat lessened. "No one said anything about a queen," complained the man who had held the knife. His sour breath was as rotten as his teeth.

"Do it," the voice commanded. "Take her below. He will

deal with her later."

Belle burned to know who was speaking. She wondered if she would recognise him, if he was a traitor from within the ranks of the castle guards.

One of them produced a length of cloth and tied it around her mouth, gagging her. She screamed against the fabric, but it was no use. A sack was pulled over her head, and the world went dark. She fought violently as a disturbing thought came to her. Could the 'he' her captors referred to be...? But no. Just because someone was untrustworthy, duplicitous and arrogant to a fault didn't mean they were capable of murder.

Still, could it be? The thought wouldn't leave Belle's mind. It pounded through her like a drumbeat.

Was it Bastien?

What if the duc had managed to trick them all, finding a way into Lio's confidence and castle both? Her logical mind rebelled against the theory. Belle had never seen Bastien be anything but supportive to her husband. It didn't make sense that he would want to kill his own blood.

But what if his support had been deceptive? What if his espionage for King Louis had been more impactful than any of them knew? Belle thought back to his trove of pamphlets, his presence at the Hôtel de Ville the day they cut off the marquis de Launay's head, his comments of support for the sans-culottes and the way he would admonish her when she criticised them. She thought of his insistence that they secede from France, how he urged Lio to think only of his noblemen when it was his commoners who needed him most, and how he had undermined Belle's efforts at every turn.

Except for when she brought forth the idea of hosting a salon, an event that would bring hundreds of strangers into the castle, making something as complicated and fraught as an assassination perhaps easier to execute.

Belle's heart stopped.

What if the duc de Vincennes had not been working to help bring the kingdom of Aveyon together? What if his intention all along had been to tear it apart?

CHAPTER TWENTY-FIVE

The men moved her from the room quickly. She tried to keep track of the turns they took through the castle, but with her head covered and her mind racing, she wasn't able to for long.

They descended a narrow staircase – Belle hit the rough stone walls a few times – and came to the bottom. The passageways beneath the castle were labyrinthine halls of cold storage and unfinished tunnels that Belle hadn't got around to exploring yet. They had been boarded up during the time of the curse, but now Belle regretted giving the order to open them back up again. If they had been used in the plot against Lio, she wasn't sure she'd be able to forgive herself. The men sat her down in a rickety chair and tied her hands behind her back, securing the rope to the chair itself, pulling tight. There would be no escaping the bonds that held her. She was a captive in the castle once more. She could have laughed were it not for the very real panic that gripped her.

They left her there without saying a word, but the way their bootfalls echoed on the walls, she could tell she was in a confined space, however much use that information would be to her.

Belle heard them close and lock the door, and felt raw terror set into her bones. She was helpless. She had no idea where she was and no way of warning anyone that an attempt would be made on Lio's life. She rocked back and forth on the chair, but the bonds were tightly secured. She didn't want to fall over and hurt herself, especially since she didn't know her immediate surroundings. If she hit her head and lost consciousness, she wouldn't be able to warn anyone about what was coming.

Stay calm.

Her thoughts drifted to Bastien. She was all but certain of his guilt now that she had put the pieces of the puzzle together. He had urged them to secede from France, had urged Lio to focus only on Aveyon's nobility in the wake of the secession, had lied to Belle about the petitioners to prevent her from making positive changes and had tried to banish Marguerite from the castle when she caught wind of his falsehoods. Everything about the duc de Vincennes was artifice: his intemperance, his overindulgence, his fatuous friends, the ridiculous clothing, the face painted bone white, the drinking – all of it was meant to deceive the beholder, to paint a picture of a spoiled, indolent nobleman. Belle could see right through it now, but it was too late.

Her mind was a mess. Sweat dripped down her forehead

and into her eyes. She wondered if she was going to die in that room. Would anyone notice her absence and go looking for her? Or would everyone be too busy with their own tasks to worry about where she was?

Stay calm, Belle.

The voice in her mind was not her own.

"Who's there?" The words were muffled through the gag pulled tight. Tears fell from her eyes and the heat of her own breath under the fabric threatened to choke her.

When Belle next heard the voice it was from a place outside her mind, almost like the voice was there in the room with her. "My name is Orella."

Something in the way the voice sounded raised the hairs on the back of Belle's neck. There was a familiarity to it, and a strangeness she couldn't quite place, like the voice belonged to someone who was both as close as family and as distant as a stranger. But panic still gripped her by the throat. *Get me out of here,* Belle thought, feeling foolish.

But Orella seemed to hear the plea. "I cannot help you in that way. I am… restricted in what I can do."

And all at once, awareness came crashing down upon Belle. The voice was that of the woman from the shop, the one she had seen in the mirror and then dreamed of. The woman had been Belle's phantom since that fateful day in Paris, and though Belle had spent the months since trying to forget the woman, it felt almost natural to find her there in a moment of great need.

Belle was far too desperate to be fearful of the woman. *Who are you?*

Was she really there, like she had been in the mirror shop? Or was this more like when she appeared to her in a dream? The chafing bonds tied around Belle's wrists and the gag in her mouth tethered her to reality. This was not a dream. It was a nightmare she could not wake herself from.

"I think I owe you an explanation, but perhaps it would be easier to show you. May I?" Belle didn't know what she meant, but finding out the truth of the mirror and of Orella was too tempting a thing. She nodded. "Don't be afraid," said Orella.

The room spun, lurching Belle's consciousness into something like a dream. She was unbound and free to move as she pleased in the endless space of white she had found herself in before. She looked up and saw the woman, Orella, standing before her, as striking as the first time Belle saw her.

"Long ago and far away, there was a princess…" she began, and suddenly they were pulled to a room of roughly hewn stone walls hung with thickly woven tapestries. The heady scent of burning cedar filled the air. Seated on a chair covered with animal pelts was a young girl with sun-yellow hair and a thick gold band around her forehead. She didn't note their intrusion, and so Belle understood it to be a vision into the past. "She was the daughter of a powerful king and a woman with a magical lineage that had long been dormant. But she bore a dark secret: the magic that had slept in her mother's blood was awake in hers, and if anyone knew she possessed power, she would be banished from her home. The princess suppressed her magic and hid the truth from everyone, fearing what would happen if it were discovered."

The vision shifted to the girl hidden under the blankets of her bed, wielding an unnatural light between her fingers. "She lost her parents to a tragic accident and became queen long before she thought she would. Her uncle pushed her to host a tourney for her hand in marriage, insisting that the only way to keep her kingdom safe was to marry the man who would emerge victorious from the contest. The young queen objected to the idea that she was a prize for a conqueror, or that she was unable to protect her people on her own, but she said nothing to oppose him, fearing she knew too little of the world to refuse him."

The vision shifted again to a wedding. The girl was slightly older now, standing before a man with dark hair cropped close to his skull and an angry scar cut across his cheek. "Her husband came from a land locked in perpetual war. He saw enemies in the faces of everyone he met, and filled her mind with dire warnings and darkness until she saw them too. When he began a crusade against the queen's former allies, she trusted he did not do so idly. And when her advisers begged her to stop him, she refused."

The vision transformed to an army marching on the

queen's home. "It wasn't until her husband died in battle that she realised his enemies had been phantoms, but it was too late. Her former allies marched on her kingdom, united in their hatred, and out of desperation, the queen called upon her nigh-forgotten magic to protect her people."

The vision changed to the queen twisting her fingers to conjure great boulders from beneath the earth, building an impenetrable wall around her kingdom. "Her magic held off the attackers, but in doing so, the queen had revealed herself to be a witch, and in her kingdom, there was no crime greater than witchcraft. So the very people she protected with her magic turned on her for having any at all."

The vision turned to the queen strapped to a pyre. Burning arrows rained down on the bundles of twigs and dried grass at her feet. Belle could feel the heat of the fire as though she were standing before the flames. "As her body burned, a conviction crystallised in her mind: she had made grievous errors that had led her to this place of darkness. The biggest of all that she did not listen to her own instincts, choosing instead to let other voices crowd her mind. If she had one wish, it was that no one else would ever make the same mistakes. The magic in her blood listened, and while her body burned to nothing, her soul transformed into something else."

Belle slammed back into her bound body, her eyes covered once more. She felt the pain of the cut on her neck from her captor's blade, and the trickle of blood that continued to leak from it. Even though she couldn't see the room, it spun without end. She felt sick.

"In a way, I am that queen." Orella was still with her, and there was a strange relief in that. "When she died, her last wish was to ensure her mistakes weren't repeated by future rulers, and her magic lived on for this purpose."

So what does that make you?

"I carry within me the wisdom of every queen and female ruler I've aided, and for that reason some have called me the Queen's Council, but in truth I have no one true form. I appear in the one most suited to those who have need of me. In part, I am an echo of the first queen's power, but I am also those who came after her. I am their weaknesses and their strengths, their fears and their beliefs, their mistakes and their triumphs."

You must help me. You must tell me what to do to be free of this place.

Silence seemed to stretch for an age. "I have done what I can for Aveyon, even when it hurt the people you love."

Belle struggled to understand what Orella meant. In the shop, in the mirror and in her dreams, none of what she said had been definitive or led Belle down a specific path. She had urged Belle to listen to her gut, to make decisions, to accept the role she had rejected. But what did she mean about hurting the people Belle loved?

And then it hit her with all the force of a lightning strike.

You were the enchantress.

Orella said nothing, leaving Belle room to figure it out for herself.

You cursed Lio and this kingdom. You let them suffer for ten long years, and for what?

"For you, Belle."

I didn't ask for this. Tears streamed down her face, and she pulled against the rope around her wrists, cutting them deeper.

"Part of my magic is foresight. I was burdened with the knowledge of what was coming for France and then Aveyon. But my powers are limited. I could not step in without someone in need of aid. I saw visions of your future, and I knew you had the power to save the kingdom, and in doing so you could bring an end to the violence. So I did what I thought I had to do. I made Lio become a man worthy of your love. I put you in his path, but, Belle, I swear I did nothing else. From the time you set foot in the castle, your decisions were your own."

Belle asked the question that had the power to change everything, and she feared the answer.

Does Lio know?

Her love for Lio was based on everything that had happened between them in the cursed castle, but that love would burn to ash the moment she found out he knew about Orella, or that he had been a part of the deception.

"He never knew. I appeared to him in a different form, letting him believe I was an enchantress."

Belle wrestled with her thoughts. *He needed love, not a curse.*

"I did what was necessary, and I have lived with my decision for ten years." She sounded hurt, and Belle hoped she was. To curse a child in order to transform him into something else, something *worthy*, was not something Belle would ever understand.

"I know it was wrong, but I've been haunted by visions of Europe burning for a long time now. Thousands dead, generations wiped out, a reign of terror. The only time my vision changed was when I cursed him and saw you with a crown on your head."

I don't want a crown. I never wanted one.

"I know, but perhaps that means you are better equipped than most to handle one." She didn't elaborate, and Belle feared Orella had seen more of a future Belle didn't want. She resisted the urge to ask her about what lay ahead; she didn't want to know. "I wish I could do more, but my powers are limited. Your future is in flux, tied with the future of Aveyon. I cannot see anything clearly. All I know for certain is that you will once again have to see past darkness and find the light hidden within."

I don't know what that means. You have to tell me more.

"You cannot see it, but I am fading. My powers ebb and flow, like the tide. I cannot take this form for long. All that I can leave you with is that you must trust your instincts."

You've said that before.

"I am sorry, Belle. But you must know that you still have the power to save the ones you love. I'll do what I can for you, in my own way."

Her last question felt hopeless. *Did we ever defeat the curse?*

But there was no answer.

Belle could sense the moment Orella left her, and in her absence, the silence of the room was deafening.

CHAPTER TWENTY-SIX

Hours trickled by before a new set of footsteps entered the room, and Belle braced herself. Her heartbeat rocked through her whole body, and her skin burned with anticipation. She thought it must be Bastien, come to silence her once and for all. A hand gripped the fabric over her head and tore it off. The dim room seemed as bright as the sun, and Belle couldn't see for a few moments as she breathed in fresher air through her nose.

When her eyes at last focused, she was looking at LeFou.

"Surprised?" he asked, waving a pistol at her. She made a noise against the gag at her mouth. "This is hardly necessary," he muttered, pulling it from between her teeth. As soon as she was free of it, Belle began screaming for help. She didn't recognise the room they were in, and fear formed a knot in her throat. "No one can hear you, Belle. Don't you know where you are?"

She chose to believe him, despite how much she desperately wanted him to be lying. "No," she rasped. The room was small and windowless. The chair she sat upon was one of a scant few pieces of furniture. It smelled musty and the air was damp, like they were underground.

"We're in the farthest reaches of your castle's cellars. Why would anyone hear you?" He laughed cruelly when she said nothing. "I want you to know we've been working against you since before you left Paris."

"Who is we?"

"Myself and my associates." He paused, but when she didn't seem to understand his meaning, he continued. "I was recruited to the cause by the duc de Vincennes, who sensed an ally in me."

So Bastien had betrayed them from the start. Fear gave over to anger. "You never struck me as a political man, LeFou."

He aimed the pistol at her. "My name is Hercule, but you didn't know that, did you?" He stepped closer to her. "And you're right. I don't give a damn about the brewing revolution. I am in this for revenge."

The words chilled her to the bone. LeFou was supposed to have forgotten everything when the curse lifted, just like everyone else who had stormed the castle that night. If he hadn't, Lio and Belle were in trouble. "Revenge for what?"

"Don't insult me, Belle. You know exactly what I'm talking about."

"I don't," she pleaded, trying to play dumb.

"Don't tell me you've forgotten, too? Do you not know who you're married to?" There was a manic glint in his eye at the thought that he would be the one to reveal everything to Belle. "Do you not remember *the Beast*?"

So he did remember when he should have forgotten. Somehow, LeFou had clung to his memories, unwilling to release them even in the face of the curse crumbling all around them. She didn't know what it meant, or why he had been able to defy it. Belle couldn't keep up the ruse.

"Of course I remember, LeFou. I remember everything. I remember you standing by while Gaston treated me like I was a prize to be won, trying to force me into an engagement I never asked for and acting like I had wronged him when I refused." The thought of him barging through the home she shared with her father still made her hot with anger. Gaston thought she should be grateful for his attentions, but he only ever made her feel small and insignificant. "I remember you trying to have my father committed to an asylum when he sought help from his neighbours. He thought he had lost me forever, and all you could do was laugh at him." The vision of her father wandering through the woods, lost and screaming for help, still filled her heart with sadness. The Beast let her go to him even though he thought it meant living with the curse forever. That sacrifice had changed everything for Belle. And what came next had only solidified the feelings in her heart. "I remember you storming the castle." When she closed her eyes, she could still recall the villagers of Plesance locking her and her father away and taking up arms against something they didn't understand. She remembered the helplessness that threatened to take her over, and the rush of defiance that set her free. She remembered racing back to the castle that had been her prison. "And what was it all for, LeFou? What did the Beast ever do to you?"

He stepped away from her. "Why should a monster be allowed to live in a castle?"

"He was never a monster, but Gaston was, and you are."

He shook his head, unwilling to accept any responsibility. "He took everything from me, and now you're going to suffer like I did." The gun looked heavy in his hand.

Belle was frantic. "What does that mean? What are you going to do?" LeFou had mentioned associates, so even though he was down there with her, others could be executing the larger plan to kill Lio.

But he wasn't listening to her. "No one believed me when I told them what happened here that day. People called me crazy." A dry laugh escaped his throat. "I'm used to people laughing at me, dismissing me, but this time I knew what had happened. I had the body to prove it."

And then Belle remembered. "You mean Gaston." It wasn't a question, but the pain that crossed over his face at the mention of that name was confirmation enough. "He tried to kill Lio," she said, her mind travelling to that moment when she and the Beast chose to fight back once she had returned. She rode Philippe through the ruined castle, pushing him all the way up the West Tower as fast and she could. "I watched the Beast let him go, even after Gaston had shot him with an arrow, but he came back and stabbed Lio from behind like a coward." She recalled watching the light leave his eyes, and the sudden realisation that she had been lying to herself for weeks. She remembered loving him and mourning him in equal measure, her heart so full and so broken all at once. "Gaston fell to his death; Lio had nothing to do with it."

But LeFou still wasn't listening. His back was to her when he spoke. "I watched the castle transform as if by magic, back to its former glory. I waited for Gaston to emerge from within, but he never did. Hundreds of people did, their minds wiped clean, but I remembered everything." He turned to face her. "I had seen him up on the tower with the Beast, but by the time I got up there, he was gone. I walked all the way down to the bottom of the gorge to find his body. I had to see it for myself." He took a shuddering breath. "And there he was, broken but still beautiful." LeFou looked at her, his eyes emptied of everything but pain. "I lost everything that day, and now you're going to lose everything, too."

All at once, Orella's incomplete vision made sense. LeFou was living in darkness, and it was up to Belle to pull him back into the light. She had done it before, when she saw past Lio's monstrous form to the man he was inside. But Belle had fallen in love with Lio. She wasn't about to do the same with LeFou. How would she pull him back? And did she even want to?

"I didn't know you felt that way for him," she said. It was weak, but she didn't know what else to say.

He shook his head. "I pushed those feelings down for so long, I didn't know either. It all came rushing back to the surface when he died. I was always too late – too late to tell him the truth, too late to save him." He laughed darkly, passing his gun from one hand to the other. "But what could I have done? If he had known how I felt, he would have hated me for it, and if I had made it to the top of the tower, I would have died, too. I should have stopped him in the village, before he even thought of marching on the castle. It's my fault he's dead."

"Hate put Gaston up in that tower, not you."

He sat on a desk across from her chair. "The war in America changed him. You didn't know the Gaston from before; you only knew the one who came back."

"Gaston was a complicated man." It was the best she could offer LeFou. "I am sorry that your friendship wasn't enough for him."

He looked up at her, and his eyes darkened. "Maybe it could have been, but now I'll never know."

She was relieved that he seemed at least willing to talk to her. Perhaps his heart wasn't taken over completely by hate if he was still willing to listen.

"You spent years by his side, but did he ever call you by your real name?"

Pain creased his features. "No," he admitted. "The worst of it is that Gaston was the one who first christened me with my nickname when we were boys."

"Why did he do that?" Belle prodded.

"We grew up beside each other and became friends, maybe out of necessity, but we both had vast imaginations and played games for years until he became more interested in swordplay and fighting with the other boys in the village. But I couldn't let go of my fantasies and I think I embarrassed him. When he dismissed me to his new companions as 'LeFou', it hurt, but I decided to be whatever he wanted me to be rather than losing him." He tugged at his collar. "I played the fool for years, until it was all I remembered being."

"That doesn't sound like friendship, Hercule."

He appeared stricken. "Gaston cared about me in his own way. Perhaps to you it seems like he was cruel, but I was happy to simply remain in his orbit." He looked to the ground. "I know he wasn't a good man, Belle. I know all of the dark things about him, but you can't help who you love."

Belle sighed. "I would know that better than most."

He glanced up at her and gave her a small smile, placing his gun on the desk. "I suppose you would."

She decided to take hold of the part of him that was reaching out to her. "You don't need to make the rest of your life a shrine to his, Hercule. You can have loved him, and you can move on from it. He died under tragic circumstances, but they were of his own making." Tears welled in his eyes, and Belle sensed she was getting through to him. "The greatest tragedy was that Gaston died not knowing how much you cared for him, regardless of whether or not he returned those affections."

LeFou hesitated. "I don't know who I am without him."

"Wouldn't it be nice to rediscover yourself? To cease being 'LeFou' and become Hercule once more?"

His eyes lit up at the thought but then went black once more. "I've done terrible things —"

"I know. But causing someone else's pain will never heal your own, Hercule. Killing Lio won't bring Gaston back."

What followed was silence. Hercule stood and paced in front of her, wrestling with her words and his feelings both. She didn't know what to do but decided to let him contend with everything on his own. She had done what she could, and short of begging him to let her go, there wasn't anything left to try.

The look he gave her was one of sorrow. "I wish I could take back everything I've done."

"You can, Hercule. You know who is behind this plot against Lio. You can stop it before the worst happens." She tried to steady her voice. "You can prove that Bastien means to kill the king of Aveyon. You can set me free so I can at least *try* to stop it."

"But, Belle, I cannot. I am LeFou. No one would believe

me, not when I accuse a *duc* without any proof. He is far too clever for that sort of ruse." He swallowed thickly. "If you escape, or if I set you free, Bastien's men have orders to kill the king on sight, damn the consequences. He wants the assassination to go cleanly, but he isn't above achieving his goal the hard way."

Her heart raced at the thought. "Can you get Lio? Or at least get a message to him? Surely he's worried about me."

"He doesn't know to be worried. Bastien had him ushered away to the garrison at Faverges to discuss the latest news from Paris with his commandants. He believes you are making last-minute arrangements with your assistant and unable to attend. He doesn't even know you're missing. I was left in charge of your keeping until the deed is done."

"So what do you suggest? That I do nothing?" she snapped, fighting against the bonds that held her. Hercule stepped back from her, frightened by her sudden anger when she had tried so hard to be calm. She had done what Orella told her she must do; she had reached to the deepest part of Hercule and forced him to shed the anger that ruled him. But for what? What use would he be if he was too afraid to help her? And how was she going to find someone willing to stand up to the duc de Vincennes when she was tied up in a forgotten cellar?

"Belle, I am so sorry," he began before Belle interrupted.

"You said you had associates," she said, thinking back to the men who had captured her. "Do you know who they are?"

"We don't use names. They're mostly sans-culottes with the occasional bourgeois as far as I can tell." He paused, thoughtful. "Though there is a new arrival who speaks as finely as Bastien. I don't think the duc found him among the rabble."

"Describe him to me."

Hercule hesitated. "He's tall, has dark skin."

"And when did he arrive?" she asked, but she knew the answer.

"Yesterday morning." He looked at her curiously. "Why, do you know him?"

"I think I do," she replied, a plan forming in her mind. "Hercule, I need you to do something for me."

He hesitated. "What?"

"I need you to bring me my mirror."

• • •

Hercule left her tied up in the dank cellar in case another one of Belle's captors came to check on her. It wasn't worth the risk that one of them might see her unbound and decide to take drastic action to fulfil the plan.

Hercule was gone for what seemed like an eternity, and it took everything in Belle not to lose her composure completely. When he returned, he deposited the mirror into her lap and got to work freeing her.

"What is a mirror going to do?" he asked sceptically over

her shoulder.

"Don't you remember?" she replied. "I used this mirror to show the village that my father wasn't lying about the Beast." She didn't need to remind him of what came after – an angry mob storming the castle to kill the man she loved, led by the man he did.

Her wrists fell against the sides of the chain, free at last. He came to stand before her, looking sheepish. "So it's magic?"

"Yes."

His eyes lit up. "You can use it to prove Bastien wishes to kill the king!"

"No, I cannot. Revealing the existence of magic to the kingdom would do more harm than good. How could I explain it without having to explain the curse?" She shook her head. "We can't rely on magic, and we can't risk playing our hand without proof to back us up. Lio would believe me, of course, but how can we guarantee that Bastien's men won't shoot him before any of us got a word in edgewise? I would imagine that since they're dressed in guard uniforms, they're tailing him everywhere he goes. If we can't get to him, we need to find another way."

Hercule looked at her appraisingly. "You've thought of every angle."

"Let's hope I'm not drastically off the mark on this one." She held the mirror aloft, letting the soothing warmth of magic spread to her hands and up her arms. The acid-green tendrils glowed all the brighter in the cellar. Hercule held his breath as she made her command. "Show me Aurelian de Lambriquet."

The mirror flared to life, transforming to a vision of a room Belle recognised as Bastien's. Aurelian stood at the desk, rifling through piles of parchment, looking desperately for something. His hair was messed up, his guard's jacket discarded. He looked wild and afraid.

"That's the new arrival," whispered Hercule.

"He doesn't look like someone on Bastien's side, now does he?" The vision faded, having served its purpose. Belle lowered the mirror and turned to Hercule. "We must go to him."

"Is that a good idea?"

She looked at him and sighed. "It's the only one I've got. But we're going to need your gun."

● ● ●

They moved through the castle like ghosts, fearful of detection, but the halls were mostly empty. At first Belle didn't understand it, but then she remembered Orella's fading promise.

I'll do what I can for you, in my own way.

She guessed that their clear path came down to her, and she was grateful, though Belle was aware that with each passing minute, her window to stop an assassination grew smaller. If someone went down to the cellar and found her missing, she could lose her chance entirely. It was not a comforting thought.

They arrived at Bastien's door and tried the handle. It was locked. Belle gave Hercule a look, and he heaved against it with all his weight, bursting through.

Aurelian was too shocked to move, save for raising his hands defensively. "Sacré," he swore, though he relaxed a bit when he saw they were not Bastien come to discover him searching through his things. "What are you doing here?" Belle recognised the voice as the captor who insisted her eyes be covered.

Belle trained her pistol on him, well aware of the fact that she had no idea how to operate a gun. But the marquis de Lambriquet didn't know that. "What do you know of Bastien's plan to kill my husband?"

He lifted his arms again. "Vague details, but enough to know I had to try to stop him."

Belle stepped closer. "Why should I believe you?"

Aurelian looked down at the desk he had all but destroyed. "I'm not doing this to *help* Bastien. I'm looking for proof of his plans. Proof I can bring to someone who can stop him."

She raised a brow. "Why did you take part in my capture?"

He bowed his head, shame colouring his cheeks. "I didn't know what else to do. Bastien is a loose cannon. I worried if I deviated in any way he would act. I am sorry for that."

Belle read the guilt in him, but she had one more question.

"Where is your sister?"

He grimaced. "Similarly locked up in the chambers I was provided. I knew she'd get herself killed if I told her what I was up to."

Belle sighed and lowered the gun. "She'll probably murder you for that," she told him. She looked at Hercule. "Do you know where his chambers are?" He nodded. "Go get her. We need her."

As soon as he left the room, Aurelian moved back to rifling through the papers on the desk, and Belle joined him. "So you came to Aveyon to make amends with Marguerite?"

He held a parchment close to his eyes to read the small script. "That was my intention. But when Bastien revealed a bit of his plot, I knew I would have to pretend I wished to aid him in his goals in order to know more." He looked up at Belle. "I hope you've got a plan, because as soon as someone realises you're gone—"

"My husband will be killed," she finished for him. "I don't need to have the stakes explained to me."

He paused. "So what's your plan?"

"We have no option but to find proof Bastien has been working against Lio from the start. And so long as he still thinks you're with him, we have one small advantage. I can't walk into the ballroom without putting Lio's life at risk, but you can."

Aurelian nodded. "So the search continues?"

"Yes, but Bastien isn't stupid enough to keep proof of his treachery somewhere obvious. We need to think like him."

He tossed the papers he was holding aside. "Then is he stupid enough to keep it at all? Who is to say he doesn't burn anything that might implicate him?"

Belle pondered that possibility but found it didn't sit right with her. She pictured his meticulous collection of pamphlets and papers back in Paris. "Bastien is calculated. He would want to keep evidence against others, should he ever need to use it. He has no loyalties to speak of, and he would most certainly use his collected information against his supposed allies if he thought it would save his neck." She moved to the desk and started feeling for a secret latch. "His desk in Paris had a hidden compartment. We should try to find something like that."

The two of them had nearly torn the room apart by the time Hercule returned with Marguerite, who looked shaken but determined.

"He's told you everything?" asked Belle, and her friend nodded.

"Belle, I'm sorry I didn't see Bastien's deceit earlier. I know him; I should have suspected him, but I avoided him because of our history in Paris. Perhaps if I had been closer—"

Belle stopped her. "We've all been tricked by the duc, and the blame lies solely with him. The distance he placed between you was all a part of his plan; you couldn't have changed it if you tried." The search was proving fruitless, and Belle was beginning to panic. "I don't know what to do. Without proof, Aurelian has no standing to accuse Bastien of anything. Maybe I should take the risk and go myself."

Aurelian slammed his hands on the table in frustration. "There are guards posted at every entrance with very specific orders. If you walk in there, it'll be a bloodbath."

"There has to be another way," Marguerite interjected.

"Time isn't on our side."

"Bastien's men must have a sense of self-preservation. Surely they know that shooting the king of Aveyon can only result in their own deaths."

Hercule shook his head. "Their desire to spread the revolution eclipses every other concern. They would die for the cause."

After what she had witnessed in Paris, Belle believed him.

Aurelian moved towards the door. "I'll go and confront him, try to talk him out of it."

"And be killed yourself?" Marguerite protested, stepping in his path to stop him.

"Without proof, what choice do we have?"

Hercule looked to Belle, his eyes hopeful. "Why not use the mirror?"

"What?" asked Aurelian and Marguerite in unison.

Belle shook her head, ignoring their confusion. "The mirror has only ever shown me the person I most desire to see.

I don't think it will show me an object." But even as she said it, she knew it wasn't true. In Paris, she had asked the mirror to show her the future, and it had given her a vision of Aveyon burning. She had dismissed it for so long, unaware that Bastien would be the one fanning the flames.

Hercule continued. "You don't think, but you don't *know*. Surely it's worth trying."

He was right. A part of Orella was in the mirror, magicked to survive after the curse had been broken. She didn't know what it was capable of. Belle pulled the mirror from the pocket of her skirts and held it up. She didn't even wait for it to warm in her hands before she made her demand. "Show me how to stop Bastien."

But the mirror didn't flare to life as it had done before. It remained inert, the surface only reflecting her own face back at her. Belle was crushed.

"Did it… work?" asked Marguerite, clearly unsure of what Belle and Hercule were waiting for.

"No," Belle replied bitterly, but as she spoke, a curious feeling took hold of her, like a thread tied around her heart, pulling her somewhere she didn't know.

It was a great deal like the feeling that had propelled her to the mirror shop in Paris, only this time she knew not to fear it. Orella was aiding her, in whatever way she could. Belle understood that she needed to follow the feeling, the thread that tugged at her. It would lead her to an answer.

"I can't explain it, but I know where to go," she told them. "Hercule, can you go to the ballroom and scout how many armed men within are loyal to Bastien? I'll need to know what I'm up against." He nodded. "Aurelian, you should go to the ballroom and pretend like all is well. Try to stall Bastien if you sense he's getting impatient. The ball is surely under way by now, so the room will be chaotic. Wait for me before you do anything reckless." He nodded as well. "Marguerite—" she started.

"I'm coming with you." It wasn't a question.

Belle didn't bother arguing. "If this... feeling is correct and I'm able to find proof of Bastien's treachery, I'll bring it to the ballroom. What happens after will have to be decided in the moment." She took a deep breath, banishing the fear that threatened to drown her. She didn't have time for it. "Let's hope we can maintain the element of surprise."

The blood in Belle's veins was on fire. Everyone moved to the door, but just before they left the room, Marguerite spoke.

"Is no one going to tell me what that business with the mirror was about?"

Belle paused at the threshold. "Marguerite, I swear to you, if we survive the day, I'll tell you everything."

CHAPTER TWENTY-SEVEN

The mirror hadn't shown Belle what to do, but Orella's magic still guided her out of the castle and to the stables, which were just about the worst place to be for two people who didn't want to be spotted.

Carriages and horses had arrived in high numbers all throughout the day, ferrying in guests for the welcome ball. Belle was in a daze and didn't care who saw her. She was hell-bent on getting what she had come for. Marguerite was the more sensible of the two of them and forced Belle to move more methodically.

"This whole plan will be for naught if Bastien catches wind of it," she hissed as she pulled Belle back from walking clear across the courtyard, driven by the certainty clenched tight around her heart that she would find what she was looking for in the stables. "You have to assume the duc has eyes everywhere, waiting to report to him."

"You're right." Belle pulled her hood over her head, thankful for the chill in the air. The sun set early in Aveyon in

October. "I'll be careful."

The two of them stuck to the shadows, making their way slowly to the stables. It was full of grooms and hostlers, but most were too attentive to their tasks to pay any mind to two maids hurrying through. Belle was so attuned to the feeling that urged her forward she hardly paused until they reached the back wall. There were no other people that deep in the stables, just some empty stalls reserved for the next day's arrivals.

She stopped and studied the stones of the wall, waiting for Orella's magic to give her the answer she sought, but nothing came.

"What are we looking for?" asked Marguerite.

"I'm waiting to feel something." Mercifully, Marguerite didn't call her mad for that. Belle stepped closer, reaching a hand out to touch the worn stones. She ran her fingertips over them, seeking some sort of confirmation.

"Well, hurry," whispered Marguerite.

And then Belle's finger caught a sharp corner. The stone beneath was loose, but you wouldn't know just from looking at it. Belle's blood warmed as she pulled it from the wall and handed it to her friend, who winced at the weight. The dark gap in the wall revealed nothing, but Belle stretched her hand into it without hesitation, procuring a leather satchel from within. Satisfaction filled her as she unwrapped it, finding envelopes inside.

"What is it?"

Belle rifled through the first. "It's... information," she replied.

She pulled an envelope labelled *MONTARLY* to the top of the pile and rummaged through it. Inside was written testimony from a maid in the seigneur's household swearing that he had fathered her illegitimate children. Other envelopes were labelled with the names of Lio's other advisers and high-ranking Aveyonian officials. The satchel was full of proof that Bastien was gathering information in order to extort them. It dawned on Belle in that moment that there was likely never any truth to the report of noblemen planning a revolt. The duc knew how bad it would look to have Lio's first act as king be placating his nobles. The advisers went along with it because Bastien had compromising information on them. Their corruption ran deeper than she thought.

"What else?" prompted Marguerite. Belle dug through the rest of the contents until she found unlabelled envelopes. She pulled out a folded piece of parchment and scanned the contents.

Do plans in Aveyon remain the same? Does L still trust you?

I've sent replica guard uniforms; the tailor insists they are as near to perfect as can be.

Is B still proving difficult to manage? Get rid of her if you must.

Belle's heartbeat quickened. "The proof we need."

It was a curious thing, she thought, to read what amounted to her own death warrant and feel relief. It was proof that Bastien had been acting against them from the start. Orella's magic had given Belle what she needed to take down the duc. For the first time since leaving the dark cellar, she felt like it might be possible to stop him.

Marguerite straightened and looked back at the castle. "Then let's go put an end to this."

• • •

They decided to approach the ballroom from the balcony, hoping to catch Bastien unawares, but climbing the trellis was not an easy feat for either of them, especially not in skirts. When they reached the top, they hid themselves among the potted shrubs that lined the edge and tried to see what they could through the window.

"You trust Aurelian?" asked Belle, straining to see through branches and leaves.

"I wouldn't be here if I didn't."

"It's just…"

"I know. He came out of nowhere to help us. Seems a little too convenient. But I spoke with him for hours yesterday, Belle. He was heartsick over our parting. He couldn't have faked it, not my brother, I know him too well."

The people milling about inside were dressed impeccably. Belle wasn't sure she recognised anyone, but Marguerite had been the architect of that part of the guest list. They were not Belle's guests; these guests were chosen to add to the pedigree of the salon itself.

"Surely the scene inside would be a tad more chaotic if someone had shot the king of Aveyon," Marguerite offered.

"What a comforting thought. I shall cherish it as we work to prevent my husband's assassination."

"I'm sorry. I say stupid things when I'm nervous." She squeezed Belle's shoulder. "I'll go see if I can spot Aurelian. No use going in if he's not in there."

She left Belle in her hiding place alone with her thoughts. Now that she was still, all her fears came crashing down at once. She was one misstep away from losing Lio, and she didn't know if she'd be able to prevent it. Saving him would not come down to her knowledge or cleverness, but rather chance. If she provoked Bastien too early, if she placed her trust in the wrong people, even if she did everything right, she could still lose him. Her dark thoughts coalesced into one realisation: she would have been able to protect Lio and her kingdom better if she had accepted the title of queen. By not doing so, Belle had left room for people to question her, to doubt her devotion to Aveyon. Marguerite was wrong when she said that Belle was a queen in all but name. By not taking the title, Belle ensured that her authority would always be questioned. She had not thought herself worthy of that authority, but what she had not understood was that in her absence, someone else would swoop in to take it.

Bastien had been successful in Aveyon because of Belle's fears. But now she understood what she feared the most was letting her kingdom be overrun by people who did not care for Aveyon. And the only way to combat that particular fear would be with strength. Belle would have to be strong enough for her kingdom, and despite her fears, she felt for the first time that she was.

Marguerite poked her head back in. "He's there and keeping close to Bastien. Lio is across the room with a group of old Paris favourites. Can't wait for them to witness another entirely overdramatic display from me. They're surrounded by guards." She reached for Belle's hand and pulled her up. "But I don't think we'll have a better opportunity."

"I'm ready." It felt like the truest thing Belle could have said. She *was* ready, and she prayed Bastien was not.

They walked as confidently as they could through the glass balcony doors, emerging into a room that buzzed with chatter and lively music. Marguerite and Belle were hardly noticed, their plain gowns lost in a sea of finery. Most who eyed them likely thought they were errant servants absconding from their duties. Despite how eager Belle was to expose Bastien, she couldn't stop herself from shaking as they walked deeper into the room.

It was as lavishly decorated as Belle had ever seen it, and it was hardly a space that required much effort. Belle had seen the chandelier lit a few times by then, but the sight of hundreds of candles shining through thousands of fine crystals still took her breath away. She distantly thought that if it weren't for Bastien, the night would have been an immense success.

A group of people broke apart in the centre of the room, and Belle saw the duc de Vincennes for the first time. He didn't notice them. Aurelian had done a good job of keeping Bastien calm and unaware of the fact that his plot against the king was going amiss. She studied Bastien at a distance, noting the return to his powdered bone-white skin, the manicured wig, fingers dripping with jewels and the finely tailored clothing, all of it a part of his mask.

Marguerite nudged her. "I've counted about forty guardsmen, and surely at least some of those are actual guardsmen and not infiltrators."

Belle looked up to the top of the grand twin staircases and spotted Hercule, but only because she was looking for him. She didn't think anyone else would have noticed him there. He held up his fists and opened them twice. She nodded, and he moved back down the stairs, hopefully to tail the men he had just informed on.

"At least twenty are loyal to Bastien."

"It's a risk," Marguerite conceded. "Sacré, can't we just pull Lio away from this? Worry about the consequences later?"

"We don't know how many men loyal to Bastien remain

in the rest of the castle, or how far those we are aware of will go to achieve their goals. I won't put everyone in this room at risk." Belle stood straighter. "The only way to stop Bastien is to take away every inch of his control. I'm going to walk right up to him as if nothing is amiss. Go find your brother, and keep Lio away from the fray. He's going to be very confused."

She walked away from Marguerite before her friend could stop her, each step ratcheting up her heartbeat until she felt certain it would burst out of her chest. Just the sight of Bastien filled her with rage, but rage wouldn't help her now. He seemed to sense something was coming for him, and when he turned and saw it was Belle, the look on his face almost made everything worth it.

The duc de Vincennes was very rarely surprised. He thought Belle was tied up in a forgotten cellar, hidden away until he could achieve what he had come to Aveyon to do. For once, Belle had been the one to trick him.

Still, he managed to recover quickly.

"Belle, what an *interesting* outfit choice for a ball." He reached for the easy teasing that existed between them, as if he could force her into submission by charm alone. She was tired of him thinking he was in charge.

Belle couldn't speak lest she ignite the nerves that threatened to burn right through her skin. So many things could go wrong, and she had put her friends in danger to boot. She couldn't give in to the anger that coursed through her. She had to be smarter than that.

He gave her an evaluating look, still underestimating her. "Come, dance with me." He pulled her tightly by the wrist to an open space. No one else was dancing – it was early yet – but Belle let him, if only to lull him into a sense of control.

He raised her hand in his high in the air. "Surely you know how to dance a minuet?"

She curtsied diminutively, holding her skirt out. "Of course."

They began the courtly dance that Lumière had endeavoured to teach her before her wedding. Belle was rusty; the duc, graceful, having spent most of his life dancing in the French court.

The steps kept them apart for a time, and Belle knew that Bastien was calculating with every move. When they stepped close together once more, he whispered in her ear, "What has Aurelian told you? You know he's as unstable as his sister."

She gave him a playful look. "Oh, Bastien, I would hardly think myself a good judge of someone's apparent instability."

She spun away from him before he could reply. By now, a crowd had formed. A few couples had joined nearby, but mostly, Belle's guests seemed content to watch the situation play out, not understanding what was actually at stake. It was not a mark in her favour that Bastien looked as polished as ever while she wore an absurdly plain gown to a ball, her hair a mess, an unwashed cut on her neck, and rope burns on her wrists. She knew Lio hadn't seen her yet. He would have wanted to know what was wrong right away. The fact that Bastien didn't even mention her wounds spoke to his desperation.

They danced close again. She let Bastien dig the hole deeper. "You cannot believe a thing he told you. Did you know he's a revolutionary? He lived most recently in Philippe Égalité's palais in Paris, plotting the spread of the bloody movement. It's why he came here. I never should have let him pass through the castle gates."

Belle gave him a curious look. "But who passes through the castle gates is not within your purview, Bastien."

He blushed for the first time that she could recall. It took her a moment to understand that it wasn't shame that reddened his cheeks but rather anger. He seemed to understand that Belle was not going to fall for his trickery any longer. He was a wounded animal caught in a trap, reaching desperately for something to hold on to. He glanced at her bloodied neck and gasped in mock surprise. "Belle, what happened? You're hurt." He spoke loudly, hoping others would hear him.

She stopped their dance and had to silently commend him for his acting skills. Bastien had not captured Belle and taken her to the cellar, he had not tied her wrists or gagged her, and truth be told, she never once saw him throughout the whole ordeal. Bastien kept his hands clean, if not his conscience. Had

Orella's magic not led her to proof of the duc's treason, Belle would have nothing to back up her accusation.

Some of the crowd gasped belatedly, noticing Belle's injuries. Bastien snapped his fingers, calling some guards to him. "Please escort madame to her chambers, she is not well."

Belle knew she had this one chance to ensure Bastien did not leave the ballroom without fetters locked onto his wrists. He was too charismatic, too slippery for her to manage outside of that moment.

She forced her voice to be clear. "Bastien, allow me to formally accuse you of a plot against the king of Aveyon."

The crowd could hardly contain itself. Belle was rooted in place as chaos erupted around her. She caught Seigneur Montarly's eye and watched the man clutch at his chest. She thought unkindly that she wouldn't miss him if the shock of it killed him.

She watched a smug smile develop on the duc's face. He thought all she had was her accusation. She'd allow him to think that a bit longer. "I have no earthly idea what you're talking about, madame, but to accuse me of plotting against my cousin, *my blood*, goes beyond the pale."

Aurelian stepped forward, Lio and Marguerite at his heels.

"I second the accusation," Aurelian said. "The duc de Vincennes is in Aveyon on a mission to spread the revolution past the borders of France, starting with the murder of the king."

Bastien threw his arms up in the air. "And without proof, all you have is malicious slander." He looked to Lio now, letting vulnerability play out in the line of his brow. "Cousin, you must not believe this. I would never do anything to harm you. We've been through so much together all our lives." Belle watched as he let his lip quiver. She could have spat on the ground before him. "You hardly know your wife – how could you say for certain that *she* isn't the phantom revolutionary you seek? Is it not possible that they accuse me of their own crimes?"

Lio was perplexed, but Bastien was at a disadvantage. He did not know what Belle and Lio had been through together. He did not know how destroying a curse with the power of their love had forged a bond between them that went far deeper than blood.

It was time for Belle to use her trump card. She pulled the leather satchel from her skirts and held it so that the duc de Vincennes could see that she had him.

The transformation of his expression was swift. Gone was any false vulnerability, any lingering smugness or superiority. All that was left was raw anger. It was not an expression Belle recognised on him, but she had enough sense to fear it. Bastien had lost, and watching him come to understand his position was not the triumph she thought it would be. There was no victory in tearing apart the only family Lio had left, in marking Bastien as the villain she had long suspected him to

355

be. But Belle had done what she had to do in order to save her husband and her kingdom.

Time slowed to a trickle as she watched Bastien pull a pistol from within his overcoat. Hercule's words echoed in her mind.

They would die for the cause.

Bastien aimed it at Lio, whose false guards had fled his side. People fell to the floor. Belle could hardly move, could hardly see. Her blood pumped through her body with the force of a hurricane. Bastien's mouth was moving, but she heard nothing over the roar in her ears.

He pulled the trigger. She watched the spark ignite.

But Hercule came out of nowhere to push Bastien's arm skyward, where the bullet shattered the chandelier into a thousand pieces, raining shards of crystal down upon them, some sharp enough to cut skin.

And then the sound of the room returned at full volume. Screams pushed against Belle as she watched Aurelian lead the few men loyal to Lio in tackling the duc de Vincennes to the floor.

"Belle, are you all right?" Lio was at her ear, but her attention was fixed on Bastien as he struggled against the men who held him down. "Belle?" Lio held her before him. "Belle, talk to me."

She looked to her husband, who was mercifully unharmed and entirely confused. "Sacré, Lio. I didn't let myself think of how I'd explain everything to you if we somehow managed to succeed." Her mind swirled under the weight of everything she had to tell him.

He looked up to where the chandelier had been, then back at his cousin. "I think I comprehend at least some of it. But what happened to you? Was that LeFou who saved me from an untimely death?"

Bastien interrupted them with the last cries of a condemned man.

"Vive la révolution! Death to the king! Death to the monarchy! We must rise up!"

But the ballroom was not the atelier d'ébénisterie at the end of a long day of work. It was not the tavern in Mauger with ale-loosened tongues. Bastien was in the castle, and he had tried to kill the king. His message meant nothing in that moment, but Belle knew it was not the end.

She looked to one of Lio's men. "Rouse the magistrates in Mauger. We cannot trust that the ones in the castle haven't sworn false oaths." The man nodded and left. Lio gave her a concerned look. "I'll explain later," she told him.

Cogsworth and Lumière appeared beside them. The majordomo was beetroot red and out of breath, as if he had run the entire length of the castle. "Sire, madame, we must remove you both from this place. It isn't safe for you here."

Lio began to protest, but Lumière interjected. "Sire, a gun is not the only thing that can kill a king." He turned to the frantic crowd and put on his most charming voice. "Mesdames et messieurs, let me assure you that the situation is under control. We would ask that you remain here, safe in this room, free to imbibe and enjoy everything our kitchens have to offer, while we search the castle. Thank you." He bowed congenially at them, and somehow, a sense of calm spread through the room. He looked to the still-red Cogsworth and grinned. "See, mon ami? It is me who should be called upon to work a crowd."

Cogsworth rolled his eyes so hard, Belle worried the expression might be permanent. He looked to Lio. "Please, let us remove you from the ballroom and place you under heavy guard until we can be certain the castle has been thoroughly searched. I don't mean to worry you, but there's a very good chance some of the duc's associates mean to finish the job." He said 'duc' the way some might say 'cockroach'.

Belle considered for a moment. She was exhausted, and the hunger she had been ignoring while being held captive for most of the day had suddenly reappeared. "We can go to the kitchens," she offered. She thought of Mrs Potts's sage wisdom and Chip's mischievous grin, of the warm ovens and the hearth, and of the mountains of pastries going uneaten.

"The kitchens?" Cogsworth choked out incredulously.

Belle gave him a look. "If we are in mortal peril, I would like to at least fill my belly."

CHAPTER TWENTY-EIGHT

They almost made it to the kitchens without incident. The intoxicating scent of freshly baked bread lulled Belle into believing the danger was over. Bastien had been apprehended, they were surrounded by loyal guards, and no one had been injured in the chaos.

And then a bullet ricocheted off a suit of armour and buried itself into the wall beside Lio's head, and chaos found them again.

Guards sprang to action, muskets raised, searching for the source of the bullet. The fear that Belle left in the ballroom returned to her once more. She reached for Lio's hand as Cogsworth put himself between them and the direction the bullet came from. Lumière was at the head of the detail, brandishing a weapon for the first time since the mob stormed the castle.

Shouts echoed in the distance, and Lumière spoke. "Cogsworth, get them away from here. We will root out the traitors."

"I'm coming with you," Lio protested as more shots fired in

the distance.

A guard shook his head. "You will be more helpful to us by hiding somewhere safe, sire."

Lio accepted reluctantly, and the detail went on the offensive. Cogsworth pulled the two of them down another hall and ushered them into a broom cupboard.

"Sire, forgive me, but I cannot think—"

Belle reached her hand out to him. "It's fine, Cogsworth, though I do not think there is room for all of us."

He stood at attention. "My duty lies elsewhere, madame." Muffled gunfire reached their ears, and Cogsworth produced a candlestick from his pocket, lighting it with a sconce just outside the cupboard. "Do not open this door for anyone you do not trust."

"We won't," Lio assured him, taking the candle.

And then Cogsworth shut them in. The space was intolerably cramped and smelled very strongly of vinegar, but all that mattered to Belle in that moment was Lio holding tight to her hand, alive and unharmed. They found a place to sit together on a dusty crate.

"Are you all right?" she asked, though the question felt too small for the day they'd had.

Lio pulled her hand closer to him. "How did LeFou get tied up into this?"

Belle was surprised that his mind had latched on to that detail first. "He came to me when I was held captive."

"Held *captive*?" His tone was stricken, but she wasn't about to mince words after what had happened to her that day.

"I left you this morning to check up on progress in the library, and I came upon Bastien's men planning your assassination. They captured me before I could escape, and they took me to the cellars. Eventually LeFou came to me, revealing his role in it all."

"Which was?"

She paused, unsure of how best to put it. "He was seeking revenge."

Lio was incredulous. "Revenge for what?"

"Gaston's death." Lio opened his mouth to speak, but Belle continued. "He loved him, Lio, as I love you. We don't have to condone his actions, but we can at least attempt to understand him." She squeezed his hand. "Try to imagine how you would react if you believed someone else had killed me. Of course, I spent a great deal of time explaining to him that you didn't kill Gaston, but vengeance is a thorny thing. I think he just needed someone to blame."

"How did you escape?"

"I didn't; he set me free. Listen, it doesn't matter. He may not have been in it to start a revolution in Aveyon, but Bastien certainly was. If I hadn't been able to reach through LeFou's pain to find the decent man buried deep, I'd still be in the cellars and you'd be dead."

It was all too much information for Lio to handle after

an attempt had been made on his life by his own blood. He dropped his head into his hands. "What have I done?"

Belle felt a pang of sympathy. "You did what you believed to be right."

"And look where it got us," he said. "I never should have listened to Bastien. I shouldn't have wasted my time with my noblemen. I should have listened to you when you said to focus on Aveyon's commoners."

The words should have been a balm to her, but Belle chafed at his belated acknowledgment. "Yes, you should have."

The extended pause that followed suggested he had expected more sympathy from her, not chastisement. "It's not as though there are instructions on how to be a good king," he offered.

"Certainly not, but there is nothing to be gained from only listening to certain perspectives."

"What do you mean?"

She took a deep breath. "You were raised to rule the people of Aveyon as a prince, yes, and that coloured your perspective from the start. Your advisory was similarly raised to be above the common class, and that has coloured theirs." She reached her hand to her chest. "I was raised to live among Aveyon's commoners. I *am* a commoner. I was the only one who could represent their many thousands of voices, versus seven men who represented the voices of Aveyon's aristocracy. How is that fair? How can your advisory be balanced when it is seven voices to one?"

Lio was chagrined. "I suppose I thought we would have time to fix our problems. I didn't think I'd ever be king of this country. I didn't think it would all fall to me so quickly."

"*I* can understand that, but your people don't have the benefit of knowing your innermost thoughts. Aveyon's dual perspectives must be given equal weight."

"You're right."

"You were so concerned with making sure your noblemen were happy, but it never even crossed your mind to do the same for the rest of your people. And because of that, you almost lost everything, Lio. I almost lost you."

He ran his hands through his hair in a frazzled gesture. "I was so caught up in protecting my throne—" He paused, trying to find the words.

"That you forgot the purpose of the crown is to serve your people?" Belle finished for him.

"And I was so scared of losing you that I stopped seeing you as my partner. I could only see you as something I needed to protect." He sat back. "I let my fears rule me, Belle. I'm hardly better than the beast I left behind."

Belle softened. "That's not true," she said, poking him in the ribs. "The Beast was far worse."

He smiled a little, but it faded quickly. "I want more than anything to fix things, but I don't even know where to begin."

"Well," she started. "Be thankful you're in a position in

which you can do anything at all. Most people aren't."

Noises from the hall crept through the crack by the door. Lio snuffed out the candle and reached for Belle defensively as they stood. She wrapped her hand around the broomstick she would make her weapon if necessary, her heart heavy in her throat. She and Lio held their breaths as they heard steps approach but then fade away.

After a time, Lio pulled her to him and kissed her forehead. They sat back on the crate, in total darkness now. "I think we're in the clear," he whispered. But fear still gripped Belle, and she sensed it was time that Lio knew everything.

"I need to tell you something."

He shifted in the dark. "That sounds ominous."

Belle hesitated. "It's not… *not* ominous."

"Well, it can't be much worse than anything I've put you through. Let's have it, then."

"I think I know why your nightmares have persisted, even though we thought we defeated the curse."

He sat up straighter. "We *thought*? What does that mean?"

She took a deep breath and commanded her nerves to settle. Lio deserved to know the truth, no matter how much it would hurt him. "Back in Paris, on the day of the storming of the Bastille, I was among the rioters because I had been drawn like a moth to a flame all the way from Bastien's home to a shop I had never visited before."

"Go on…"

"Inside there was a strange woman who talked to me like she knew me. She showed me a vision in a mirror quite like the one you gave me, of Aveyon burning, set aflame by our own people. I didn't understand it at the time, but I think it was a vision of what would have come for us if Bastien had succeeded. It was enough to send me running from the shop, straight into the mob." She twisted her hands together. "I thought nothing of it until I saw her again, only this time it was through *your* enchanted mirror."

"My *what*?" He was standing now, though she couldn't make him out in the dark.

Belle pressed on. "I went to the library that night you woke to find me missing from our bed—"

"I remember." His voice was taut.

"The mirror was lodged behind the book I had gone to find. When I picked it up, she spoke to me, warning me not to wait for others to save Aveyon. I fled the library, intending to tell you about it, but when I came back, you had been taken by a nightmare and I couldn't bring myself to add to your worries."

Lio began to speak.

"Let me finish," she begged. "I put the mirror from my mind, and I had a lot keeping me busy while you were gone. But then she came to me in a dream. She told me that Aveyon was at risk of falling to revolution like France. She told me it was in my power to stop it." She pushed her hair behind her ears. "When I awoke, Bastien was trying to have Marguerite forced from the castle, and the woman's dire warnings got buried in my mind." She took a breath, but Lio was silent, waiting for her to continue. "She came to me again, when I was LeFou's captive. She told me something I had already begun to understand, albeit in my unconscious mind. She was—"

"The enchantress who cursed me," Lio finished for her.

Belle sputtered. "How did you know?"

"Someone has been visiting my dreams of late, and after a while, I began to suspect we had met before."

"Your dreams? What did she say?"

"Not so much as she said to you, but she tried to deter me from the path I was on. She told me that the only way to stop the revolution from coming to Aveyon was to return to you. It was part of the reason I rode through the night to get back to you, Belle." He reached for her hand. She reached back, feeling the pull of what had bound them together that night on the tower.

"I don't know what any of it means, but she claims she placed the curse on you in order to bring us together."

He shifted uncomfortably. "I'm never going to pretend like I'm grateful for the hell we were put through, but if that's true, then perhaps I can begin to understand in some small way why it happened."

She leaned her head on his shoulder. "I think we did defeat

the curse. What remains is just an echo."

Lio lifted the hand that was holding hers and tucked it to his chest. "As far as I'm concerned, the curse was defeated the moment I transformed back into myself. I can contend with an echo of it."

Belle's heart settled a bit. "I am sorry I didn't tell you sooner."

"I know you tried. I'm sorry I wouldn't listen."

They sat there quietly, waiting for what would come next, feeling in their hearts that they were perhaps a bit more ready for whatever it may be.

"For what it's worth, I think the enchantress was right about you."

She paused and felt the weight of what he said. "How do you mean?"

"You were always going to be the one to save Aveyon."

CHAPTER TWENTY-NINE

After a time, Cogsworth came back for them. The majordomo's cravat hung limply around his neck, his hair stood on end, and he seemed to be entirely covered in soot. It was the most dishevelled Belle had ever seen him.

He bowed as crisply as ever. "I have come to retrieve you and to make a report—"

"Cogsworth, are you all right?" Belle demanded.

"Yes, madame." He soldiered on in his retelling. "There was a skirmish, but do not fret, we apprehended the infiltrators with minimal injuries on our end."

"But there *were* injuries?" she asked frantically.

He bowed his head. "One of our men was shot, madame, but he is being tended to."

Lio grimaced. "How serious is it, Cogsworth?"

"Sire, your safety is still at risk. We have men sweeping the castle, but the work will not be done for some time. Please, come with me to the kitchens, one of the only spaces in the castle we can be reasonably sure Bastien's men have not infiltrated."

"What makes you think that?" asked Belle.

Cogsworth raised his brow. "I do not think an agent of the revolution would pass Mrs Potts's scrutiny nor meet her standards."

The trio hurried to the kitchens. Guards were posted at the entrance, but it was a haven of normalcy within. Staff moved around in a practised dance of chopping, boiling, sautéing, washing, as though an attempt had not been made on Lio's life that night. It was exactly what Belle had been hoping for. Relief flooded through her as she snatched a croissant from a passing tray.

"Goodness! I've been at my wit's end with worry!" Mrs Potts exclaimed when she caught sight of them. Everyone noticed at once that Belle and Lio were among them, but before they could make a fuss, Mrs Potts ushered them away. "Come, you lot, to the pantry. Everyone else, back to work – we've got a lot of guests eating away their fears out there."

She led Belle, Lio and Cogsworth to the small space and shut the door behind them. Without a word, she began tending to Belle's neck wound with a damp cloth. Belle was happy to let her.

"Mon dieu," Mrs Potts tutted. "Is it true what they're saying? Did the duc de Vincennes truly mean to harm you?"

Lio sat on a barrel, his eyes locked on nothing in particular. "It is," he started. "But, mercifully, he was thwarted."

The door crashed open, revealing Lumière, Aurelian

and an irate Marguerite beyond it. When she saw Belle, she launched straight into her arms.

"What is the meaning of this?" exclaimed Cogsworth so animatedly he knocked over a bushel of onions. Mrs Potts gave him an icy glare as she wrapped a length of cloth around Belle's wrist.

The maître d'hôtel gave an apologetic shrug. "I didn't have a choice, mon ami. Once the Mademoiselle de Lambriquet accosted me in the hall, she refused to leave my side until I brought her to Belle."

Marguerite pulled back and shook Belle's shoulders. "You did it, Belle. You tricked the untrickable Bastien. You stopped the assassination."

"It's not as if I did it on my own." Belle blushed. "I'm sorry we left you in the ballroom."

"You can hardly be blamed," said Marguerite. "And besides, it was worth it to watch my old friends trip over themselves trying to explain that they'd *always known Bastien had revolutionary sympathies.* Lying sycophants, the lot of them."

Belle's eyes went to the weeping cut on Lumière's cheek.

"What happened?" she demanded.

His hand floated to the wound as if he had forgotten it was there. "I caught the wrong end of a bayonet, madame. It is nothing."

But Mrs Potts began cleaning the cut as she had done for

Belle, and the maître d'hôtel gladly accepted.

"How bad is it out there?" asked Belle.

Marguerite plopped down on a sack of flour. "Your aristocratic guests are having the time of their lives, truth be told. An attempt on the life of Aveyon's freshly minted king? It will be the talk of the Continent."

Aurelian sank down to sit beside his sister, and Belle noticed for the first time how alike in manner and appearance they were. "Your guard is working hard to find Bastien's men throughout the castle, but clearing out rooms and wings takes time. It would seem the duc was preparing for war."

"There's much I don't understand—" began Mrs Potts, the words dying before she could finish them.

Lio took a long swig from the dusty bottle of cognac he had pulled from a shelf. "Shall we start at the beginning?"

And so the seven of them began the work of unravelling everything that had happened since Belle and Lio arrived in Paris. Everyone contributed to the telling of it, but Belle kept all talk of mirrors and Orella out of her version. When she got to the part where she realised Bastien had been working against them all along, Marguerite interrupted.

"What I don't understand is why Bastien was on the side of the revolutionaries? He's a nobleman. He stands to lose everything in the event of an uprising."

Belle drummed her fingers on the barrel she sat beside. "Back in Paris, I found a hidden stash of revolutionary documents he had collected, and he revealed his sympathies towards the sans-culottes to me on more than one occasion. But I never had enough cause to accuse him of anything. He had the perfect cover."

"Which was what?" asked Cogsworth.

"He was acting as an agent of the French crown, infiltrating these rebel groups to gather information and inform on his would-be comrades. Evidently his allegiance switched at some point."

Aurelian shifted. "Bastien didn't share everything with me, but his disdain for France's nobility became more obvious the closer we got. It was like he couldn't hide it any longer, which only made him try all the harder to do so. There was a time when he didn't paint his face like a prince du sang, but sometime in the last two years he picked it up, along with the wigs and the jewels and the ivory cane."

"To use as a mask," Belle offered, and Aurelian nodded.

"Events in Paris and Versailles changed a lot of people's views this year, my own included, but I would never sink to using murder as a means to spread a message or achieve a goal."

Lio sighed. "I thought I knew him." He looked around the pantry at the faces of his closest allies, incredulous now that the magnitude of what happened that day was hitting him. "I trusted him, and he manipulated me into thinking my instincts were wrong and a nobleman from Paris knew better than I did about what my kingdom needed."

Mrs Potts offered him a sympathetic pat on the shoulder.

Belle sighed. "I don't think anyone was as deceived by Bastien as I was. I spent the most time with him and let him burrow into my head and make me doubt myself on countless occasions. Hell, he managed to make me wonder if *Marguerite* was the secret revolutionary I should be watching out for." Lio and Aurelian looked at her like she had grown another head. "It's a long story," she offered.

"Too long," Marguerite agreed.

"The point is, I should have listened to my gut when it was screaming at me not to trust him." Orella's dire warnings made sense now that Belle had the benefit of hindsight. Orella had told her the revolution was closer than she thought, but Belle allowed herself to be manipulated by the very man who would bring bloodshed to Aveyon's doorstep. "I feared causing a rift between Lio and the only family he had left."

"He's not the only family I have left." Lio touched the back of her hand. "But I guess we've all learned to trust your instincts."

• • •

Belle awoke with a start, surprised to find she had made a pillow out of a sack of flour. The pantry was pleasingly warm as Marguerite and Aurelian slumbered in a heap nearby.

She knew she hadn't slept for very long, but a lingering

373

thought had risen from the depths of her mind, one that would not be ignored. Belle rose and stretched her aching muscles as she made her way to the voices back in the kitchen, emerging from the pantry to find Lio, Mrs Potts, Lumière and Cogsworth debriefing over a pot of tea.

"What happened to Hercule?" she asked no one in particular.

"Who?" asked Lio.

"LeFou," Belle corrected. "I lost track of him after the gunshot."

Mrs Potts paled. "Why should you want to know where he is?"

Belle felt a pang of defensiveness. "He's the reason we were able to stop Bastien."

Lumière cleared his throat. "He was taken to a cell for his part in the plot against you and the king." His features softened when he saw the look on Belle's face. "He went willingly, madame."

Belle took a deep breath. "May I remind everyone that he stopped a bullet from hitting Lio."

"That is true," Lio confirmed, as though they hadn't witnessed it themselves or heard the story told ten different times from other people present during the attempt.

They seemed to consider that a mark of his capacity for change. But then Belle thought of the worst of it. She looked back at the pantry and spoke lower this time. "He also remembers everything."

Cogsworth gave her a steely look. "Everything?"

"Everything. The curse. The Beast. Gaston falling to his death. I don't know how. But he didn't just save Lio today; he saved me, and I don't think he deserves to be imprisoned for it."

No one had discussed the curse so directly since Belle and Lio destroyed it. Belle knew she was breaking an unspoken rule among them all, but after what had happened under their very noses, she found herself less willing to pretend everything was fine in Aveyon.

Lio broke the silence at last. "I don't know—" he began.

"Can we at least go to him? And you can speak to him for yourself and see that he's changed?"

Lio curled his hand into a fist on the table. "Fine." He stood. "But I am only doing this for you."

• • •

Belle hadn't been in the castle's dungeon since she briefly occupied a cell in place of her father. As she and Lio climbed the tower staircase, she had to force her feet to keep moving as bad memories threatened to pull her under. So much good had happened since then, she kept reminding herself. But after the assassination attempt on Lio, it was hard to remember.

The cells, usually empty, were filled with men loyal to Bastien and the revolution. They jeered at Belle and Lio as they passed, shouting "Vive la révolution" and spitting at their feet. Lio pulled her close, but he didn't try to stop her from going farther. For her part, Belle was unbothered by their insults. The men didn't know her, they didn't know Lio and they didn't know Aveyon.

They reached a guard seated at a table, recording the names and offences of the prisoners arrested that day. Soon the magistrates would formally charge them and they would be moved to the prison in Mauger to await trial. The guard stood quickly at the sight of them and bowed. "Sire?" He inclined his head at Lio, unsure of what the king of Aveyon was doing in the dungeon.

"We're here to see a prisoner named Hercule…" But they didn't know Hercule's surname.

A voice leaked out from a nearby cell. "Garoutte. Hercule Garoutte."

Belle walked over and peeked in through the bars. "Hercule?"

He looked up from where he sat crouched on the cramped, straw-covered stone floor. "Belle?"

Belle stepped closer to the bars. "I wanted to thank you—"

"Please, Belle, don't thank me."

Belle continued, undeterred. "Without you, this day would have turned out quite differently."

"Without me—"

"Bastien would have found another way," she interrupted.

There would be time to contend with the sins of the day, but Orella had made it clear to Belle that finding the good in Hercule had been the only way forward. She wouldn't turn her back on him now.

Hercule swallowed, and though it was dark, she could see his cheeks turn red. He looked up and his eyes widened when Lio appeared behind her. He moved to stand, brushing the straw from his pantalon, but both men were silent. Belle knew well enough not to push her husband to speak.

Eventually, Lio spoke. "It would seem I owe you my life." It wasn't gratitude, but it wasn't a challenge either.

Hercule wrung his hands and stared at the floor. "Think of it as a small step towards repaying the immense debt I owe you." Neither of them had to say aloud what he meant by that. Hercule had been at the centre of two plots against Lio. It was a darkness that hung over them all.

Lio surprised them both by speaking. "I can think of another way for you to do that."

Hercule looked up, almost hopeful. "How?"

"Will you testify against the duc de Vincennes? I know we have plenty of witnesses who watched him try to shoot me, but I'd like for him to face consequences for his less... overt treachery as well. You were privy to his plot – perhaps you can help to build a stronger case against him."

Hercule nodded. "Of course, Your Majesty."

Lio took a deep breath and motioned for the guard, who

rushed to answer. "Please release Hercule and drop the charges against him."

The guard bowed and produced a ring of keys from his pocket. He stepped forward and unlocked the incredulous Hercule's cell.

"Why?" he whispered. "Why do this? Why set me free after everything I've done to you?"

Lio's mouth was pressed into a grim line, and Belle understood that setting him free had not been an easy decision.

"Because I know what it is like to live with hate in your heart, and how difficult it is to let go of it." Lio stepped into the cell and held his hand out to Hercule. "And besides, what's the point of being king if I cannot pardon someone every once in a while?"

Hercule took his outstretched hand and shook it, and all at once the tension dissipated.

"See to it that Hercule has a room to stay in tonight," said Lio to the guard.

"I—I cannot thank you enough," Hercule stammered.

Lio nodded. "Thank *you* for setting Belle free, and for saving my life."

Hercule bowed at them both and followed the guard back down the staircase, eager to put some distance between himself and the cell that he had been freed of.

"I didn't expect that," said Belle.

Lio shrugged. "I'm just trying to be a bit more like my wife by seeing the good in someone instead of only the bad." He reached for her hand, but she did not take his. "Hercule helped us save this kingdom. I cannot ignore that." He looked down curiously at her hand, still hanging at her side. "Let's leave this place."

She hesitated. There was a feeling in her gut that wouldn't allow her to simply walk away now that she was in the dungeon. "I think I want to see him, Lio, but you don't have to come with me."

He didn't need to ask whom she meant. His mouth was a grim line once more, but he nodded, letting her lead the way.

Bastien was being held alone in the cell at the top of the dungeon tower, the very same one Belle's father had been held in not so very long ago. Their ascent up the spiral staircase made her dizzy. When they reached the landing, Lio stayed back in the shadows. Belle couldn't blame him. She wasn't sure she'd be able to face him if she were in Lio's shoes. But Belle was more than willing to confront the architect of her suffering. The space was lit only by the pale moonlight shining in through the keyhole window in his cell and the candle Belle carried. She stepped up to the cell and let the light leak over the prisoner within.

The duc de Vincennes was not surprised to see her.

"You've got the wrong man. I've been framed. I'm the duc de Vincennes," he said without emotion, as if by rote. He knew

Belle wasn't about to believe a word out of his mouth. He was doing it to taunt her. He turned his head lazily her way. "Come to weep over the mistakes you've made?"

She looked at him there, slumped in a cell, devoid of all the things he had used as a mask in Paris. His brown hair was messed up, taking years off him. He had been stripped of his fine outer garments, leaving him in a white undershirt and black breeches, the most subdued she had ever seen him. This was not Bastien, duc de Vincennes. This was a broken man.

"My only mistake was trusting you."

He stood and walked to the bars, a curious glint in his eyes. "Want to know *my* greatest mistake?" She was silent, but he continued anyway. "My greatest mistake was my belief that you needed to be kept alive. I could have had you killed so many times, Belle. But I was certain that your death would only hinder my goals. I thought the people loved you too much, and I needed Aveyon to rally behind the revolution, not a dead queen gone too soon." He reached his hands out to grip the iron. "But now I understand that all I needed was chaos; the people would have done the rest."

"You have so much faith that the people of Aveyon would have revolted?"

He gave her a pitying look. "You were there in Paris, Belle. You know that a crowd merely needs a spark in order to burn."

"Aveyon is not Paris, but you never seemed to comprehend that." He tried to speak, but she interrupted him. "And you're wrong, Bastien – your biggest mistake was believing that things must be broken before they can be fixed."

She turned away from him, having got whatever small bit of closure she had come there for.

But he continued to speak. "Where is my dear cousin, the petit lionceau? Hiding away with his nobles? You must know he'll never really love you, Belle. You're a peasant. A title won't change you. Lio will always see himself as being above you."

Belle paused just before the shadows that concealed Lio, her blood boiling. She wanted nothing more than to yell at Bastien, to tell him every wretched thought she had about him, to do everything she could to make him hurt. But then he would win.

Instead, Lio stepped out of the shadows and into the pale light. Belle was nearly overcome with the memory of when she demanded he do just that when he was the Beast and she had offered herself to him as his prisoner.

But this was different.

Behind her, Bastien choked on his laughter and cleared his throat. "Lio, so unexpected of you to join us."

He was deathly calm when he spoke. "When I leave here, Cousin, I will endeavour to forget you." He stepped closer to the cell. "When I become worthy of the crown you thrust upon me in the hopes that it would be my end, it will not be because of your efforts." He paused and let the words settle between them. "Your legacy is nothing but ash and ruin, and your greatest punishment will be never witnessing Aveyon grow into the kingdom it should be, the one you imagined it could be. Pity for you that such things cannot be felt from inside a prison cell."

Bastien, man of constant ploys and manoeuvres, had no reply for him. Lio turned his back on his cousin and took Belle's hand. The last expression she saw on the face of the duc de Vincennes was one of emptiness.

Darkness swallowed the cell once more, and Belle thought perhaps she understood the duc at last. She had believed him incapable of being loyal to anyone save himself, but she was wrong. Bastien was loyal to one thing above all else. Oaths sworn to his king didn't matter; the blood he shared with Lio didn't matter. All that mattered was furthering his cause, furthering the message of the revolution. It would have been admirable if it hadn't taken him down the darkest path.

As they descended the stairs from Bastien's cell, she wondered what could have been if he hadn't been so married to violence as a method of reaching his goal. If he had come to Aveyon with a desire to work with them instead of against them, then perhaps some good could have been achieved. She knew there had been a time when Bastien would have been her ally, but he only saw her as his enemy.

Belle and Lio both knew what happened in France was a mistake on the part of the king, and they were both going to do everything in their power to make sure they didn't make those same mistakes in Aveyon.

But Bastien couldn't see past his own hubris, and now all he would see was the inside of a prison cell.

CHAPTER THIRTY

By the time they left the dungeon, Belle was near collapse. She hadn't a proper sleep since leaving Lio in their bed that morning, and everything caught up with her at once. She wobbled on her feet before Lio pulled her into an alcove.

"Belle," he said. "Are you all right?"

She hadn't known she was holding so much pain inside her until she let herself weep in Lio's arms, releasing the stress and woe that had followed her from Paris. But they were also tears of relief. Somehow, despite the odds stacked against them, they had survived. She cried in his arms as he rubbed her back, feeling that being able to hold her husband was a gift she should not squander. She let the last of her tears fall, soaking Lio's shirt, feeling a great deal lighter than she had before.

"What are we going to do?" asked Lio in a whisper.

"About what?" It was a ridiculous question; she knew that.

"Everything. I don't even know how to begin to repair the rift I made between myself and my people."

"You have a starting point to work from," she offered.

"And what is that?"

"In France, the National Assembly is fighting for a constitution and a two-chamber system of parliament. Louis refused until it was too late, but what if we didn't?"

Lio mused on it for a moment. "We could get ahead of any unrest in Aveyon by simply giving our people what others have fought and bled for in France."

"Exactly. Monarchies everywhere need to be held accountable, and the common people of the world deserve to have their voices heard. Let's get rid of archaic French laws and establish modern ones that make sense in Aveyon."

Lio kissed the top of her head. "I can't imagine what this kingdom would look like if we had never met."

Belle thought of Orella, who had set them on a path towards each other some ten years before. Belle was beginning to understand why Orella had done what she did. Sometimes sacrifices had to be made to turn the world into a better place, and while Belle could not speak for her husband, she knew in her heart that she wouldn't have changed a thing.

A guard hurried past them, backtracking when he realised he had overlooked them. "The castle is clear, Your Majesty, but there's been a disturbance in the gardens."

"What's happened?" Belle asked, expecting the worst.

He cleared his throat. "If I didn't know any better, I would think all of Aveyon had gathered on the grounds." They stepped past him and moved in the direction of the ballroom. "It isn't safe, sire!" the guard called after them, but they ignored his warning.

They strode through the crowded room, ignoring the shouts of their guests. Guards flanked them on either side and prevented anyone from following them through the room.

They could hear the crowd before they set foot on the balcony.

"Should we wait? Do they sound angry?" asked Belle.

Lio shook his head. "I refuse to fear my own people."

They took each other's hands and stepped out. The sun was only beginning to rise on a new day, painting the castle grounds in a pale light. The crowd surged and shouted, but it wasn't until Belle and Lio went right up to the railing that the shouts gave over to cheers. There had to be thousands of people below them, drawn to the castle as news of the assassination attempt trickled through Aveyon's villages and towns.

Lio waved down at them and turned to Belle. "There's nothing like an assassination attempt to endear a king to his people, no matter how much of an ass he's been."

Belle laughed at him and waved down, too. Before long, chants of "Vive le roi" spread out over the crowd, reaching them with the force of a wave at high tide. Lio tightened his grip on her hand, and Belle's heart grew. Right now, the cheers and chants were an almost involuntary reaction to seeing their king, but soon the people of Aveyon would know what they had decided that night, hidden in a dark alcove. Soon

Lio would earn those cheers, proving them right, and Belle couldn't wait for the rest of her kingdom to know how worthy he was of them.

But then a curious thing happened. The chant transformed, slowly at first, fractured over the many thousands of people, but it became clear soon enough.

"Vive la reine!"

"Vive la reine!"

"Vive la reine!"

Lio looked over to Belle, perhaps expecting her to recoil from the chant. But if anything, she found she didn't chafe against the title like she once had. Belle was beginning to understand that becoming a queen wasn't just putting a crown on her head – it was a tool that could be used to make the lives of her people better. It was not something she needed to fear; it was something she could embrace and make her own.

She squeezed his hand but said nothing, and Lio seemed to understand.

Belle had come a long way from her desire to leave Aveyon behind forever in search of adventure like those she had read about in her books. Now she understood that adventure didn't have to mean chasing endless horizons. Adventure could be gathering brilliant minds like Marguerite and her father and others to her court so they could challenge her. Adventure could mean travelling to every corner of her kingdom and meeting people from all walks of life in order to learn from them. Adventure could be working to make her kingdom a better place for everyone in it, with the man she loved by her side.

She leaned in to whisper in Lio's ear. "The people of Aveyon seem willing to give us another chance. Let's not waste it, shall we?"

EPILOGUE

Belle didn't grow up wanting or wishing for a crown.

In all her dreams, she left the kingdom she was born in far behind her, chasing adventure on an endless horizon. Aveyon had always been too small for her, too married to tradition, too quiet. It took leaving it to realise how very wrong she had been. Now she was to be its queen.

The sun shone through the stained-glass windows of the eastern wall and painted the throne room with colour. It was a stark contrast to the first time she had set foot in it, back when it was filled with a decade's worth of dust and decay. But like everything else in the castle, a broken curse had restored it to its former glory in the blink of an eye. Each soul within the castle walls had been similarly transformed, forged by the fires of Orella's ancient magic into something stronger than they were before. Belle was different now too, changed from the poor, provincial girl she had once been to a queen in her own right.

She stood tall in a gown as golden as the sun. It hearkened back to the dress she had worn the night she dined and danced with the Beast, when he had shown her a vision of her father and let her go to him, despite the fact that leaving meant an eternity as a monster. It was hard to understand how much had changed since then, and how far they had come.

Even though she couldn't see them, she felt hundreds of eyes pressing into her back. Her heart was a steady drumbeat against her ribs as she repeated the words that would make her queen.

"I swear to serve the kingdom of Aveyon and to govern its people in accordance with its laws and customs."

They were the same words she had written with Lio a few months before, on the eve of his own coronation. So much had changed since then. It had only been a few weeks since Lio had ratified Aveyon's first constitution, cementing in place the inalienable rights of every citizen of their kingdom. Soon, elections would be under way to choose representatives from every town, village and hamlet that would make up Aveyon's first parliament. And the cataloguing of Belle's library was almost complete, with Marguerite and Cogsworth overseeing the necessary preparations to open it to all of Aveyon.

"I swear to perform my duty faithfully and to uphold justice and mercy in all of my judgements."

The bishop anointed her forehead with oil and murmured a prayer as attendants presented him with the crown he was to place on her head. It was a simple gold diadem inlaid with small rubies that had once belonged to Lio's mother. Belle's husband had offered to have one made for her, but she insisted on wearing Delphine's, knowing it meant a great deal more to him that she would be wearing the same crown his mother once did. Maurice had arrived home from his travels just in time to present her with a piece of gold used as a conductor in one of his old inventions, now braided along the base of the crown. Her father had sacrificed so much to make sure Belle had more opportunities than he did, and the crown meant more to her now that it had a piece of her father in it. "I'd like to see anyone call you odd now," he'd whispered to her just before she walked the length of the throne room to the dais. She'd let him think she was somehow changed from that funny girl she used to be, but she knew better.

The bishop placed the crown upon her head as she spoke the final words of her oath.

"I swear my allegiance to Aveyon, above all else."

The room seemed to hold its breath as the bishop announced her.

"Long live Belle, queen of Aveyon!"

The crowd roared to life as she turned and looked out to find her father in the sea of people. He and Mrs Potts were holding each other up, both with tears streaming down their faces. Chip looked up between them in amused bewilderment. Cogsworth stood next to them, a look of unrestrained pride on his face, and Lumière to his left, weeping like a babe. Marguerite stood with Aurelian and Hercule, the three of them beaming up at her. Belle's heart swelled at the sight of her family, the one she was born into and the one she had made for herself. Belle and Lio had dissolved his advisory the day after she had almost lost him to a radical, but that didn't mean she and her husband would be ruling Aveyon on their own. They knew a kingdom was best served by a tapestry of voices and viewpoints. The future of Aveyon would not be determined by the voices of a few any longer.

"Vive la reine!" boomed the bishop, and the crowd answered just as a flurry of blood-red rose petals fell from the ceiling like rain.

Her eyes found Lio's amid the chaos. She had fallen in love with his soul long before she knew him in this body, but the eyes were the same. He smiled at her through the petals, and she quirked a brow subtly. He shrugged and cupped his hands together to collect them. The curse had no claim over him any longer. Lio's slumber had been undisturbed since the night they took to the balcony and promised each other they would work to make Aveyon a better place.

She could just make out a familiar figure in the back corner of the throne room, one that had followed her from a mirror shop in Paris all the way to the cellar that had become her prison. But she was not there to deliver dire warnings or visions. Belle understood now that magic did not flow through her kingdom like a swollen river; it was confined to the spirits of all the queens and female rulers who came before her, bound to Orella so she could help those in need, as Belle had been.

Belle watched as Orella faded from view like a flame extinguished, and found she didn't feel enmity towards the enchantress any longer. Orella had done what she needed to do in order to spare Aveyon from the storm; Belle and Lio had done the rest.

She looked up at the portrait of Lio's father and grandfather, who wore their heavy crowns like they weighed nothing at all. They were born to rule, whereas she was born to nothing. The oaths they swore were to the French crown, but her oath was to her kingdom alone.

She knew in her heart it would make her a better ruler.

And they all lived happily ever after…

THE END

Acknowledgments

I can't remember a part of my life without Belle.

Being that I was two years old when the movie came out, this makes sense, but it's deeper than that, too. I grew up with Belle as a sort of archetype – I felt she represented both the person I was and the person I wished to one day become. I, like countless others, saw parts of myself in her stubbornness, her empathy, her outspokenness and her courage. Belle told us all that it's okay to be odd, to be different, to be ourselves even when the world wishes we'd be someone else. I am so grateful to have been given the opportunity to tell a part of her story.

My first thank-you is for my tireless champion of an agent, Suzie Townsend, without whom none of this would be possible. Thank you for never letting on that my panicked emails are, indeed, as over-the-top as I suspect. Thank you to Dani Segelbaum for your assistance in all matters big and small. A big thank-you to everyone else at New Leaf who has helped me on this journey.

A gigantic thank-you to my editor, Jocelyn Davies, for taking a chance on me and for connecting so fully with my vision for this story. This book (and its author) would be utterly lost without you. Thank you to everyone at Disney Hyperion for all that they have done to bring this book to life – specifically, thank you to Cassidy Leyendecker, Kieran Viola, Emily Meehan, Jamie Alloy, Marci Senders, Guy

Cunningham, Sara Liebling, Lyssa Hurvitz, Melissa Lee, Seale Ballenger, Tim Retzlaff, Elke Villa, Dina Sherman, the entire sales team, Steve Borell, Lauren Burniac and Alison Giordano.

I would be nowhere without the writing friends I have made along the way. Thank you to my VIPs: Alexa Donne, Emily Duncan, Rosiee Thor, Rory Power, Christine Lynn Herman, June Tan, Kevin Van Whye and Deeba Zargarpur. Special thanks to Rory and Christine for the sprints that got this book written. Thanks to my sub crew: Hannah Whitten, Tori Bovalino and Jessica Bibi Cooper. Thank you to my AMMFam, but most specifically to Leanne Schwartz. Huge thanks to my ride-or-dies: Suzie Samin and Brendon Zatirka. Big thanks to Kelsey Rodkey, Kat Dunn, Dante Medema and Rachel Griffin for always being supportive in the DMs. Innumerable thanks to Alwyn Hamilton for being here since the day she helped me write my query. Massive thanks to Elizabeth Lim and Alexandra Bracken for their support and advice. To my gorgeous agent sisters: Laura Steven and Claribel Ortega, thank you for always inspiring me. And special shout-out to my pal/mushroom/American twin Victoria Aveyard for putting up with me since 2013.

Thank you to my friends Tarek, Kerstin, Carrie, Jon, Steve, Michelle, Ted, Jennifer, Brandon, Celeste, Emma and Max for your enthusiasm and attentiveness even in the face of my exhaustive explanations re: the publishing industry.

Thank you to Biz and Kelly Williams for your constant

love and support over the last decade, and to the rest of the Williams family for being the best cheerleaders a girl could ask for.

Thank you to my dad and Anna for your unwavering encouragement. Thank you to Uncle John and Tee Wei for your love, felt all the way from Australia.

Thank you to Lauren and Wade for never failing to remind me what a tyrant of an older sister I was in our youth. Love you both so much.

Huge thanks to my mom for believing in me from day one and for rewarding every single one of my accomplishments with a trip to the bookstore.

Thank you to Byron, the bacon to my eggs. My books wouldn't get written without you in my corner. Thanks for being the world's best cat dad to Harriet and Gatsby. (And thank you, H & G, for being the world's greatest cats, period.)

Lastly, my biggest thanks are for you, reader. Books are just words on a page until someone decides to read them. Thank you for choosing to read mine.